VIRAL GLYPH
THE ROSETTE REBELLION

A GATSBY DONOVAN *PARADIGMS LOST* MYSTERY

ELLERY STONE

Verbatim
Publishing

Verbatim Publishing
Portland, OR USA

Copyeditor: Linda Grimsson

Ordering Information:
Quantity sales. Special discounts are available on quantity purchases by corporations, associations, and others. Orders by U.S. trade bookstores and wholesalers.

ISBN13: 978-0-9658835-7-3 (pbk.)

1. Main category—Fiction
2. Other category—Action & Adventure
3. Other category—Mystery, Thriller
4. Other category—Psychological Suspense

First Edition

Manufactured in the United States of America

ALSO BY ELLERY STONE

DEEP STRUCTURE
The Stonehenge Quantum
Where are the mysterious symbols coming from? Why have they appeared in an Egyptian tomb, a Peruvian palace, and a shape created by a fakir's squirming snakes?

Dr. Gatsby Donovan's career at the British Museum has made her an expert in decoding ancient glyphs, but solving this linguistic puzzle is the greatest challenge of her life. Will her knowledge unearth the answers, or are they secreted within the very source that she dare not decipher? As she spirals into the universal "deep structure," she finds herself dangling from the edge of everything she once believed about reality.

ALPHA OMEGA
The Holy Drug
In a London suburb, a cult disciple gasps, dying in a pool of his own blood. The only clue is the holy scripture that he clutches.

Who would kill for the Librah Vae-ta? What secrets are hidden within its pages? Do the leaders of the Omega cult know of the terrible violence it can spawn, or was that the intention?

Dr. Gatsby Donovan's abilities to decipher ancient writings pull her into the vortex of a treacherous mystery. Revealing Omega's most powerful secrets will be deadly—the question is not the salvation of her soul but whether she will survive the night.

www.ellerystone.com

ACKNOWLEDGMENTS

My thanks to the following fine people:

- The Administrator at Hellenism.net Forum for Greek translation
- Taylor Gilmore for custom illustrations of glyphs
- Linda Grimsson, Northwest Independent Editors Guild, for copyediting
- Debra Hartmann of The Pro Book Editor (www.theprobookeditor.com) for expert publishing guidance
- Antonios Tsagkaratos for details about Athens
- Monica Villa for descriptions of chemistry labs and equipment

Valuable information was found in Chapter 3 "How the Linear B Script Was Used" in *Linear B and Related Scripts* by John Chadwick (Berkeley: University of California Press, 1987).

Hieroglyph

A hieroglyph (Greek for "sacred writing") is a character of the ancient Egyptian writing system. Logographic scripts that are pictographic in form in a way reminiscent of ancient Egyptian are also sometimes called "hieroglyphs"…The word *hieroglyphics* refer to a hieroglyphic script. (Source: "Hieroglyph," *Wikipedia,* https://en.wikipedia.org/wiki/Hieroglyph)

Phaistos Disk

The Phaistos Disc (also spelled Phaistos Disk, Phaestos Disc) is a disk of fired clay from the Minoan palace of Phaistos on the Greek island of Crete, possibly dating to the middle or late Minoan Bronze Age (2nd millennium BC). It is about 15 cm (5.9 in) in diameter and covered on both sides with a spiral of stamped symbols. Its purpose and meaning, and even its original geographical place of manufacture, remain disputed, making it one of the most famous mysteries of archaeology. This unique object is now on display at the archaeological museum of Heraklion.

The disc was discovered in 1908 by the Italian archaeologist Luigi Pernier in the Minoan palace-site of Phaistos, and features 241 tokens, comprising 45 unique signs, which were apparently made by pressing hieroglyphic "seals" into a disc of soft clay, in a clockwise sequence spiraling toward the disc's center.

The Phaistos Disc captured the imagination of amateur and professional archeologists, and many attempts have been made to decipher the code behind the disc's signs. While it is not clear that it is a script, most attempted decipherments assume that it is; most additionally assume a syllabary, others an alphabet or logography. Attempts at decipherment are generally thought to be unlikely to succeed unless more examples of the signs are found, as it is generally agreed that there is not enough context available for a meaningful analysis.

Although the Phaistos Disc is generally accepted as authentic by archaeologists, a few scholars believe that the disc is a forgery or a hoax. (Source: "Phaistos Disk," Wikipedia, http://en.wikipedia.org/wiki/Phaistos_ Disc)

PROLOGUE

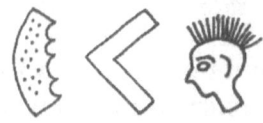

RUZ WER DAN

You haunt me again—why now?

How will I ever know you intimately?

I know your sound but not your meaning, your shape but not your face.

I search the sources over and over, interrogate experts, scour the Internet, leap to every ridiculous conclusion imaginable, run into brick walls and dead ends, give up, despair, and start all over again.

RUZ. Rose, rise? Red wine?

WER, DAN. Surname or given name? Nickname? Company name? Abbreviation or initialization, palindrome, anagram? Encrypted message? 3+3+3 = 9? WTF?

I know that I must find you out, no matter what it takes, no matter how long it takes.

She warned me not to look for you, in that split second of compassion.

She said that the day I find you will be my last.

Considering the source, I must believe it.

But I won't give up. I can't.

RUZ WER DAN

I'm coming for you.

CHAPTER 1

The engineered toxin stopped the heart in less than sixty seconds.

Darkness—black as the hair tumbling to her waist—blanketed her as she crept toward the entry of the Spiti Deka Apartments. A softshell jacket offered her lithe body some warmth against the evening chill, unusual for Athens in September.

She ran her fingers over the nylon fabric pack strapped around her hips, feeling for the small glass box that held a toxin-infused patch.

All DOLIUM tested and functional.

She pulled a universal keycard from her pocket and swiped it through the security system pad mounted on the wall. With a beep, the door unlocked. She pushed it open, stepped into the lobby, and spotted the elevator.

At the second floor, the doors slid open, and she walked out into a long hallway. When she saw the room number plate 202, she took out the key and opened the door.

RUNNERS always have security systems.

On the left wall, rather than a standard electronic security panel, she saw a grouping of framed photos. She glanced at the STAR SEED—the Circle-engineered smartphone—in her hand and read the last message from the BOAT.

Twelve minutes.

As she moved down the dark entrance hall, she spotted the bathroom door. She moved inside the room and sat on the edge of the bathtub, again checking the smartphone.

Three minutes.

She spotted a ceramic soap dish sitting on the tub ledge, picked it up, wriggled behind the vinyl curtain that hung over the tub, and folded into a tight ball. She slipped one hand into the hip pack and pulled out a pair of nitrile gloves.

Beyond the racing adrenaline—focus. Readiness.

The lumbering city bus moved along Kleomenous Street; the advertisement on the side beckoned Kolonaki visitors to enjoy garides giouvetsi at the St. George Lycabettus hotel. It pulled to the curb, unfolded its doors, and deposited a woman in a tailored suit. A laptop carrying case swung by her side as she stepped onto the sidewalk. The bus belched black exhaust and rumbled down the street. The woman started down the sidewalk. In a minute, she turned onto a walkway that led to the front doors of Spiti Deka.

The elevator took her to the second floor, where she stepped out into the hallway, walked toward unit 202, and pushed against the door. She turned on the lights and wandered into the kitchen. With a long sigh, she pulled a tumbler from a cabinet and reached for the counter-top wine rack.

Οι αθώοι δε θα γλυτώσουν. *The innocent are not spared.*

The intruder held her breath, listening to footsteps in the kitchen, a drawer yawning, silverware chiming. She squeezed the soap dish in her hand and then threw it against a storage cabinet on the opposite wall.

The woman jumped at the BANG and spun toward the noise, eyes wide. She set the glass on the kitchen counter and walked toward the bathroom.

Footsteps padding closer.

It was the moment that destroyed distraction. Dacea did not feel the hammering of her heart, did not taste metal on her lips.

The handle turned; the woman stepped into the dark room.

As she reached for the light switch, something solid hurtled toward her and pinned her against the wall. She gasped, but a glove slapped over her lips. The arm wrapped around her body was a vise; fingers crushed her windpipe. She struggled violently, eyes bulging. Her chest bellowed as she tried to scream.

Her free hand flew to the pack that held the DOLIUM. She tugged it from the protective container, touching only the safe edges, and slapped it onto the woman's neck. Thousands of microbarbs pierced the skin; wings expanded like molly bolts, crushing any hope of removal. The toxin that stopped the lungs and heart cascaded into her bloodstream.

The woman howled. Her hand flew to the patch as if she might try to pull it off, but she shook her head and slumped to the floor, staring up with dull eyes. "HAMMER?!"

She studied the woman—her eyelids were already drooping, leg muscles twitching. *SWORD, you HORN.* "You broke the law of the Circle. RUNNERS do not survive."

A salvo burst from the woman's lips, spraying the underside of the sink with blood. She collapsed into a disjointed S-shape on the tile, her hair a splayed Rorschach pattern. One of her high-heeled shoes bobbed, like a dingy, in the toilet. As she convulsed, her feet pumped against the tile, and one heel smacked hard against the intruder's calf. She gurgled on the saliva that pumped from her lips, jittering as if electrocuted. When her head dropped to the tile and a sluggish breath pushed the last air from her lungs, her hands opened and shut as if to grasp it.

Hunkered over her, she reached into a compartment of the hip pack; the plastic protector inside it held a razor blade.

Left wrist—two centimeters above the lunate, 1 centimeter deep, 7 centimeters long. Right wrist—1 centimeter above lunate, 6 centimeters long.

Two red trickles flowed, glistening across the white tiles that smelled of bleach. As she stared at the blade, memories washed over her.

...the Maratti knife that tore her skin

...the faces of Badra and Jaleen, burning with anger

...her punishment for spilling, for forgetting to pick up bread or sweep the floor, for a bewildered look

...the children skittering to the other side of the street to avoid her

...the anxious faces of the fish sellers at Souk *al-Harajb*

...the slash on her cheek that had become gangrene and carved her face into a rictus of bone

Her other hand rose; a fingertip stole under the black qunae and across the raised scar tissue. The rat's nest of twisted flesh extended from her temple across her cheek, nose, lips, and upper neck. Hate clogged there like a tumor.

A single tear trickled down her cheek.

She set the blade on the tile by the woman's hand—dead, but her fingers still twitched—and walked out of the bathroom.

As Dacea Bayoumi headed south on down Kleomenous Street, she reminded herself to return the keycard and door key to the BOAT in the morning. She turned west, heading for Veranzerou Street, wondering why she felt a knot twisting in her throat but nothing else.

CHAPTER 2

"But whoever translates it—the glory, the immortality! Can you imagine it?"

Gatsby ran her fingertips across the spines, luxuriating in leather and vellum and antiquity, as she paced the length of the bookcase and ignored him. The office was cramped with dark walnut bookshelves. Sunlight poured in through ceiling-high windows that he had propped open at the bottom edge. The University of Cambridge spring term was in full swing. She heard a soccer team punting and shouting with exuberance, and remembering the same enthusiasm of her undergraduate years at Blake brought a smile to her face.

Ram Balasubramani—Roman to his friends—puffed on a briar pipe that still had the price sticker on the bowl, and the office began to darken with Borkum Riff Bourbon smoke. As he propped an elbow on the desk, bumping the computer keyboard askew, his expression hinted at verbal jousting. "Goes without saying. The language has tormented translators for almost four thousand years."

And one phrase has tormented me for four decades. RUZ WER DAN. Livia's face, Hollywood perfect, flitted through her mind.

She shoved it away and felt herself submerge in the book titles: Sumerian pottery. Iron Age peat corpses. Egyptian hieroglyphics, the "sacred writing" system developed around 4000 BCE. Paleolithic tools. The solstice markers at Stonehenge. The bath houses of Mohenjo-daro. It was his world and hers: all things buried, dusty, and dead, methodically resurrected with horsehair brushes and software.

Among the innumerable shards and mummies and tablets, there was nothing equal to it. *One Disk, across all human history and treasures. ONE.*

She stopped, slowly sucking in air as she saw it. At eye level, stashed between *The Great Egyptian Pyramids, Vols. I–II,* the ceramic plate stood vertical on a brass tripod. Her gaze moved over the easily identifiable symbols—flowers, birds, fish, dogs, boats—and those less literal, portraying what might be fire or water, a cave or a robe, a fork or a serpent's tongue. When Luigi Pernier discovered it in 1908, researchers learned that the clay type was commonly used in the city of Phaistos, and they dubbed it the Phaistos Disk.

Would a scribe in 1850 BCE be so driven to record on this small clay tablet? And what the hell do I have to do to unlock its message?

Roman cleared his throat. "As I said, I appreciate your drive all the way from London. My new course is contested archeology. Slated for the spring. A full segment focuses on the Phaistos Disk, and there was only one person to call on as a guest expert."

She turned, giving him a wan smile. "That's what I am, an expert?"

"False modesty, GM?" He rolled his eyes "Unseemly, and I've known you long enough to recognize it." Sitting taller in the chair, he propped the pipe on his lower lip and seemed to be trying for stateliness. He pulled in his stomach muscles. His daily runs around the campus kept him trim, even though he was known among the faculty as a bottomless pit when presented with his favorite Indian dish, tikka masala with paneer. Since joining the Office of Archeology at Cambridge two years ago, he maneuvered his way into Gatsby's orbit and pestered her with lunch invitations.

As she looked down the shelf, something caught her eye: a program from an academic conference, nestled between the cartouche bookend and a hardback on medieval artillery. The cover included a photo of a forty-something woman with hazel eyes. Her hair, dark as organic cocoa powder, fell to her shoulders. She wore a fitted suit and taunted the lens with a look that said *but I never got caught.*

She skimmed the credits below the photo: monographs for the *American Journal of Archaeology, Archaeology Magazine, Review of Archaeology*, and *The London Museum of Archaeology*, contributions to three textbooks that were adopted at six universities, and the title of lead consultant for the British Museum's Department of Orthography and

Translation. The sidebar noted, *Dr. Donovan is a ten-year member of the Vanderbilt Racquetball Club and has consistently achieved Gold Circle standings.*

But not an Aeon. Her smile faded. Livia's precious Aeon, her Nobel and crucifix and Iron Maiden all in one.

She tugged the program free. "For god's sake, Roman."

Smiling a little, he looked down into his lap. "Well. I have been known to keep memorabilia of my colleagues. Come on, have a seat and tell me how many years this damn artifact has possessed you." He pointed at her daypack.

"Too many. It's all my free time, when I'm not writing for the societies or attending conferences. The American Society of Epigraphy is hounding me for a third lecture at its summer symposia, did you know that?" She stretched her hand toward the Disk but, just before her fingertip connected, drew her hand back and stuffed it in the pocket of her jeans. "It may take a lifetime to decipher the bastard, or it may never be deciphered, because there are no other samples."

The only one of its kind. Like the last of a species that could disappear in a blink. Extinct. The thought made her swallow. She stared at the object that had become her life's singularity. Her gaze wandered over the spiral of symbols that, after almost four millennia, remained a mystery. "The most perplexing message of all time, but I'll go to my grave before I give up."

(Never give up!!)

Her hand crept to the pendant that lay against her breastbone: a hematite disk the diameter of a liquor shot glass, hanging on a fine gold chain. She gently tugged it from the neck of her polo shirt and held it toward him. "Roman, did I ever tell you the story about this?"

He waved toward a damask wingback chair by the desk. "Sit. Tell."

The daypack hanging from her shoulder bulged with books from her home office. She sank into the chair and let her pack slide to the floor. As she moved, he watched her separate the air, as if parting warm water, noted how her hair flowed around her neck, immersed in the supple curves of her shoulders and waist. A sigh pushed its way up his chest and dissipated.

"A week after I turned seventeen, a package arrived. No name, no return address, no note, nothing but a small box with this inside." The tip of her index finger lightly brushed the engraved markings: a circle with seven dots, a flower with eight petals. "My father and Livia," she felt her lips tighten, "my stepmother, wondered if I had some secret admirer, but I didn't. No one in my family knew anything about it or what the marks meant, but it was so mysterious that it ignited my interest in ancient writing. I've worn it ever since. When I attended Faucounau's symposium on the Phaistos Disk, I learned that these same marks are found on the Disk. That was it—a lifelong obsession." She gave him a tight smile. "We all need one, right?"

(What is your place in history?)

(What will YOU be remembered for?!)

For surviving teenagehood with you, *Livia, you gold-plated bitch. Leave me alone.* A cramp flared in her belly. *When will I exorcize that voice? Christ!*

A memory flashed through her: storming out the front door of her family home in West Seattle, fiery with teenage angst. "Gatsby, stop!" The shift in Livia's voice—muted, almost trembling—as she murmured, "RUZ WER DAN..."

That was the only time she ever spoke to me with tenderness. Was it sincere or just one of her manipulative mind games?

She glanced at Roman's desk; the mountain of paperwork spoke of curriculum design rather than vacation. She could imagine him, over the next few months, banging away on a medieval Selectric typewriter while she emailed PDF documents to the *International Journal of Language and Epigraphy.*

Roman pushed up the sleeves of his sweater and picked up a pen as if preparing to take notes. "The Disk. Now tell me, what are the extant theories?"

She rolled her eyes. "How long do you have? There are hundreds of theories, and every would-be Champollion..."

"Who?"

"Jean-François Champollion, credited with decipherment of the Rosetta Stone. Every linguistic wannabe claims that his translation is indisputable. It could be an alternate Mycenaean Greek or ancient Minoan. It's claimed to be a prayer, an epic hero poem, a calendar, a board game…let's see, a language primer, a call to war, an astrological map. Some nutcase in Australia says it's a portal to a parallel universe." She snorted. "Shall I go on?"

"Absolutely!" He scribbled on a ruled notepad. "And the spiral design? Most writing systems are horizontal, right to left or vice versa, but how did the artist draw the symbols in a spiral shape? More important, why?"

She propped one boot atop the opposite knee. "He could have affixed the tablet to a wheel with a hub. Most likely, it was turned by hand, because the symbols weren't drawn, they were imprinted with stamps, the same way that the metal keys punched out letters on manual typewriters. It's the first movable type. The first typewriter, you could say. Staller has some good color images. Here, I'll show you." She hefted the backpack from the floor, pawed through it, and lifted out a book.

As she pushed the papers on Roman's desk into a pile and opened *The Mystery of the Phaestos Disk*, the pipe between his lips bobbed like a conjurer's wand. "Amazing." He gazed at a full-page photo of the artifact. His finger traced across the spiral of symbols: plants, warriors, trees, faces, animals, temples. "Clearly not Egyptian hieroglyphs, and not cuneiform."

Gatsby leaned over the desk. "It's dated about 1850 BCE, the same time that Linear B was coming into use."

He frowned. "Remind me."

"It's a syllabic script, the proto-Greek that predated alphabetic Greek by several centuries. Michael Ventris and John Chadwick are credited with the decipherment, and their efforts were confirmed—supported, at least—by tablets inscribed in Cypriot and Linear B."

"Something like decipherment of the Rosetta Stone?"

"In a way. It's the same process. Writing the same message in differing scripts allows apples-to-apples translation."

"What would proto-Greek look like?"

Gatsby reached across the desk, tugged the yellow notepad from his hand, turned it sideways, and sketched a series of symbols.

"Ai-ku-pi-ti-jo—the syllabic presentation of *Aiguptios*, translated as *Egypt or Egyptian*. About eighty symbols have been translated, but the jury's still out on a few."

"Impressive!"

She looked down at the photo of the Disk. "Impressive will be when I crack the symbolic language of Disk, if it even *is* a language. Archeolinguists around the globe will shit themselves."

Roman's eyebrows popped up as he stood to walk toward the bookshelf. "While singing your name or cursing you?"

"It's the *last* undeciphered script, Roman." The heel of her boot connected to the floor with a *bam*. "The last bloody one! You know what that means!"

He nodded. "Some epigrapher's brass ring."

"It's an Aeon, the most prestigious award in antiquities sciences. Big Athens party, funding for life, the whole shebang."

He turned on her with a frown. "My god. You're *that* determined to follow in her footsteps?"

Her hand dropped to the notepad, but rather than releasing the pen, her fingers tightened until they flushed. "We both know—"

(What is YOUR place in history?!)

"—that there's no second place in this field, Roman."

A buzz broke her thoughts. She fumbled in the pocket of the backpack for her smartphone, and a message appeared on the screen.

```
The ancient chakra did align
To bring the argonauts new wine
Captives now with shields do
   Escape the thistles 242
Hark a dog can bark in vain
The lioness in endless chain
```

Άνοιξε τα μάτια σου στην αλήθεια
Ο γραφέας είναι ψεύτης
Ο κόσμος εξαπατήθηκε

"What...what the bloody hell is this?"

Roman walked over and stood at her side, and her eyes flew over the words. "*Chakra* is Sanskrit for wheel. Argonaut, shield, thistle, dog..." She stared at the screen, mouth working silently, until Roman poked her arm.

"What is it?"

"These are symbols from the Disk. The Godart sign names!" Her breath hitched. "Some researchers refer to the Disk as 'the wheel,' and two forty-two is the total number of symbols."

Roman swiped at his forehead with the back of a brown hand. "Good lord."

"But these three lines are Greek." She studied the words and mouthed the words slowly as she translated. "Open your eyes to the truth. The scribe is a liar. The world has been deceived."

They glared at each other like predators.

"Has to be a prank. Some archeologist wannabe tracked down my cell number. Damn it!"

Roman leaned in and pointed at the screen. "Hang on, I think there's more. Scroll down."

As she scrolled with a fingertip, two lines rose into view.

```
      M. AFFIATO
63A BREWER STREET W1F 0LA
```

They blurted in unison, "Soho?"

Gatsby jammed the phone into her backpack and slung the pack and her jacket over her shoulder. The heels of her boots slammed into the Persian rug and then pounded the oak flooring as she sprinted toward the door.

He leaped up to run after her. "Wait!"

The Volvo lurched as she sped down the M11 toward Soho, London's district of ethnic restaurants and recording studios—the razzle dazzle of Carnaby Street, the sticky titillation of sex shops and strip clubs, and the thriving gay scene comingled with theater critics.

The scribe is a liar? The world has been deceived?

Her chest billowed as her fingers tightened on the steering wheel. *Who has the balls to make cryptic, anonymous claims about the Disk? Is someone else as intent on it as I am?*

A dark pang struck at her mind and gut at the same time. *Or intent on me?*

CHAPTER 3

She clambered from the car and hurried down Shaftesbury Avenue, a busy boulevard intersected by pedestrian-only streets. Shoppers wandered by as evening-hours shops and bars began to turn on their lights.

She shoved past them and turned onto Brewer Street. The bright, neon signs of an adult store announced SEX! MOVIES! FUN TOYS! Tucked between a Chinese pharmacy and a vintage clothing shop called Big Bang, she spotted a tiny store with 63A etched on the front door. The sign above it read in spidery, gothic script THE SORCERER'S APPRENTICE.

She leaned against the door and stepped into a carpeted lobby. Muted lighting reflected off glass cases containing a dizzying assortment of paraphernalia: gold rings, cups, ropes, silk scarves, dice, feathers, crystal spheres, playing cards splayed as if merrily tossed and then abandoned. The walls were heavy with Oriental tapestries and posters.

She spotted an antique cabinet sitting against a wall at her left; tinkling sounds seemed to be coming from it. Stepping closer, she placed it as the sort of maniacally happy organ music heard on an amusement park calliope, spinning with rainbow horses. Under the melody, she heard metallic ticking, like the sound of a toy train chugging around a track.

The doors at the top of the cabinet opened with a *pop*.

While the ticking continued, a puppet dressed in harlequin garb emerged. Its black plastic eyes blinked; its watch-work legs bounced with the music. The white tunic fluttered; the silk pantaloons, checkered with red, black, yellow, and green diamonds, billowed in time. The clicking slowed and became a steady tick-tock as the puppet's arm raised and its hand stretched forward, clutching a slip of paper.

Gatsby inched closer to read THE ATHENAEUM.

Only one route was available to her left and down a shadowy hallway. *Alone in a weird novelty shop in Soho? At night? Oh boy.*

She wobbled at the edge of her safety zone, groaning as curiosity and anxiety churned through her. It hurt more to resist than to give in. Digging in her shoulder bag, she pulled out her smartphone. After the recorded greeting, she whispered, "Roman, I'm at 63A Brewer Street. It's some weird novelty shop called The Sorcerer's Apprentice. If you don't hear from me in one hour, call the police." She ended the call and gripped the phone as she walked forward.

Speakers hidden somewhere above quavered with the opening triplet of Bach's "Toccata and Fugue in D Minor" for pipe organ. At the end of the hallway, she stopped before a solid black door and read the sign above it: *THE ATHENAEUM.*

She pulled in a deep breath and pushed. At first, there was nothing but blackness—then, a few meters away, a gold light began to flutter, like turbulent firelight. A shape wavered within the light. Like a developing photograph, the shape slowly emerged. A human form floated as if standing atop a platform, and as the contours of the head and face became recognizable, the sphere of light erupted.

She jumped back with a shout as the shape was engulfed in fire. As quickly as they had burst into life, the flames died into a circle of clusters, glowing like coals, on the marble floor.

The overheads magically rose to full, flooding the room with light. It was stunning—as gleaming as a Venetian ballroom, adorned with crystal chandeliers and sconces, Sotheby's-worthy Persian rugs, a Pramberger grand piano, settees, and Greco-Roman statuary that stood as stoic as kings. The white marble floor with an undulating pattern glistened as if every inch had been lovingly polished by hand.

Standing within the glowing circle, the man appraised her with a toothy smile. "Impressed?"

She saw bushy, black hair and a Van Dyke beard-mustache combo, highlighted with wisps of grey, a judicious forehead, and eyes that tugged upward at the edges, giving him the look of a man who took joy in crimes of passion. As he drew a hand to his neck, the floor-length cape—

burgundy, susurrus, and sensual—surged around his body. Gold buttons and trim on the cape and trousers caught and reflected the lights like hand-cut crystal.

She stared, rooted, and finally tested her voice. "Sh— should I be impressed?"

Around the room she saw armchairs and long Chesterfield couches covered in a velvety fabric, red as sangria. The walls, covered with velveteen paper, were crowded with framed, Vaudeville-era posters—elephants and skeletons, spheres floating in space, winged doves, vixens draped in diaphanous gowns, roaring tigers hurtling from cages, top hats and turbans, white gloves, black tuxedos, coiled snakes, stylized drawings of spirals, and myriad mechanisms of capture.

Alexander, Crystal Seer: Knows All, Sees All, Tells All
Hermann the Great: World of Mystery!
Carter: Enchanted Palace
Thurston, Master Magician: Europe's Greatest Sensation; Million Dollar Mystery
Chung Ling Soo: Conjurer of the Ages
Malini: Astounding Illusionist
Kellar's Greatest Wonder: The Most Daring Illusion of the Age!

"You're a magician?"

"I have numerous titles, but that is one of them. Populus vult decipi ergo decipiatur." He winked as if he'd cheerfully revealed a national secret.

"The people wish to be deceived. Therefore, let them be deceived."

He nodded.

A frown creased her forehead. "I think I'm starting to underst..."

"Dr. Donovan, do not presume to understand anything you see or hear in this place."

The text message flashed through her mind. "How do you know who I am?"

As he crossed the room, he moved with the fluidity of the man who knows his charm can draw blood. The wake of his cape rippled as he strode to a liquor bar that overflowed with stemware: carafes, decanters, toasting flutes, tumblers. The mirrored cabinet behind it held a lavish collection of spirits. He wrestled open a bottle of Courvoisier and hoisted two brandy snifters.

"Ahh, but I know much about you." As he poured, his expression shifted to appraisal. "How delicious. You do not look anything like I imagined. I pictured freezer burn in Versace." His eyes caressed her from collar bone to pubis while his tongue clucked. "Entirely wrong. You are extraordinarily fit. Field hockey? Lacrosse? Some pitch where sweaty amazons chase each other, no doubt. Who could know that such an athletic housing contained a world-class mind." He held out a glass. "But my apologies, I have not made a proper introduction. Macèo Affiato."

The liqueur, dark as death, quivered in the glass in his outstretched left hand. Where the small finger should have been, she saw a scarred stump.

She snatched the glass from him while scanning the room for something heavy enough to crack his skull. "What the hell was that message about?"

He flourished an arm toward the claw-foot Chesterfield sofas arranged in an L shape. "Come, let us sit." They settled in the cushions as Affiato twirled his snifter. "Now we may converse like civilized persons."

Without taking her eyes off him, she sat her glass on the mahogany table, carved to resemble a trumpeting elephant, by her left arm. "Dandy. Now who the fuck are you?"

He roared with laughter. "Brilliant and passionate! Oh yes, I like you already. An excellent beginning for a business relationship."

"A *what*??"

"Venerable Dr. Donovan, tell me." He sat back, legs wide, cape undulating around him, and swallowed a mouthful of cognac. "What do you want more than anything? What have you *always* wanted?"

"Jesus. I've had enough." She rose.

"Wait, wait, sit, and let me explain everything."

She slowly sank back onto the couch, barely restraining the need to throttle answers out of him or sprint for the door.

"You have thirty seconds to explain what I'm doing in your little shop of horrors."

"You deserve to know. As I said, I am a magician, but that is not my sole pursuit. More important than legerdemain, I am on a quest, a hunt for the artifact of which you have made a very thorough study. You do know the prize of which I speak." He gave her a look that invited treachery.

"The Phaistos Disk?"

He threw his arms out as if to embrace the universe. "Ecco!"

"What do *you* know about it? Or my interest in it?"

"You have made your interest, as you say, in it well known. Your innumerable monographs. The many conferences and organizations for which you are a key advisor or speaker. Anyone researching the Disk can learn your love affair with it with ease." He exhaled softly as if teasing a concubine's nape.

I have worked with archeological societies, scholars, amateurs, linguists, and libraries, so my fingerprints all over the place, but who IS this madman?

"Dopo tutti, you are the world's foremost expert on the attributes of the Phaistos Disk. That is why I need you."

"For what?"

He leaned forward to run her through with a stare. "To find the real Disk."

The scribe is a liar, the world has been deceived. "What are you saying?"

"As I suggested in my message, the Disk on display at the Heraklion Archeological Museum—the one that is to all the world such an astounding mystery—is a fake. I must find the real Disk. With your help, I will do so."

Gatsby squeezed her eyes shut, fighting the urge to succumb to the embrace of the velvet sofa. This unbelievable claim, juxtaposed against a series of bewildering events, felt like a lucid nightmare. Her weirdness bubble was about to burst. *I've tripped into fucking Wonderland.*

"A fake? Right." She downed a gulp of Courvoisier. "Says who?"

As he leaned closer, she smelled his breath, sugary from the liqueur but laced with something even sweeter, something viscerally intoxicating, the perfume of candlelight and sweat and ritual defloration.

"Of course. My burden of proof, the story that must convince you. How could I know that it is a forgery when the world's top curators do not?"

She glanced at a poster on one wall. A gentleman wearing a jeweled turban held up playing cards while a red-jacketed figure with pointed ears, crazed eyes, and curved horns glared from the other side of a card table. The caption above the turban blared CARTER BEATS THE DEVIL!

"Ancient history is my passion. Throughout my life, I have traveled the world as an amateur archeologist and anthropologist, learning the fields through my travels. As you can see, I am also something of a collector of antiquities. When I lived in Greece, I befriended a businessman named Kyro Doumas. I learned that he had become involved in a plot to steal the Disk from the Heraklion and replace it with a fake. He later told me that the switch was indeed a success, and the museum never detected the crime, but he did not reveal the hiding place of the real Disk before he died." He lowered his chin. "I believe he was murdered for what he knew."

She snorted. "*That* is an imaginative story, but if it could possibly be true, and you know who stole the Disk, wouldn't you know where it is now?"

"I do not, and that is precisely the question I bring to you. Maybe Doumas gave the Disk to an associate. Maybe it is hidden in a private library. Maybe it is buried in the sand. Who knows."

What the hell is his connection with this? Why would a magician be interested in artifacts, lost or not?

He fondled his goatee with the four fingers of his left hand, and the gold rings chimed like tiny Tibetan gongs. "No doubt you question my fascination with the Disk. As I said, archeology has long been my passion. Learning that the Disk was switched for a fake and the price was Doumas's life, *and* that the real Disk is missing, I determined to find it. It *must* be recovered."

The alcohol was making her eyeballs jitterbug.

"Imagine holding in your hands this object of such astounding power and mystery. Who could not leap at that opportunity? It is the world's most unique treasure, and my objective is to find it and return it to its rightful place."

A poster emblazoned with nightmarish pink and black swirls caught her eye: *Kellar's Greatest Wonder: The Most Daring Illusion of the Age!*

Or the most daring delusion *of the age?*

"Affiato, listen, I'm a translator, a good one, but I'm not a bloody treasure hunter. Why the hell would you waste your time—and infinitely worse, *my* time—with this load of bullshit?"

His smile flared, displaying inhumanly white teeth. "Indeed. To recover the real Disk, I need a keen professional who knows her way around archeological artifacts. One who knows the right questions to ask. It must be a person with a strong desire to preserve renowned artifacts, especially *this* one. Travel will be necessary, so the seeker must be fit and not saddled by traditional employment or children." His hands moved continuously, his fingers rippling in patterns as if shuffling a deck of cards.

She mentally replayed the message that she had left for Roman.

His face darkened to sober intensity. "The Disk is not only my Holy Grail, Dr. Donovan, it is *yours*. I know of your publications. I know the professional societies that you have dumbfounded with your ability to decipher ancient inscriptions. I know that *you* know the Phaistos Disk is the single sample of its kind and may well be the last undeciphered script in the world—the *last*. If you are credited with recovering the real Disk, can you imagine the accolades? I have no doubt that you can. You will be the new Howard Carter, the Richard Leakey, the Indiana Jones of the millennium." He burbled laughter. "Foundations will clamber to fund you. The acclaim will provide you with a lifetime of opportunities. Imagine walking across that stage to accept your prize. Imagine the thunderstorm of applause!"

The scene materialized in her mind:

...the International Institute of Archeological Sciences in Athens, the packed auditorium, the tuxedoed audience standing to applaud as millions across the globe watched on screens

...striding toward Minister of Academia Hellenique Dimitri Petrou and bowing

...Petrou gracing her shoulders with the indigo sash

...the radiant gleam of the Aeon medal

The voice charged through her like a manic-depressive drill sergeant.

(PUSH HARDER, then push some more! Never stop, never give up! Never settle for second best! The best opportunities come only once, so you grab them before someone else does, hear me? NO MATTER WHAT IT TAKES, you little stoat, do you understand??)

I'll take that bloody award, just like you did, Livia. She grimaced at the bitter taste on her tongue. *But even that wouldn't be enough. I'll win the recognition that was your heroin and then tell you why I endured the hell of your...*

Affiato's voice broke through her thoughts. "...will be allowed greater access than anyone else, making *you* the person most likely to decipher it, and there it is on a clay platter—your immortal glory."

Her heart pounded so hard that she winced. *If there is an iota of truth to his insane story, this is a once-in-a-lifetime opportunity. More than that. For the person who recovers a stolen Disk, the world will stand still, but for the person who deciphers it? Breaking a code that has baffled every scholar who tried?*

Dizziness swelled over her, as if she were spinning, air rushing over her face, thousands of eyes straining to catch a glimpse of the woman whose lifetime of research yielded both an Aeon and the discovery of a lifetime. Of the century. While every part of her leaped to shout *YES,* everything about Affiato, his velvet sofas and Courvoisier, his Daliesque spectacle of fire, and his story about an undetected museum theft screamed *HOAX*.

She leveled a stare at him. "What makes you think that any of this sounds remotely plausible? This ludicrous story you've thrown at me—how am I supposed to believe a word of it?"

His grin made her think of macaques baring their incisors before a brawl. "Improbable stories are the best stories. I don't care whether you believe it or not. I'm concerned only with your actions."

She pulled in a breath and slowly blew it out. "I have to think about this."

He raised an arm as if to pluck something out of the air. Sweeping his hand out and toward her, he presented a white business card and draped into the sofa, the cape undulating like a wave machine. His voice was a rumble.

"Don't think too long, Dr. Donovan. A clock is ticking."

CHAPTER 4

She moved through the lobby of Polemistís Myaló, the trendy new dojo on Dinokratous that was overflowing with students. Her muscles ached from the spinning hook kick that had been added to the taekwondo class; her thoughts fluttered around feints, combinations, attacks, and counterattacks. She leaned against the front door.

Just before it closed, they blasted forward and tackled her.

She used the first man's momentum to spin him clockwise as she dug her fingers around his collar bone. While she stomped on the navicular bone of his instep, she ducked right. He fell to the ground. In the next instant, she grabbed the elbow of the second attacker flying toward her and flipped him so that he sprawled face down. She crashed onto his back, wrapped her legs around his neck in a chokehold, and squeezed until his face flushed. Gasps popped from his mouth.

Hassan slowly sat up. He panted as he rubbed his foot and shot her a pissed look. "Sharmoota! Shit! I was going dancing tonight!"

Dacea uncurled and rolled off the second man, checking her elbows and palms for scrapes. She tucked her t-shirt back into her jeans. In the attack, the *qunae* had slipped down to her neck. The plain scarf of black cotton, knotted at the back of her head, was the mask that kept her face hidden, the armor that protected her from ridicule. She tugged it upward to cover everything but her eyes and the top half of her nose.

Niko rolled over on the asphalt and flopped onto his back with a groan. "Auugggh! Not bad, Saja. For a beginner."

"Ευχαριστώ." *Thank you.* She gave Hassan a snarky look. "You need more lessons, bint il-kalb." *Daughter of a dog.*

Hassan laughed as all three wobbled to their feet.

She smiled at Niko's frayed t-shirt—the consolation prize in the dojo's level 1 competition, more a badge of shame than a reward. He panted, "How long…have you trained…to defuse attack?"

Since my wretched birth. "A while."

"Are you in the tournament?"

"Maybe. I have other training that week."

"In what?"

"Krav Maga."

The young men exchanged glances, their eyes widening.

Dacea gave them a dismissive nod, and they traded jokes as they watched her walk down the street, headed for Xenokratous.

By the time she reached Dionysiou Areopagitou, she had to push through noisy crowds. The district was chaotic at the end of the business day—bustling with workers, white collared or brown suited, all ready for dinners of lamb and pita bread. Buses moaned, cabs honked. Kolonaki merchants reviewed the day's profit off their tourists; they chattered in Greek and English as they tugged curtains closed, locked their doors, and set security alarms.

The apartment in a northeast neighborhood was less than a kilometer from Dove4 in Plaka. Two members of the BOAT—the ruling council of the Circle—lived at Dove4. Tess Miranovski was the executive lead. Anastasia Hoda directed IT networks, and the third member, Jayna Dhar, the tactical and weapons lead, lived at Spindle5. Although the BOAT paid the SWORD's rent and living expenses, they did not know her address. They did not know her real name or even her multiple aliases. They had never seen her face.

She pushed her door open and walked into a living room furnished with Spartan chairs and tables, all neutral shades with no pattern. Dropping onto the couch, she stretched out on her back with a sigh and tugged off the black percaline that covered the lower half of her face. When her fingers stroked the scars, the ridges spoke of a soul that had been excised. The first faces she had known rose in her memory: brown and wrinkled as walnuts, their eyes fluttering with suspicion. Badra's voice whistled through her like a winter wind.

...a heap of discarded clothing and rags, someone's garbage, but we saw it move

...you were wrapped in a fabric bearing the image of the ROSETTE

Then Jaleen's voice, dark with scorn.

...Someone wanted you in the Circle. Why, I will never know.

Badra and Jaleen had shared a one-bedroom apartment in Souq al Jum'aa, a neighborhood east of Tripoli. The city of one million was called "the bride of the sea" in travel guides, but even after the Arab Spring and Gaddafi's death, it was still a war zone. Government leadership was disjointed; shortages of food, gasoline, and cash led to shootings, but the residents had learned to not depend on police for protection. The two women had been best friends since childhood, and while many Circle members believed that they were lesbians—frowned on but not illegal in Libya—they insisted that the relationship was platonic.

She never attended public school. While barely more than a toddler, the BEEHIVE began teaching her history, arts, biology, chemistry, sociology, and computer science. She became fluent in Arabic, Greek, and English, but most importantly, she learned WATER. All members were required to master the syllabic language, and all were forbidden to reveal or use it outside the Circle.

As she was trained and progressed through her lessons, Badra and Jaleen could not have overlooked Dacea's mastery, but they never commented on it.

Who had wrapped her in the fabric, imprinted with the image of the Circle, but left her on the street to die? She wondered. Exposed at birth, they might have said in ancient Rome. She asked her guardians too many times to count, but they did not know or would not say. They only knew that the child they had been ordered to raise was a brat. Their disdain for her was illustrated by the scars littered across her skin. Her body became the map of their anger. Cuts from knives, too shallow to cause permanent damage, only anguish. Bruises from beatings.

A moan wavered on her lips. Age five. The BEEHIVE began my training in martial arts, guns, and poisons. They didn't protect me from the threat behind closed doors.

When she was twelve, she came home from the souk with the wrong fruits. The gash that Badra sliced into her cheek became infected. The ulcerative gingivitis she had endured for more than a year, aggravated by lack of dental care and dirty drinking water, turned into fusospirochetal gangrene, also called Noma. The disease ate away the flesh and destroyed the left half of her face.

No doctors or hospitals. "Not important enough," they said. Children, shopkeepers, strangers on the street…the terror on their faces. They assumed leprosy. It may as well have been. Her fingers grappled at the cloth that had covered her face for nineteen years. They treated me like a slave until…A strangling sound pushed through her lips. Fifteen years old with no money. No friends or family. Nothing but anger and the will to survive.

Her fingers churned against the cloth of the couch until it began to shred.

They will KNOW how well they trained me. She whirled from the couch and dashed to the bathroom. Retching over the toilet, she squeezed her eyes shut as bursts of hot air rippled the water.

They will pay. I add them to the list of WHITE BIRD targets. They will PAY! She smacked her hand against the toilet seat. Out! How do I fucking get OUT of this life?!

The two-line message sizzled through the OAR network, marked for delivery to the SWORD and the BOAT.

```
The infinite chakra serves the Guardian
The Guardian decays in the cage of time
```

CHAPTER 5

"He said *what*?!" Roman's voice cracked.

Gatsby switched the phone to her other ear, squirming to get comfortable on her artichoke-green loveseat. She reached for a wool throw near her feet and pulled it up over her legs. "He's claiming that the Disk in Crete is a fake and wants me to help him find the real artifact."

Sputtering popped over the line while she sipped from a black mug, the one she had picked up at the Musée du Louvre gift shop. Outside her flat, she heard foot traffic picking up on King's Road. Finches made kamikaze dives in the birch trees.

"He's fabricating this rubbish to pull you into some kind of black market trade, GM. Archeological bounty hunters around the globe work without a trace of ethics. If he's a master of deception, as any magician worth his salt would be, he will play you like a toy and then toss you in the dust bin!"

She set her mug on an end table. "Evidence is the first order of business, of course, so I have to convince Alexiou to test the Disk, and I've…"

"Who?"

"Stephanos Alexiou, the curator at the Heraklion." Memories of past conversations with Alexiou seeped through her mind like an oil slick. "I get him to do a thermoluminescence test, it shows whether the Disk is genuine, and that's it. Affiato and his bag of tricks go packing. End of story."

Roman's voice was a whisper. "What if it's *not* genuine?"

She huffed. "Roman, what are the chances of that? I have every reason to think that his story is designed for his own amusement or some illicit purpose. Perhaps there's no doubt about the authenticity of the Disk and *he's* planning to steal it, and if that's the case, he's given himself away, and someone should run a stick into his wheel, which is exactly what I'll do."

More grumbling over the line. "If you collaborate with this insane yobbo in any way, be very careful." A pause. "I don't want to see anything happen to you."

A smile tugged at her lips. "Thanks for your concern." Out of nowhere, the ghostly phrase slid through her, and she pulled in a breath. "Roman, you like deconstructing mysteries. Ever play around with cryptography?"

"Ahm, on occasion. Why? I thought that was your area of expertise."

"Translating ancient languages is a far cry from encryption, especially in the digital era. I'm trying," she paused, "trying to unravel this three-syllable phrase, RUZ WER DAN. Something my infamous stepmother said when I was a teenager, but I've heard it repeatedly for years."

"RUZ WER DAN? No idea. Why do you feel it's worth investigating?"

Her toes curled under the wool throw. "Because of the way she said it. The look on her face, sound of her voice. As if for one second, a decent human being was hiding inside."

"Did she ever say it again?"

"No. A one-time occurrence."

"Sorry, GM. I'd put you in touch with a colleague in the math department, but he deals only with computer languages."

She sighed and closed her eyes. "Never mind. I must be trying to distract myself rather than deal with Affiato."

"Exactly what he wants you to do, most likely, so don't give in. Keep me posted."

"I will."

They said goodbye, and Gatsby sank lower into the loveseat.

Since the internship offer from the British Museum and the move to London ten years ago, her flat had been a juxtaposition of simplicity and overfilled bookshelves. On the coffee table, two books lay sprawled: *The Mystery of the Phaestos Disk* and *Linear B and Related Scripts: Reading the Past*. She flipped them over and stared at the stylized images of the Disk on the covers. The symbols stared back at her as if desperately trying to speak.

She shivered.

A short walk up Sloane Street, and she was at Hyde Park and wandering through the lawns, trees, fountains, manicured flower beds, and walking paths. As she meandered, she saw the symbols everywhere.

An elderly woman, meandering down the walkway, her Jack Russell barking and tossing against the lead. *DOG— A110.*

A hill of pink and orange tulips. *FLOWER—A1, A13, A76, B70.*

A landscape crew, spreading fresh sod and pulling weeds. *THISTLE—A7, A56, B83, B109.*

A flock of pigeons circling in lazy spirals. *BIRD—A32, A78 and B55.*

A couple, both holding the hands of their chortling toddler. *CHILD—A5.*

A jogger, adjusting the settings on his iPod. *RUNNER— A4, A19, A41, A66, A83, A118, B44, B58, B69, B86, B94.*

The glyph for woman. *A29, A94, B20, B57.*

His voice rumbled in her like echoes in a deep-sea trench: *The Disk is not only my Holy Grail, Dr. Donovan, it is yours.*

And of all the treasure seekers who have tried to find it, how many met a particularly nasty end? She turned abruptly and headed back to King's Road.

Inside her flat, she finished the leftovers in the refrigerator—perhaps a macaroni-and-cheese bake, but it was hard to tell—rinsed out the bowl and reached toward the dish drainer. Her hand stopped in midair. *Where did I see it? In his...what the hell was it called? THE ATHENAEUM. I saw something that looked like the Disk. What was it?* She sat the bowl into the drainer, frowning. *I saw something important there, I know it.*

Shaking her head, she wandered from the kitchen and headed to the living room. Once nestled on the loveseat, she palmed her phone and dialed. The line connected.

"I knew you could not resist my charm." His voice dripped with arrogance.

"There's *nothing* about your narcissism that I can't resist, Affiato. My only question is whether the Disk at the Heraklion is genuine. We answer that, and our business is done. Understood?"

"Of course, but if it *is* a fake, you vow to help me find the real artifact." Affiato paused. "Do you agree?"

"Do you have any idea what you're proposing? No matter how famous it, locating an object that's only twenty-five centimeters will be impossible unless someone points it out on a neon-lit billboard. It could never make its way into a museum, because any curator, even one with even the most rudimentary knowledge of Grecian antiquities, would identify it. It could have been sold on the black market. Hidden in a private art collection or a basement. Dumped as trash or buried in the Sahara. It could be anywhere on the bloody planet!"

"Indeed, and because of that, I will provide you with extremely good clues and set you on the hunt."

"*Set* me? What are *you* going to do?"

"I will deliver pertinent information but leave the legwork to you, therefore leaving the credit to you. I don't care about the accolades, but you do. I only want to see the Disk recovered."

He's lying. The reasons to refuse collected in her mind. *Collaborators get in the way, and they lie and steal whatever they can.*

"Fine. I work better on my own."

She heard music in the background. Her mind tiptoed back to The Sorcerer's Apprentice, the fiery illusion, the Courvoisier. Her neck muscles tensed.

"The best minds operate thus. Geniuses have no need for interns."

Who is the genius here? Her foot tapped rapidly against the leg of the loveseat. "*If* the disk in Crete is a fake, and *if* through some miracle of luck we find the real Disk, I get unlimited access. I can remand it to the Heraklion or any other museum. Its dispossession is my call." She heard a sound like liquid sloshing into a tumbler.

"I cannot imagine you would want it any other way. Marvelous! We begin. You will contact the Heraklion."

She felt him breathing down her neck and Livia's voice skittering through her like a wolf spider. "I know the curator, Stephanos Alexiou. I'll call him tomorrow."

The tone was slick as ice. "Do it now."

CHAPTER 6

Aria Vlahos quickened her pace, pushing by the shoppers who meandered down Voukourestiou Street and peered in the window cases at Italian fashions and antique rugs. "SHIP?"

Tereze trotted to keep up with her while fielding rapid-fire questions. "A potential threat to the Circle. A RUNNER is a deserter."

"PEDESTRIAN?"

She scanned the concrete under her heels as if the answer might be hidden there. As a stout woman grappling a bouquet of blood-orange tiger lilies hurried by, the petals stabbed against Tereze's face. "A person unconnected with the Circle."

Vlahos fired volleys. "HELMET."

"An immediate alert."

"BOAT."

"Three-party council, the ruling committee."

"SHELL."

"Country commander."

"RAM."

"Regional commander."

"MAIZE."

"A metro commander."

"BEEHIVE."

"The general membership."

"CAT."

"New recruit."

"OAR."

"The Circle-exclusive server."

"GRASS."

"Reward for work well done."

"HORN."

She glanced away, weighing her word choice. "A very insulting term."

Vlahos slowed, allowing Tereze to coast to her side. "You've done some homework. Now the THISTLE training. Describe the structure and function of the TIARA."

Tereze bit her lip and framed an answer. "It's a weapon, projectile at short range but silent. The material is *Semiarundinaria* bamboo. It fires a dart loaded with the same toxin as the DOLIUM."

"How does the DOLIUM work?"

"It's the Circle-engineered patch. Mimics the action of the sea wasp jellyfish and uses TUNNY."

"Details."

"A toxin synthesized from the sea wasp poison. Toxicity level 6 or supertoxic."

"It's deployment?"

"Attach near a vascular area. The microneedles pierce the dermis. Trying to pull it off accelerates heartbeat and aggravates the barbs to release more toxin. It floods the neuromuscular system and paralyzes the heart, lungs, and brain."

"How fast?"

"Not more than sixty seconds, or rarely."

"Antidote?"

Tereze glanced at her mentor. "There is none."

"Correct. Good. This way."

They dodged Athenian drivers and careened past the five-star restaurant I Kriti. Along with the exuberant chatter of the diners, the smells of lemon, saffron, and cardamom flowed from the doorway and windows.

"What are the Laws of the Circle?"

"We are air—invisible and everywhere." The shoulder bag bumped rhythmically against Tereze's hip as she jogged. "Circle teachings are passed orally, only between members. All members learn WATER and use it only with other members. Members move up by selection of the one leaving the post." She quickly ran her tongue over dry lips.

Vlahos turned on her with a stern look. "One more."

Tereze's smile melted. "RUNNERS do not survive."

The woman's face revealed neither agreement nor judgment. Now navigating Solonos Street, they turned onto

Ippokratous, and Tereze hustled to turn with her. Rows of custard-yellow apartment buildings rose into view. Kids scampered or zoomed by on skateboards; well-kept housewives sat on their balconies, eating lunch and jabbering in Greek.

Vlahos stopped at the second building and opened the security gate; they stepped into a courtyard filled with olive trees and yellow primrose. Water burbled down a stone fountain as they approached the front door of Crab6. "You did pretty good, CAT. Any questions?"

Tereze locked eyes with her. "When do I start?"

Dacea stared at the computer, drumming her fingers impatiently as it booted. *The building is quiet today. The whole city is quiet. Is Kolonaki on holiday? Where did everyone go?*

She sipped from a can of Red Bull. *That dispatch from the HAMMER, out of the blue. The old message about the infinite chakra, the guardian in the cage. Disturbing, especially given the timing—BOOMERANG is live, WHITE BIRD in six days.* The infamous riddle had circulated through the Circle for years. Some guessed that it pointed to the location of the Disk, but no one reliably knew its meaning or origin.

It's far too vague to guess at. Why bring up that hoary riddle now? I don't like it.

Vlahos's notes cascaded onto the screen.

PRIORITY 1 Communications
SHELL, RAM, MAIZE commanders—update HW/SW, STAR SEED
OAR—access code QAM
TEMPLE—hack scans 24/7
Members—WATER, oral and sign language

PRIORITY 2 Labs
Inventory
Manufacture training for CATs

PRIORITY 3 Defense Training
BEEHIVE—defense training, weapons, escape
Truth detection, method acting, body language

Who has the deepest skills? She typed "Tap Tokada" and then thought, *What was the term Sanchez used for the THISTLE division? Right. Wet work.*

She glanced at the on-screen clock; a bell-shaped icon on the screen was glowing. A teleconference program loaded, and panels filled the desktop with multicolored rectangles that morphed into live webcam feeds. The BOAT members logged on and gave the updated password.

"Dhar. Tan ruz."

"Miranovski. San tot."

"Hoda. Ker sil."

Dacea clicked CONNECT so that all four saw and heard each other. "Convened. THISTLE installations. Dhar, your report."

Jayna Dhar's reserve showed in her flat, robotic voice. "Training and installations complete except Belfast and Palermo. I want to distribute expanded e-learning packets and fine-tune WATER acquisition. Ten more CAT candidates coming in tomorrow."

"Networks. Hoda?"

Anastasia Hoda scratched her cheek. "All functional. Stations in Bern need replacement hardware because some arrived damaged. All upgraded STAR SEEDs have been distributed."

"Don-muz. Miranovski, the status of the labs?"

Tess Miranovski said, "Chemical shipments confirmed for delivery in Mumbai tomorrow."

Dacea nodded. "Next item. This morning—the message from the HAMMER. You all received it?"

In chorus: "Yes."

She recited, "The infinite chakra serves the Guardian, the Guardian decays in the cage of time. That crazy old riddle shows up out of nowhere. Comments?"

All three shook their heads.

"A cryptic message from First Commander, which is an anomaly, and on the surface it looks innocuous, but WHITE BIRD is in six days. The timing can't be arbitrary. Miranovski, follow up and report by 2100."

Miranovski said, "On it."

Dacea scanned the faces, reminded that two feeds streamed from less than a kilometer away, the third from Sicily, yet none of the participants knew her location. "Donmuz. Ser oh san-til un." Accepted. Authorization to sign off.

They logged off. One by one, the feed panels went black.

She took another sip. The caffeine-taurine buzz throttled into a pounding at the back of her head. The chime of an IM made her jump.

HADAD SIGHTED IN BARCELONA

Badra? Her hand crept toward her cheek, the scars hidden beneath the qunae, as the gruff voice wafted through her mind.

(a heap of discarded clothing and rags, someone's garbage)

Not now…focus! She moved on to the next lines.

WHITE BIRD
DOLIUM / BE, PA SHIPMENTS CONFIRMED

Glancing at the clock again, she thought, *Five o'clock in Tel Aviv. THISTLE 1 operation of BOOMERANG is complete.*

She rose, walked to the living room, and grabbed the remote on the low table in front of the sofa. Looking toward the television at the other side of the room, she pushed ON. The newscast was in progress. Synagogue spires rose behind a reporter who spoke breathlessly into her microphone.

"...was arson or an act of terrorism. We are told that Benjamin Tzadok was leading a *minchah* prayer service at the Bet-El Synagogue when the fire broke out. The intense heat sealed the doors shut, trapping more than fifty people inside the building. Most escaped by smashing out the windows, but four people died, including Rabbi Benjamin Tzadok, who was rumored to be linked to Al-Qaeda or the recently revitalized Tzrifin Underground. Municipal investigators are scouring..."

Dacea felt for the pack strapped to her hips and pulled out the STAR SEED. She typed *FIRE A49*

The reporter pushed fluttering strands of hair off her face. "No organization has claimed responsibility. For i24 News, Deborah Aronson reporting from Tel Aviv."

She clicked the TV off and went back to her desk. Settling before the computer, she opened a document and began to type. The WATER syllables pulsed through her mind.

```
             PER-RAN-+TER B113
    WAN-UN-SIL-TUZ5 WUZ-SER> A24
             7KAN-EN-SER
         WOT-DER-MUZ0 WAN-SUZ
             KER-DAN!-AN
         DER& POT-MER-PAN-WER3
```

WATER B113
DOLIUM A24
Install LIONESS in Jerusalem
Confirm Maiduguri 8
Reinsert Palermo 2
Fortify BEEHIVE in Lima

She shook her head. *Invisible and everywhere, just as invisible as the First Commander. Since the fifth year of the Circle, no one has seen the HAMMER face to face. THE mistress of espionage.* She cradled her chin in her hand. *That message with no explanation. It's too odd. There has to be an underlying reason. What game is she playing at? Could it be an outside threat? Our systems are impenetrable.* She took another sip. *Has she detected a SHIP?*

She sent her notes to the BOAT members via OAR. The monitor scuttled with activity; panels opened and disappeared.

It will be soon, and it will be bloody. Will the HAMMER's revolution be as successful as she intends? It must. There is far too much at stake.

CHAPTER 7

Gatsby clicked away from the website. How many sites related to the Disk I have bookmarked? Hundreds, probably, over twenty years of studying this riddle stamped in clay. Leaning back in her computer chair, she watched the finches darting outside the living room window and glanced at the clock on the screen.

Noon. Her foot tapped rapidly on the leg of her chair. She opened the updated videoconferencing program and wheeled her chair toward the camera; its READY light blinked steadily. As she typed the numbers on the keypad, the wording of the email whispered through her mind.

Stephanos:
Two months ago, I provided details for your research on ArchNet. As you know, I have been researching the Phaistos Disk for many years. I believe the Disk must be reexamined and request thermoluminescence testing to verify the dating. More details will be provided when I call tomorrow.
Gatsby Donovan, PhD, CCBE
Lead Consultant, Dept. of Orthography and Translation |
British Museum

Her heart shifted into high gear as the image appeared, slightly pixilated at first and then in sharp focus: a burgeoning second chin, russet eyes hugged by crow's feet, an abbreviated beard, and a cream dress shirt, lazily open at the collar.

"Gatsby!" His voice was as animated as the mop of black hair. "What a pleasure to speak with you again."

"Hello Stephanos. I heard about the tide storms there two days ago."

"Luckily, the damage was mostly in Agios Nikolaos and Chania. Lucky for the museum anyway." He paused. "Now you surprise me with this question about testing. The Phaistos Disk? What is this about?"

She combed her fingers through her hair. "I know it's an odd request, but I have good reason, so hear me out. The Disk may have been stolen and replaced with a fake."

His eyebrows popped, and one side of his mouth curled. "Stolen and replaced with a fake? Ha, that's good. The Disk has been guarded around the clock since it was installed in the Kavvadous Wing fifteen years ago. During our last security audit, CISCOR inspected all systems. Every vibration sensor, inventory control number, infrared and microwave motion detector, every closed circuit camera and temperature control—everything was checked and upgraded." He coughed and managed to make it sound condescending. "Where has your information come from?"

A highly questionable source. "Sorry, I can't reveal that, but the argument was persuasive enough for me to make this call. You need to do the TL test and confirm the age."

He shook his head vigorously. "Impossible. I don't know how the ridiculous rumor has come to you, but it's absurd."

She felt the blood rushing to her cheeks and pounding at the back of her head. "It's a simple TL test, Stephanos. You have the staff and the equipment."

(Never give up, never settle for second!)

She heard blips of static over the London-to-Crete connection.

(Do you understand??)

"A *simple* TL test? Without an extremely good reason, it is not simple. Absolutely not. My security measures are better than the Louvre, and we have never had an incident."

This is too important!

(Are you listening?!?)

The image of herself—eighteen years old, two weeks from moving out of the home she grew up in, leaving behind her father and sister—bloomed in her mind, so intense that it was painful. The nauseating mix of lavender air freshener and Clorox that assaulted her sinuses as she hunkered on the edge of the tub, cradling her head in her hands, imagining her stepmother dashing into the traffic on Fairway Drive. *BAM! Livia pâté! She's the reincarnation of Livia Drusilla, the third wife of Caesar Augustus, who bribed politicians and priests, hated everyone, destroyed families, lied and libeled, killed her family members, even murdered her emperor husband. The embodiment of cruelty in the name of power. Did Dad's trophy wife pick her own name in infancy?*

She smacked her hand against the edge of her chair, and the pain brought her back to the conversation in progress. "I need that test, Stephanos. It will quash the rumor before it goes anywhere, before it defecates on your reputation, because if there's a one-in-a-million chance that it's true, who do you want making the discovery—you and me, quietly, or the International Council for Museum Security?" Her pulse stabbed at her temples. "We both know that even suspicion of fraud is the kiss of death for a world-class museum."

"For god's sake, Gatsby, what the hell are..."

"I'll have the test done, with or without your cooperation, Stephanos. I don't care what it takes."

(Never let go!)

"Oh, you can't be..."

"Will a personal call from Livia Rudden be necessary? Shall I arrange it?" The steel in her voice made her stomach flip-flop.

He sat back, lips tight and eyes darting. "You wouldn't dare."

"Try me."

He blew out a stream of curses in Greek and crushed his arms over his chest. "Αι γαμισου! Christ! Fine! Saulos is out this week. When he's back, I'll have him do the fucking test. Satisfied?"

Are YOU satisfied, Livia?

"Yes."

"I demand complete confidentiality. I cannot allow even a rumor that my museum is storing a forged artifact. Send an NDA before the end of the day, am I clear?"

The thudding in her ears bloomed. "Crystal."

CHAPTER 8

What a dump Crab6 used to be. Crumbling, scheduled for demolition.

When the members at Dove4 in Plaka found it, they agreed that it was suitable as a second location in Athens. They scheduled the renovation and added state-of-the-art security systems. Crab6 transformed into a safe house, meeting site, and training center.

Dacea walked down the stone path toward the entrance.

At fifteen, after a decade of training in martial arts, self-defense, escapes, poisons, and guns, she left the hell of Tripoli and sheltered with Circle members in Libya and Egypt. She quickly moved up the ranks despite her age, became the SWORD, and took up residence at Crab6.

Ellyi Goutala, the SWORD who appointed me. She said I had "fearsome" abilities.

She brushed away the sharp bamboo leaves that brushed her face. To her left, water trickled from a bamboo deer chaser into a granite basin. She gazed up at the eaves. *The cameras are well hidden. No doubt plenty of GRASS went to the installation team.*

She pushed the door open and stepped into the foyer decorated with abstract art. The flooring was an elaborate tile mosaic of swimming fish. The hallways leading left and right were dark except for spots of light rising from frosted sconces. A side door opened with a snick, and a slender woman with cropped, black hair stepped into the foyer. Her silk shirt and trousers rippled against her body as she approached.

"Mil wan ruz-tan oh." Vlahos pointed.

They moved down the right hallway and into a meeting room where rattan chairs were nestled between potted sword ferns. A fire flickered quietly in a gas fireplace.

The message from the HAMMER ghosted through her mind.

```
The infinite chakra
serves the Guardian
The Guardian decays
in the cage of time
```

The message that followed was for Dacea's eyes only.

```
TWO SHIPS IN LONDON
ROSETTE GAUNTLET
IVY9 RECONNAISSANCE
```

The meaning had blazed. *Two infiltrators in London. Threat to the ROSETTE. Assign agents at Ivy9 to investigate and report.*

As they sat, Dacea said, "What did they find?"

The woman's gaze moved over Dacea's face: the black fabric that covered a gnarled cheekbone, the flesh that twisted like rotting meat. Her lips began to shrivel in disgust, so she shifted her gaze to the fireplace. "Browning and Bashir reported this morning. SHIP-1 is an American. An accomplished scholar. She translates inscriptions on archeological artifacts, consults primarily for the British Museum. Two days ago, she went to see SHIP-2, who is a stage performer, an illusionist." She paused. "A male."

"Male?" Dacea jumped at the impulse to voice her shock, but her lifelong training held her back. "That's a first."

"And the woman is the first PEDESTRIAN in my experience."

"Which speaks to the reach of the Circle. We are invisible and everywhere except for the anomalous pockets." She frowned. "What is their connection to the ROSETTE? What would they want?"

"Theft. What else?"

"It wouldn't be the first time."

"Cambier?"

"Our most infamous RUNNER. She managed to steal the ROSETTE twice and elude the THISTLE for decades—she has to be credited for her ingenuity." She paused. "If they even *think* they could acquire it! If they did, we would have to do all we can to *help* them." She pressed a thumbnail against her lip, trying to connect strategic pieces that seemed abrupt and disjointed. "BOOMERANG 1 complete. WHITE BIRD is only days away. The old riddle resurfaces. Two SHIPS, and one of them is male." *And a GAUNTLET on the ROSETTE.* "All at once? What the hell is going on?"

Vlahos shook her head, eyes clouded with confusion.

"I want the follow-up report from Ivy9 before BOOMERANG 2."

"In forty-eight hours? That's a very short window." Vlahos sputtered.

"You heard me. Go."

Vlahos rose, crossed the room, and disappeared down the hallway.

Dacea thought, *My lead LIONESS is very useful but still new. No room for questioning orders, especially from the SWORD. It must not become a pattern.*

She stared into the wavering flames in the fireplace, letting her mind race. *SHIPS, two of them, in London. If necessary, THISTLE agents know how to deploy the DOLIUM.*

The frozen face of the RUNNER rose in her mind. Spiti Deka. White tile, the acrid smell of bleach, a Blahnik strapless bobbing in the toilet.

Dead in eighty seconds.

CHAPTER 9

Gatsby reached toward the carafe in the coffee machine, poured a few ounces of something tar-black and tepid, and sipped. She made a face that mirrored the taste and exiled the mug to the corner of the desk. She glanced out the window, surveying the courtyard: marigolds, ferns, lily pads, and koi fish meandering in a shallow pond. After eight years with the British Museum, Nelson Clevis gave her the office, but she ended up doing most of her work from home and used the museum office only when needing access to certain databases.

Her mind turned back to the meeting with Affiato.

...the heady Courvoisier

...*Kellar's Greatest Wonder: The Most Daring Illusion of the Age!*

...his rumbling voice: *And there it is on a clay platter— your immortal glory.*

A beep signaling a call jolted her. She combed her fingers through her hair, positioned herself in front of the camera, and pushed the ACCEPT button.

"That was quick."

"We had to dismantle five systems just to remove it from the case." Alexiou's expression and ragged breathing matched the feeling that gripped her stomach. "But Saulos managed it. He did operational checks on the TL equipment with two supervisors present. He called me, and when I got to the lab, I told him to run the test again."

Gatsby felt muscles knotting in her lower back. She waited an eternity for his next sentence. "And?"

"And we ran it a third time. The results were consistent each time and well within the standard range of reliability." He pulled at his hair as if watching his career go up in flames and spoke so fast that the words ran together. "It's about thirty years old, made of baked clay comparable to that found in Kamares. The symbols were made with stamps, probably some type of hard rubber, obviously not the material used for the original. Whoever did it had an impossible eye for detail. Every symbol is in the correct space, the right order, on both sides, even the imperfections are recreated—the chip that defaces part of the symbols at A97 and A98 and the scratch overlaying the bow of the BOAT at B103." A muscle beside his mouth twitched. "They knew how to recreate not only elements visible to the eye but the irregularities of the incised radial lines, even the indentations on the edge."

Gatsby saw the thunderclouds gathering in his face.

"A forgery! A goddamned *forgery!*" A bead flew from his lips; his hands did a Saint Vitus dance. "I don't know whether to thank you or have INTERPOL throw you in a bottomless Turkish prison!"

She spoke with the control of a bomb dismantler. "Stop. Stephanos, calm down and think about this. I had nothing to do with this. I *couldn't* have anything to do with it, and you know it." She pulled closer to the screen and stared him in the eye. "Would I be stupid enough to lead you to a forged artifact if *I* had stolen the original? Don't insult me." She struggled to breathe evenly; the sweat from her palms formed dark swaths on her jeans. "Confirm everything. Get third, fourth, fifth opinions, whatever it takes." *The bastard was right! Was it Doumas? Was it HIM?* Her fingertips dug into her thigh.

"I have been..." His voice was leaden. "I have been trying to analyze this without going mad, and I remembered the Cyclades earthquake in 1980, just before Bena was born. There was massive destruction throughout the islands. Four halls were badly damaged, and the museum was closed for eight months. When the renovation was complete, the new security system was installed. Twelve million euro." Quivering slightly, he gazed into space, his eyes dull.

"In the chaos of the earthquake and rebuilding, you think the thief took the opportunity?"

The dark circles around his eyes said that he hadn't slept well for several days. "It's the only explanation that makes any sense, but why?! Why take it and secretly replace it with a fake?! When famous artifacts or artwork are stolen, the museum is always contacted, and the criminals demand the amount for which the piece was insured…"

"And threaten to destroy it if the ransom isn't paid."

"Gatsby, how did you know about this?" The fire in his eyes could melt sand into glass. "You have to tell me!"

She tipped back in her chair and shook her head. "Page two, first paragraph."

"What?"

"The contract we signed, Stephanos. Page two. The findings of this test are as airtight as that case in your museum holding a fake Disk *and* as tight as the identity of my source."

He stared down as if into hell. "I must contact ICMS and IARA." He swallowed. "And explain."

The agony on his face stabbed at her, but the feeling faded as they logged off and the screen went dark.

She turned to face her computer and, with a few clicks, was scanning the BBC news. The lead story flowed around a lurid color photo. The headline read "Fire Destroys Tel-Aviv Synagogue."

A fire destroyed the Bet-El Synagogue in Tel Aviv. The intense heat sealed the doors shut, trapping more than fifty people inside the building. Most escaped by smashing the windows, but four people died, including Rabbi Benjamin Tzadok, who was rumored to be linked to Al-Qaeda or the recently revitalized Tzrifin Underground. Municipal investigators are trying to determine whether it was arson.

She clicked away to other news stories—the new Canadian Prime Minister, cleanup work after an oil spill near Florida, a bombing in Luxor—but realized that she was reading without engaging. Her thoughts revolved like the spiral of the Disk itself.

So much passion devoted to this thing, and it's a fake, while the real Phaistos Disk is lost, somewhere on the planet, hidden and silent. Adrenaline made her heart pound. *Waiting for its liberation. Waiting for ME.*

CHAPTER 10

The subway train screeched to a stop, the doors opened with a Star Trek *wshhhh*, and a robotic voice intoned, "Mind the gap."

Gatsby pressed through a gaggle of midday commuters and up a flight of stairs. She emerged at street level to station signs reading OXFORD CIRCUS and turned east, heading toward Soho.

When she pushed against the door of The Sorcerer's Apprentice, she was surprised to see a young woman hovering over the glass cases filled with magic accoutrement. Petite, platinum blonde hair, haute couture ensemble, and the high-born scent of Crabtree & Evelyn. Gatsby imagined that she was an assistant, a show-biz ingénue with pragmatic morals and a gilded stage name like The Beautiful Demetra. She dissected Gatsby with mascara-lidded disdain.

"I need to see Affiato."

The girl tipped her head as if thinking made it hurt and floated down the hallway.

Charming.

The cape had been traded for a black tuxedo jacket and trousers, and the collar of his ivory shirt was pulled open to reveal a tangled garden of hair. Arms outstretched, Affiato brandished his nine fingers, laden with heavy gold rings, and bounced toward her. He nodded to the girl. "Thank you, Felicity. Why don't you take the afternoon off?"

She gave Gatsby a scowl and slid, like a false memory, toward the front door.

Turning to Gatsby, he murmured, "Dr. Donovan, mi fa molto piacere. Voudriez-vous me joindre dans l'autre salle?"

She followed him down the dark hall, and they stepped through the door into THE ATHENAEUM. Stage props had been hauled in and chaotically stashed about the room: lacquered tables, trimmed with gold acrylic and brass handles; a black box impaled with swords; a dresser piled with locks and keys; a tall contraption resembling a guillotine, complete with a glittering blade; cabinets, crates, and vintage travel trunks of all colors and sizes.

Affiato scampered across the room, bending frequently to adjust knobs and pull levers.

"You're cheery."

"Certainly, and why not? Ars longa, vita brevis, yes? Hippocrates."

She stopped before a curious prop, tall and boxy enough to hold an average-sized adult, that stood upright. The lid was carved to resemble an epicene face. The eyes and mouth expressed neither joy nor sorrow, and a cape of straight hair fell behind its ears and down to the breast. The rest of the container was carved with images of snakes, owls, and hieroglyphics. Three heavy brass locks secured the lid.

He moved toward it, pulled a key from his pocket, and inserted it into each of the locks. They popped, one by one, and Affiato tugged on the lid, grunting from the effort. He placed one foot inside the cavity.

"You see here? The illusionist, or his assistant, is placed inside this beautiful coffin and locked in. Buried alive." He pressed the toe of his shoe against a button at the base of the cavity, and the hidden escape panel silently opened.

"Nice." A pinguid feeling floated on the surface of her thoughts, and she huffed in exasperation. "How can I talk to you when you're fiddling with that thing?"

He patted the lid as if it were a faithful dog and stepped to the Chesterfield sofas at the center of the room, motioning for her to follow. The cushions sighed as they sat. "There. Happy?" He set to fondling his goatee with two fingers. "What have you found?"

"I found that one part of your story is true. Alexiou's team ran the TL test. Three times." She gave the details of the forged artifact's composition. "He thinks it may have been there since 1980 when an earthquake hit and they rebuilt."

His fingers wriggled; his face remained flat.

"Well? What do you have to say?"

"I will say that this news obliges you to trust me. I told you that the disk at the Heraklion was a fake, and you now know that it is. I should also say that the discovery is a dual-edged sword. The crime was committed, and the whereabouts of the real Disk are unknown," his face lit up, "which means that we are in the perfect position to find it."

"How is *this* the perfect position? How do we fine-tooth comb the globe to find it?"

"I promised to provide you with clues, and I shall." He bounced across the room to a roll-top desk, snatched something that looked like a shoebox, and lightly brushed the dust from the lid. "Before these infernal Turing machines, people wrote letters, and I have a number of letters that were written to Doumas. After the theft, he gave them to me. Quite surprisingly." Affiato rifled through a stack of yellowed envelopes in the box. "As you see, they are all postmarked from Marseilles."

Gatsby walked to his side, pulled out one of the envelopes, and nudged a dainty sheet of paper from it. Though the paper was not ruled, the handwriting ran across the page with almost mathematical uniformity. Greek and French alternated, most of which she translated with ease. At the bottom of the last page, she spotted a name. "Eloise Cambier? Who is she?"

"His paramour. From the writing, it is clear that she was deeply in love with him. The solvent that can melt the most indestructible safe box. He may have talked to her, confided in her about the theft. He may have even told her where the Disk was stashed. You must speak to her."

"That's a hell of a long shot. He had to know the risk he was taking. What makes you think he'd confess something like that to a lover?"

He dropped his chin, eyeing her with condescension. "How did you live to middle age and not know the answer to that? In the fulgent spectacle of human experience, only one emotion surpasses the ecstasy of holding a secret: the ecstasy of divulging it."

She gave a small shrug of agreement. "True."

"There is no guarantee that Cambier is still in Marseilles, of course, or even alive, but it is a reasonable place to begin."

She felt him studying her face, and her cheeks flushed as if she were in the throes of a racquetball match.

The smile tugged at his lips. "Hmmmm, yes, I see it in your eyes. Come this way. I must show you something." He set the box of letters on the desk and walked over to a standing cabinet at the other side of the room, again motioning for her to follow. The oak cabinet held twenty shallow drawers; it was the type of organizer that a retail business owner might use to store small tools or expensive jewelry.

"The Disk beckoned me, and now it is beckoning you. It wants to be found as badly as you want to find it. It will suck you in. It will hold you as firmly in its embrace," he opened the top drawer of the cabinet and withdrew an object that glittered, "as this." The flexible cylinder, about ten centimeters long, was decorated with tiny glittering stars and moons. He grabbed her left hand and slid one end of the cylinder over her small finger.

"Hey!!"

Before she could pull away, he had grabbed her right hand and pushed the tip of her other small finger into the opposite end of the tube. "It is a philosophic question, and once posited, some questions hold you forever."

She tugged at the device, which tightened its grip on her fingers. Her heart began to race. "Bravo. How amateur."

"Perhaps not. You see, there is no release mechanism." He slid to the bar at the opposite side of the room. "Like the Okinawan Death Trap, the puzzle of the Disk has caught you, and it will never let you go."

Pulling violently against the grip of the tube, Gatsby swept across the room toward him. "Get this fucking thing off me, Affiato."

He calmly poured Drambuie into a tumbler.

"Get it off. Now!"

He bolted, darting around the room, tails flying, and she chased him like a kid pursued by schoolyard bullies. Running with her hands shackled threw her balance off, almost tripping her, and she felt her cheeks burning. He slipped right and left until she dropped onto the Chesterfield sofa, panting.

Crouching behind the sarcophagus, he chortled. "You move like a thoroughbred. Pure poetry in motion!"

"Goddamn it, Affiato!" She tipped her head back against the sofa.

"Are you ready for release?" He stepped closer.

"Get it off!"

"Yes, yes, yes. Stand up."

She teetered to her feet, and as he slid up behind her, a shiver trickled down her spine, pricking the hairs on her neck.

"Now show me your hands."

She raised her hands—eight fingers splayed, two imprisoned—to eye level.

As he encircled her with his arms, his hands folded over hers. A gold key the width of a penny appeared from between his fingers. He inserted it into an invisible hole on the underside of the cylinder and turned it, and the tube expanded, releasing her fingers. She brusquely rubbed her hands together.

His torso pressed fully against her back; the gold rings glittered inches from her face. "You were never in any danger. This device is one of my own invention and extraordinarily made, as I'm sure—"

She cocked her right fist and slammed it into his face. He staggered back into the bar. A bottle of retsina plunged to the floor and shattered; the resinated liquid and shards rained across his trousers. The rosacea patch blooming on his cheek began to swell as he goggled up at her, cursing in three different languages.

She hovered over him, eyes blazing. "Asshole."

As she charged down the hall and through the front door, she heard gales of laughter.

CHAPTER 11

She's perfect. At long last, the Second Commander I have been seeking.

The image of her enticing face and body moved through him, especially the intensity of her hazel eyes when she was angry. The vision provided a sweet moment of distraction, but he pushed it away to focus on the business at hand.

Move more THISTLE agents to this location? No, Zagreb is fully covered. His hand raised as he stared at the world map on the monitor, thoughts darting from one operational division to another. The tech recruits that experienced agents were training in identity theft and credit card skimming, the forgery team that was developing a new type of counterfeit cyber money and distributing it via the dark web. The planted C-level officers who extorted corporations for kickbacks. The fresh recruits placed in positions that allowed them to embezzle from any organization, whether legitimate or black market.

He ensured that each RAM and MAIZE had the funding to buy the best minds from the best universities and tech schools. He called for access to top-secret information in private, military, and government intelligence organizations. His eager trainees got it for him.

One day there will be no more PEDESTRIANS.

Over the last year, the ranks had grown exponentially. Women were not just poised for revolution, they were screaming for it. Given the opportunity to join a network that severed the reins of patriarchy and put women in power, they grabbed it with manic enthusiasm. The fact that the powerhouse of the Circle was secretly led by a man filled him with glee.

The illusion of the ages! The instant they find out, my life will be over, but that will never happen.

He stood and crossed the room, moving between consoles, kicking through the chaos that littered the floor— paper, power cables, coins, ropes of various materials and thickness, bolts of velvet, playing cards, pyro fireshooters, sponge balls—until he stood before an enormous whiteboard mounted on the long wall of the room. His eyes crept over the rows of face shots, each with the name below.

Amira Jazazi
Rachel Moskowitz
Sabeen al-Naid
Farida Sharraf
Ishtar Wahin
Carol Young
Devin Blaine
Maria del Scorro
Franca Volante
Marta Obsanje
Jun Tokada
Rose Perrin

They're all perfect. So lovely, so useful, and so willing to serve in my army.

Next to these twelve was a chaotic collection of photos, each seven centimeters square. The hair and skin color were of all types. South African, Japanese, Peruvian, German, American, Indian, Greek, Balkan, Iranian—all nations represented. All ages from those just beginning to walk to those who would soon be buried. Their shadowed eyes said *don't fuck with me.*

Who is leading them out of their misery? What savior will wrench them from poverty, oppression, subjugation? Who is the unsung, the unknown hero? Me! Will they one day thank me for it? Will they??

A dark memory stole into his awareness, the one that could not be named other than *She*. His fingers twitched. The Ghost smoldered, threatening to rise again, but he grunted and shoved his hands deep into his pockets.

Once they prove their loyalty, I will give them what they've never had, the power that was torn away or plundered or never there from the start. Will they ever thank me?? I show them how to TAKE what they need and want, what they deserve. They will learn the game of power, just as I have, but they will do it with such stealth that the world will call it magic.

He allowed the smile to creep over his face as the phantoms of childhood enveloped him, visions of the people who had molded him from a young age. Though centered in Florence, his extended family spanned an enormous geography, some as far away as Sydney and Buenos Aires. His parents viewed their first-born son with a status nearing divinity, and they ensured his connections with those in power. Andre, you are born for greatness, his father intoned, as solemn as if creating the universe. A day did not go by that Andre was not reminded of his superiority and entitlement.

Today only one matches my ambitions. Only one is fit for the crusades that MUST be won, the pillage that is necessary to propel a global shift. Only one is as compelled. He chuckled. *What that infamous stepmother implanted in her! The maneuvering that took—she has no idea! Eventually, she will know all. She will see the complexity of it and understand how the threads of strategy were woven into a glorious tapestry.*

The Ghost blazed.

The burning flared, spreading like electricity up his thighs and into his belly, the throbbing that signaled her arrival. His hands clutched as a loud groan flowed from his lips. He spun and leaned back against the wall; his thigh muscles quivered.

She…She, the one who…

She was the enchantress, the one who had seduced him and left such indelible marks, the one who haunted his dreams each night.

The one who enacted such savage revenge.

After his release from incarceration, he found work as a courier, one of the few jobs available for a felon. He raced through the streets of Rome on a clattering Roketa scooter, hand-delivering confidential documents. For the young Andre, life started to move forward. Discreet customer introductions became contacts. New associates—soldiers and captains—helped him finalize the legal name change, and Andre Vinzzini was reborn as Macèo Affiato. He was set up in a well-appointed apartment adjacent Parco della Caffarella, and his niche became apparent: white-collar crime. He developed operations for money laundering, embezzlement, and bribery. "You know this turf," Carlos Maglione told him with a hearty slap on the back.

As a distraction from the stress, he practiced the simple magic tricks that he had taught himself in prison. He made balls and watches disappear, pulled currency out of thin air, and made tables and chairs levitate. He perfected the more dangerous illusions of appearing in a bank of fog or disappearing in fire.

Ten years in Regina Coeli. That gabinetto di merda. A stew of violence, but the connections were invaluable. How ironic that the Queen of Heaven was once a women's prison.

His case was touted as the most extensive money laundering scheme in Italian history, and he congratulated himself that it was the only charge that could be proven. The sentences for extortion and counterfeiting were doled out to his junior associates.

That sunny day, he stood at a newspaper kiosk on Viale Tiziano, purchasing the morning *La Repubblica.* She approached him with her devastating smile.

The images flooded his mind:

…the milky, translucent skin, her piercing eyes

…the tattoo of a blue-green phoenix on her left bicep

…the terrifying power of her hands, her lips, her tricks, her mind games

…the astounding secrets she told him

She didn't tell him all her secrets, but he uncovered them by hacking her email and phone records. When she discovered how he had used the information, she demonstrated her infinite superiority.

His left hand rose as if an alien entity. He stared at the stump of the sacrificed finger; the four remaining fingers wiggled involuntarily.

She took the finger, far from a pound of flesh, but that wasn't nearly enough. How I underestimated…

The Ghost howled. The nerve endings throughout his pelvis fired, sending out bolts of pain. The muscle memory of the toxin raging through his cells burned like a welding torch, blasting at skin and tissues. Saliva bubbled at his lip as he closed his eyes against the wildfire. *Stop it stop stop stop oh God STOP!!*

He was back in her dark room—the faint scent of jasmine, his shrieks reverberating off the walls and knowing no one would hear, his legs tangling the sheets and ropes. Her face a mask, her lips crushed against his ear. *You broke the law of the Circle, HORN.*

A cry burst from his mouth, becoming the yowl that possessed him when The Ghost descended. Memories flashed like strobe lights:

...muffled voices, fragmented, shouting

...a scream as he crawled across cold tile at Ospedale San Pietro-Fatebenefratelli

...drifting in and out, frightened faces appearing and disappearing into darkness

...white surgical masks and gloves

...tissue-wrinkling smells of alcohol, latex, chlorhexidine gluconate

...a spike of pain in his lower back

..."ottenere gli anelli...la sua arteria femorale...controllare i segni vitali...cos'è quello?" *Get the rings off...the femorale artery...check his vital signs...what is that?*

Semi-conscious, he could barely whimper when he heard the surgeon mutter, "Necrosi. Troppi Danni. Esso non puo essere salvato." *Too much damage. It cannot be saved.* The anesthesiologist checked the tubing. Nurses adjusted the lights and began assembling scalpels on a steel tray.

He collapsed to the floor, knocking over the lightweight table he used for a levitation illusion. Prone and writhing from the pain, he stared at the overhead lights of the secret room. *But she was right to do it.* His fingers clawed at the crotch of his trousers as he gasped for air. *It proved beyond any doubt the efficacy of the DOLIUM.*

CHAPTER 12

Dacea walked into Loumidis and looked around. Metal chairs and wobbly, laminate-topped tables were scattered around the café. The bookend college boys who toyed with empty cups were unshaven and too thin. They glanced up with brooding expressions as she slid by.

Vlahos sat in a booth at the back of the room. As she raised her eyes to meet Dacea's, she held herself with the iron of an elder. Her hair framed a placid face, but her eyes darted like escaping prey. She tugged a woven bag off her shoulder.

Dacea settled in the booth, facing her.

"Tan-wil-in ruz—"

Dacea brandished her palm to signal STOP. *Verbal or written, but never simultaneous.* The security rule was strictly enforced. A hard copy report was almost impossible to verify if unaccompanied by verbal communication. An oral message between members, without fixed evidence, never happened.

Vlahos slapped a hand over her lips. She quickly opened the bag, extracted a large manila envelope, and held it forward. "Dot-wer pan on ter dan."

Dacea took the envelope. "Ril-ran dotst?" *Your source?*

"Dan-wuz CAT. Sot-ter man-wil un-sher." *A new CAT. Local, young.*

"Suz-til wan un-wer kan?" *How is her work?*

"Tuz ker shin." *Reliable so far.*

"Muz-ker-pil-dot wan-dan-un London dan-suz-oh?" *All product tested and shipped to London?*

Vlahos nodded.

"Don-muz. Ser oh san-sil un." *Good. You can go.*

Vlahos rose. As she headed toward the front door, she jostled the boys' table. They hurled shouts at her, but she ignored them and stepped out onto Rizari Street.

Two minutes later, Dacea pushed against the door of the café and began walking toward the northeast neighborhood of Kolonaki.

Once inside the apartment on Xenokratous, she opened the slat blinds and windows to air out the room. Her couch sighed as she stretched out on her back, opened the envelope, and pulled out the report papers.

```
SHIP-2
Age: 49 Height: 5'10" Eye color: Brown.
Citizenship: Italy.
Education: No records.
Profession: Business. Address in Soho,
London, The Sorcerer's Apprentice
Bio: Unmarried. No children.
International traveler, frequent visits
to Asia and North America. Home
addresses in Italy, Spain, Belgium,
Libya, and Argentina.
```

Where's the rest? She shook the envelope, expecting more pages to flutter out. *No prior records? Smells of a criminal background. Apparently he knows how to remain invisible. Miranovski will have a good time with this.*

She wriggled into a more comfortable position and continued reading.

```
SHIP-1
Age: 44 Height: 5'5" Eye color: Hazel
Citizenship: USA.
Education: Degrees from Blake
University and SUNY, linguistic
anthropology.
Profession: Lead consultant for the
British Museum Department of
Orthography and Translation. Translates
inscriptions on artifacts—Aramaic,
cuneiform, Sumerian, Cypriot,
Phoenician. Eight published monographs
on theoretical translation of the
Phaistos Disk.
Bio: Unmarried. No children. Birth
mother deceased. Father in Seattle,
older sister in British Columbia.
Stepmother received Aeon Award from the
```

```
International Institute of
Archeological Sciences.
```

Aeon award winner. Sounds like some kind of academic royalty. As she read the next lines, her eyes widened.

```
Stepmother was RAM; AXE imposed for
five Level 3 violations
```

How did this slip under the radar? A PEDESTRIAN may not be a threat, but a SHIP who doesn't know she's a SHIP can be catastrophe. Given that close an association with a penalized RAM, she can't not have an agenda! As she pulled out her STAR SEED, her mind raced. *Convene the BOAT immediately.*

The STAR SEED vibrated silently, signaling a transmission on the Circle's top security channel: the direct line connecting the SWORD and the HAMMER. In the time since she took the role, it had never been used. She entered the access code, and the message rose on the screen.

ADDED MEASURES NECESSARY
GO TO LONDON NOW
INSTRUCTIONS TO FOLLOW

Another message followed a few minutes later.

RETRIEVE TOOLS AT IVY9

CHAPTER 13

"How do you endure his mania?!" His jugular throbbed.

Here we go... Gatsby knew that lunch with Roman meant well-meaning lectures that were best washed down with sauvignon blanc.

The Punch & Judy Pub, nestled in the breezeway of Covent Garden, was one of his favorite haunts. The immortal maître d', Nigel—stoic as a Tuscan pillar—wafted by their table. As he disappeared into the crowd, the clatter of stemware and conversations melded into ambient white noise. Gatsby mopped at her linguini with a chunk of bread.

Roman launched accusations like grenades. "He's a con artist of the first water! And you went back there? Alone? Are you mad?" He slammed his glass of Black Rabbit ale on the table loud enough for patrons to fire frowns in his direction.

"Mad enough to persist until I find the Disk?" Propping her elbows on the tablecloth, she leaned forward into his angst. "Clearly."

"Pah!" His elbow sent a fork rocketing to the floor. "Gatsby, the Disk is an unparalleled pursuit. That's not arguable, but don't you see the danger you're exposing yourself to? A man who plays ridiculous tricks on you like that finger trap?" His face wrinkled like an abandoned puppy. "Next time, can't someone go with you? Why must you do this on your own?"

"Because there—"

Her hand wavered in midair. Droplets trickled down the inner surface of the wine glass.

(Collaborators get in the way...they always have their eyes on you...if you're on to something important, look for an ambush)

She pawed through the reasons not to finish the sentence out loud, kicked away the needling voice in her head, and swallowed the alcohol and reasons with one gulp. "Because I work better on my own."

Roman stared at her until she blurted, "What?"

He studied her, eyes narrowed, before speaking. "*If* you managed to find the Disk, imagine it—the Phaistos Disk discovered, lost, and then miraculously recovered by a scholar in the lineage of an Aeon winner. It will be the moment of a lifetime." His face softened. "Who is the first person you'll call, GM?"

The question prompted a draw from the glass that drained it empty. She stared at the drops clinging to the side, small globes of vineyards and centuries, rippling and then melting into extinction. "CNN. I'll email a headshot before the plague of reporters descends."

He waved a hand to flag Nigel and dug for his wallet.

The clatter of the Tube was the ostinato of her thoughts as she watched the underground whiz by.

There's something like seven million websites devoted to archaeology, and every one of them would include a story of the Phaistos Disk along with my name and photo. BRITISH MUSEUM CONSULTANT RECOVERS STOLEN ARTIFACT! Exclamation points like confetti. Every archaeologist across the globe, now and future, would read it and imagine the quest, the recovery of the Disk. Perhaps even learn how it was deciphered.

The studies in epigraphy at Blake University, the brutal doctoral program at SUNY—they felt like lifetimes ago. She stared out the window as the world rolled by. A line from one of her favorite movies popped into her head: "This is your life, and it's ending one minute at a time."

What is the measure of each person's life: what you achieve in the finite decades you're alive, or how you are churned and spit out from the mill of history? Can I go to my grave having SOMETHING worthwhile enough for her to finally...

(What will YOU be remembered for?!)

(NO MATTER WHAT IT TAKES!)

She felt the whine of neuralgia and dropped her head into her hands. *Fuck.*

From the darkness of the back corner, Dacea looked out across the crowd. *Do they know the enormity of this machine? Know that they're just cogs?*

The message floated through her mind: *Added measures required. Go to London now. Instructions to follow. Retrieve tools at Ivy9.*

What added measures? What tools? No specifics given. That alone is concerning. Orders from the HAMMER are lengthy, comprehensive down to the last detail. It's a subtle change of tactics, and at that level of leadership, any behavioral change no matter how small is suspect. If the capabilities of the HAMMER falter, who must maintain the integrity of the BEEHIVE? She pulled in a breath. *The SWORD.*

The Crab6 meeting room was packed. Anxiety flickered over the faces of about thirty women who ranged in age from seventeen to sixty-five. Wide computer screens were mounted on the side and back walls. Aria Vlahos walked down the left side of the room and stopped to perch against the wall. She drew a handheld device to her ear, spoke into it, and stowed it in her pocket. As the women jostled into folding chairs and wriggled to get comfortable, Vlahos paced the perimeter of the room and down the aisles. When something caught her attention, she pulled out the device and quietly typed something.

At the front of the room, the BOAT council stood in front of a walnut table. Tess Miranovski, Anastasia Hoda, and Jayna Dhar faced the assembly.

"This is not an elite organization." Miranovski's voice was serrated. "It is *the* elite organization. You are here because you were nominated by a standing member. Everything that you hear today, you will never repeat. Your life depends on it. I'll say that again: Everything that you hear today, you will never repeat. Your life depends on it." Her eyes twitched as if she was about to pick out Dacea, but she instantly shifted her gaze back to the audience.

Dacea thought, *Reconfirms her self-control—good. The general membership never knows the identity of the SWORD or the HAMMER.* As Miranovski began outlining the agenda, Dacea tugged the black qunae across her face so that only her eyes showed. She thought about how each woman in the room was recruited and the elaborate steps of induction.

She was approached by a Circle member.

She learned the duties and dangers of joining the Circle.

She learned that the reach of the Circle extended farther and deeper than anyone beyond it could imagine, farther than even most members realized.

She learned how the Circle was more covert than any other global force.

She learned that while organizations led by men—the armies, cartels, and brotherhoods—flourished by publicizing missions and openly recruiting, the Circle grew silently.

She learned the Circle motto: "We are air—invisible and everywhere."

She learned that Circle training was passed orally, almost never in writing, and only between members.

She learned the Circle language, WATER, spoken only between members. Most details of the language's development were shrouded in secrecy, in keeping with the meaning of the word *hieroglyph*: sacred writing. Because Egyptian writings were difficult to create and learn, they were reserved for the elite classes of priests and royalty. To commoners, the writing was magical and mysterious, the words of the gods.

Every member was required to learn the syllabic pattern, the forty-five phonemes based on the forty-five unique symbols of the ROSETTE, and the twenty-one diacritics that represented a combined sound or diphthong. She learned how to arrange the syllables into meaningful morphemes, in both written and oral form, and when receiving messages, how to decrypt them.

She learned that RUNNERS did not survive.

Dhar's gaze swept the upturned faces. "You all receive manuals in the morning. Your FORK will provide the password. Any questions?"

"Yeah." The woman with her hair cut almost to baldness shifted in her seat. "I'm not clear on the network."

Dhar turned to her right. "Hoda, this is your area."

Hoda stepped forward. "The server is the OAR. It's not part of the World Wide Web or the Internet and therefore not susceptible to viruses unless we are hacked, which has yet to happen. The tech team is called TEMPLE. It designs the software and a version of hardware that is completely wireless. The digital signatures and KSA proxies ensure that no one individual ever has access to the entire system, only sections. The only way into OAR is with a STAR SEED, which only members have."

The woman frowned. "The messaging process. Could you explain that?"

"You're all learning WATER?"

The women nodded.

Hoda said, "You compose a message in WATER and use ZIPZ to encrypt it. The receiver opens the message by using the key—the decryption algorithm that changes every twenty-four hours—and the key then converts the message back into WATER. Think of it as the hieroglyphic writing system of the twenty-first century. An encryption system that is digital, global, and unbreakable." She gave a rare smile. "A viral glyph."

A Thai woman raised her hand. "When do we get the STAR SEED?"

"Two to three days."

A tattooed girl in the back row erupted with smoker's cough. She was covered with tattoos and piercings and wore a t-shirt with an anarchist's logo. "So, uh, we never talk about this group with anyone who's not a member, and we never use this WATER language except with other members?" Her expression was a smirk. "And we're supposed to keep all this hush hush? Never say a thing to a friend? Boyfriend or girlfriend? Spouse?"

Miranovski, Dhar, and Hoda exchanged looks. They knew the girl wasn't done.

"Someone is bound to break the law!" The girl, Alena, blurted it as if wrangling with a pissed-off parent.

Dacea thought, *The BOAT has seen this a thousand times. They know how to handle it.*

Holding eye contact with the girl, Miranovski took two steps toward her. "When did you meet your FORK?"

"A few days ago."

"Did you tell anyone that you were coming here?"

Alena tried to look petulant. "No."

"It's that simple." Miranovski anchored her hands on her hips. "The next year is your field test. You'll be given a shitload of challenges, and all of them require different levels of secrecy. We'll find out how good you are at manipulating and divulging new information, misinformation, and partial information. You'll learn complex coding methods and be able to do them in your head instantly. You'll be able to recognize a fellow member with a word. Some of you will be selected for the role of LIONESS—a data mule. Just being in this room means that your training has begun." She paused. "Some of you won't pass the tests. You'll be kicked out with instructions on how to delete everything you received and forget everything you have heard about the Circle. You will follow these instructions to the letter."

The women glanced at each other, murmuring nervously.

Miranovski looked across the crowd. "Here's the real question. Why are you here?"

Shuffling and rustling. The Thai woman, Suda, said, "Honor. The prestige."

Miranovski folded her arms over her chest. "Banish *that* idea. Do you think this is a sorority? Think you'll be crowned a fucking prom queen?"

Suda shriveled.

"You're here for the GRASS and the AXE, the fuel of the Circle. GRASS is reward. You will receive training like no other boot camp, including extensive self-defense and combat tactics. Access to people and places you have never dreamed of. *Access* is the key to every type of power. You need money, business partners, equipment, professional services? Inside the Circle, you are plugged into a network that connects millions of members at every level of every society. Where there are women, there are members. We are air—invisible and everywhere."

A fair-skinned redhead asked, "I can see that in big cities, but what about isolated areas? South American villages? The Australian desert or Outer Mongolia?"

"The directive of the BEEHIVE is to reach women everywhere. Hundreds of millions of women do not have computers or cellphones, so we have to be creative and relentless. All women have one thing in common: language. This is where they leave men in the dust. Language precedes devices, and often, it is superior to anything tangible." She pressed her palms together, readying for another volley. "Don't fool yourself into thinking that this is a noble cause or a quest for world peace. We don't exist for truth or goodness or equality. The Circle is at fucking war. It is the KGB, CIA, Mossad, MI6, and you are the agents. If you step onto this path, your life will never be the same."

A black woman with salt-and-pepper hair spoke in a husky voice. "If that's the GRASS, what's the AXE?"

"AXE is punitive measures for certain types of behavior. They are graduated from Level 1 to Level 5. Minor mistakes, depending on the severity of the consequences, are Level 1. Blatant insubordination brings a Level 5. Beyond that, you are considered a SHIP, a potential threat. Remember, you have a year to decide about membership, but know that security agencies around the world don't have the enforcement tactics of the Circle. We *are* a government, and membership is for life. If you join, you are a CAT—a fledgling recruit. If you go rogue, become a SHIP or a RUNNER, write your will and get your affairs in order."

Murmurs floated around the room.

The black woman, Leesha, said, "That sounds like..."

"We know what it sounds like," Miranovski cut in. "You'll get details from your FORK, but here's the bottom line. We don't fuck around."

The room was silent.

Just four, Dacea thought. Eleven years ago, two RUNNERS emerged: Nicolette Bandara, a RAM in Buenos Aires, and Jori Gromyko, who did tech repairs from Moscow. In the organization's history, only two defectors had managed to evade the ubiquitous radar of the Circle: Eloise Cambier and her daughter, Helena Girard.

Miranovski cleared her throat. "What's the First Law?" She waited, knowing that some ambitious recruit would say it.

Suda said, "We are air—invisible and everywhere." She glanced over her shoulder at Alena and then back at Miranovski.

Alena flopped against the back of her seat and scanned the room, her eyes darting. She anchored her elbows on her knees and alternately glared at the floor and the other women as if she'd been insulted.

Miranovski leaned against the edge of the table. "Sanchez will brief you about the DOLIUM—how to handle it and deploy it. The next meeting is in four days, so prep by memorizing the last chapter of your manual. Memorize it."

Leesha said, "Memorize it? Why?"

"To avoid an agonizing death."

CHAPTER 14

Dacea made her way down the concourse toward the security gate. She flipped to the back page of her passport, her gaze traveling over the kaleidoscope of stamps.

My relatives around the globe, always inviting me to their events. A funeral, a birth, a wedding, and now my ailing grandmother in London.

Athens International Airport was a stew of sounds: feet shuffling, cellphone ring tones, babies crying, newspapers rustling, impatient shouts, snoring. Her only carry-on, a canvas bag, held three well-used paperback books and a jumble of clothes. She moved a step forward in the queue of fractious travelers, all anxious to leave the overpopulation of Athens and enjoy the relative peace of a flight to Anywhere.

"Next?"

She approached the uniformed man who barked instructions from a Plexiglas cube and held out her passport.

Once on board the plane, she found her seat and hugged the bag on her lap. Her thoughts circled back to the reports that Vlahos had delivered. *Two SHIPS in London—one male, one female with a next-generation tie to the Circle. What did the RAM stepmother divulge? If the SHIPS are threatening enough to warrant the SWORD's presence...* She rubbed her temples. *Added measures necessary, go to London now, instructions to follow, retrieve tools at Ivy9.*

An hour into the flight, passengers watching the newscast on the overhead screens sat up straighter and murmured.

"...within the last hour, when the body was pulled from a reservoir at the Saad el Aali, the Aswan High Dam. He appears to have drowned, but police are conducting a full investigation to determine whether this was a homicide or suicide. Abdul ben Nassarim was a top general in Hesh al-Dalah, the Egyptian network of Hamas."

Dacea thought, *WATER B113. THISTLE 2 of BOOMERANG complete.*

The story about Nassarim concluded. Another reporter appeared on the screen in a flash of stylized graphics.

"We go now to the United States and the disturbing story of Rico Bianchi, the son of Antone Bianchi and the Don of one of the most powerful Mafia families. This morning, he was found dead in his room at the Hotel Palomar in Chicago." The reporter glanced over his shoulder at the building that dripped of luxury and then looked back into the camera. "The first reports are that he died of a heart attack, and there was an abrasion on his neck that has yet to be identified. An autopsy will take place at Northwestern Memorial Hospital, but no updates can be released until the..."

DOLIUM A24. All three BOOMERANG operations complete. Dhar will send the report in twenty-five minutes.

She shifted back to the command from the HAMMER. Which tools, and why no specifics on what to do with them?

She pressed her hands against the tops of her thighs, knowing that she knew which tools and that she knew exactly what to do with them.

CHAPTER 15

King's Road was the center of Swinging London, the epicenter of the miniskirt revolution of the 1960s, then the punk crazes of the 1970s and 1980s. Once a haven for bearded literati and anarchist radicals, it was now packed with upscale shops and restaurants.

Gatsby's three-story flat building was nestled between a quaint tavern and a recently opened Starbucks. It faced Sloane Square, an open space with a paved walkway, a flower stall, and the Venus Fountain, sometimes called "The Kneeling Nymph."

Gatsby mounted the stairs to the front door of the building and stopped before the brass knockers fashioned to look like snarling lions. An envelope was tucked behind a decorative panel at eye level, and the calligraphy in black ink formed the letters GD.

The paper bag holding her breakfast, two warm *pain au chocolat* from Panerie SW3, dropped to the bricks with a thud. She tugged the envelope free and opened it to find a note, hand-printed with black ink on ivory ecru paper.

British Telecom reveals
E. M. Cambier in Marseilles
Do not divulge that you seek the Disk. Invent
A plausible reason for speaking with her
3 441 66 23 23

There was no mention of their last meeting, the Okinawan Death Trap, or the clout to the cheek.

He's testing me. At least as much as he wants to find the Disk, or says that he does, he wants to find out if I'm a suitable plaything. He offers something alluring, but the price is the mind games! She felt her jugular pounding. *Affiato, you don't know who you're dealing with.*

She entered the building, dashed up a flight of stairs, and stepped into her flat. After tossing the pastry bag onto the desk in her office, she grabbed her smartphone and settled on the loveseat in the living room. She gripped Affiato's note in one hand and dialed with the other; with each ring, her heart beat faster.

A weak voice, dry as eggshells. "Qui est là?" *Who is there?*

She toggled into rough French. "Est-ce que vous êtes Madame Cambier?"

"Que voulez-vous?" *What do you want?* A phlegmatic cough.

Choosing each word carefully, Gatsby explained that she was a consultant for the British Museum and that she translated the inscriptions on artifacts.

"Have you been to the British Museum?"

A clatter as if a handset had been dropped, then a grunt of irritation. "Why? What is this about?"

(Do not divulge that you seek the Disk)

"I need to talk to you about the Phaistos Disk."

A sharp gasp, then silence.

"Hello? Madame Cambier, hello?"

Damn it!

Finally, a whisper. "I will not talk about that."

Maybe she's running from something or from someone. Reassure her that I am not a threat. "It is important. No one will know that we have spoken. You will be perfectly safe."

"No one is perfectly safe!" The quiver in her voice spoke volumes.

Doesn't take a magician to figure out that she has life-or-death reasons not to talk about the Disk. If she is afraid, she must want to talk to someone about what she fears, someone who understands. She dropped her voice to a murmur, as if comforting a tearful child. "If we can speak in person, Madame, there will be no trace of our meeting. I have no connections." Gatsby felt her heart pounding.

After a beat: "No trace. No one."

It was the sound of a window of opportunity sliding open. "I understand."

"How did you find me?"

By escaping from the clutches of a lunatic. "I'll tell you when we meet."

She hopped on the Tube at the Sloane Square station. It zoomed through Brompton, Knight's Bridge, and Piccadilly Circus to arrive at St. Pancras International Train Station—almost a city unto itself of arcing glass ceilings, escalators, and departure/arrival boards. The diaper stations and restaurants were packed with travelers. She stared upward at "The Meeting Place," the nine-meter-tall tribute to romantic love.

After a stop in the restroom, she wandered the Undercroft, finding it amazingly quiet, considering the hordes of people trudging alongside their wheeled luggage. Students and tourists took photos with smartphones. Starry-eyed couples sat in the austere booths, sipping coffee and pointing at maps, chattering in French, English, German, Italian, or any of a dozen other languages.

Following the bright blue signs, she found her gate and platform and boarded the Eurostar. The line bound for Paris traveled undersea through the Channel Tunnel—the "Chunnel"—at three hundred kilometers per hour. A Londoner could be walking the streets of Paris in two and a half hours.

Once in her Business Premier seat, an attendant brought her a lunch of crab cakes, butternut squash soup, and chocolate mousse, along with a copy of *The Observer.* She popped open her laptop and typed notes as multilingual staff members in grey uniforms bustled about the cabin.

Gatsby finished the mousse and nursed a can of ginger ale, deep in thought.

(Do not divulge that you seek the Disk)

(No one is perfectly safe!)

When the train stopped in Paris at Gare du Nord, she disembarked and looked for the signs to the Express Metro, the RER Line D. She bought a ticket at a kiosk and headed to the platform. In five minutes, the train rolled in, and she hustled on board.

The next stop was Gare de Lyon. More stairs, signs, and stopping to ask for directions. Gatsby found her way to a set of escalators and followed the signs that pointed to the Grandes Lignes. The Blue zone area was packed with colorful banners and shops.

As the serpentine Train à Grande Vitesse rumbled forward and crept to a stop at the platform, overhead speakers blared announcements in eight different languages.

She stepped aboard and was taken by the plush interior. The rows of rotating seats were upholstered in rich earth tones, and fold-down tables on the window seats and throughout the cabin allowed passengers to comfortably eat a meal or read. Most set up laptop computers to create a temporary office. She caught whiffs of coffee and cinnamon tea and remembered the website description she had read a few days earlier: "The train is as smooth as an aircraft in clear skies, and there are no vibrations at all, and so quiet you can hear someone whispering at the other end of the carriage."

The passengers settled. During a polite welcome message from the chef de train, the TGV began moving forward.

Travel time? She pulled out her smartphone and connected to the onboard Wi-Fi. *Nine hundred kilometers. Arrive in Marseille in about four hours.*

Twenty minutes into the trip, Gatsby strolled into a buffet car called Bar TGV and bought a bag of sea salt crisps. She took a seat at the window counter and tugged open the bag.

At the end of the counter, two women chatted over porcelain cups of coffee. They were whispering but seemed to be in a heated discussion. When the younger woman glanced at Gatsby, their eyes met for a second. Gatsby nodded and turned to focus back on the window, but she caught snippets of their conversation.

"…ruz-sil-der an?"

"…kot-san…oh sil-on wer…"

She felt herself stiffen involuntarily and listened more closely. *What is that? It's syllabic but only partially. Some derivative of Hindi? Farsi?* She gave them a one-second glance. *They look more Northern European than Middle Eastern.*

"...mil-on-san wil duz white bird..."

White bird? That's clearly English. Shaking her head in bewilderment, she pulled a travel guidebook from her shoulder bag and began reading.

Marseilles (pronounced mahr-SAY) is a sparkling tapestry of ancient and modern Provence. Since its founding in the sixth century BC, Marseilles has grown into France's second largest city, one that now serves as a hub of transit and commerce for the Mediterranean. You will want to get acquainted with the Panier, the historic district. Take a guided neighborhood tour on foot or by electric bike. Get lost in the shops, bars, and boutiques as you taste the city's unique flavors. From the Vieux-Port ("old port"), be sure to visit La Canebière—this kilometer-long street highlights the glory and wealth of a colonial past and has even been called the Champs-Elysees of Marseilles. When you are ready to expand your sightseeing, explore the other quartiers (arrondissement). Take a day trip to see the calanques, and be amazed by breathtaking cliffs of limestone and dolomite that plunge into the Mediterranean. The area is difficult to get to by car or on foot, so be prepared to hire a boat from the Vieux Port.

The TGV began the delicate processes of decelerating, using the magnetic induction brakes, from 160 kilometers per hour to 5. Gare de Marseille Saint-Charles was the terminus of the Paris–Marseille line. Passengers began folding their magazines, saving electronic documents, and gathering their bags.

When it stopped with a gentle thump, the two women rose, still chattering as they sat their empty cups on the counter.

Gatsby stood and pulled her bag over her shoulder, exited the train, and looked around the platform. Inside the station, spacious corridors beckoned; live trees were incorporated into the architecture. A steep staircase led toward Rue Marcel Sembat.

She hailed a cab. After a ten-minute ride down Avenue Leclerc to Rue de la Republique, she was in Le Panier, a district close to Vieux Port where narrow pedestrian avenues ran between the multicolored buildings. Clotheslines draped with fluttering laundry wove apartment balconies together like spider webs. Residents moved about on foot, bicycle, or scooter, shopping or walking their dogs. Gatsby breathed in distinctive aromas—olive bread, fish, and the briny smell of saltwater.

In the Saint Lambert section, the buildings were darker and grittier, some spray painted with graffiti. Many shop windows were secured by steel bars. Bits of newspaper blew across the street; shouts carried down the alleys, bringing a volley of barking from a few street dogs.

She turned the corner onto Rue de Cazes, stopped in front of an apartment building, and pulled the notebook from her bag. *35 Rue de Cazes…this is the right building, but* this *neighborhood?*

She mounted the stairs and pushed the call button for apartment 35, preparing to announce herself. Instead of a voice, she heard the rattling buzz that unlocked the main door.

At the center of the rectangular building, she saw a courtyard filled with failing sunflowers. *35…where is 35?*

A tiny sign had the numbers of the second level and an arrow. Once at the top of the staircase, she spotted "35" on the first apartment.

Show time. With a deep breath, Gatsby knocked on the door, and it opened with a dramatic screech.

"Madame Cambier? Je suis…" She stared skyward at a figure swathed in indigo wool and pewter buttons. The equine face held sunken eyes; scattered wisps of hair seemed to weigh on the skeletal shoulders.

"Est-ce que vous est seule?" *Are you alone?* His tone melded apathy and catastrophe.

She nodded, staring.

He allowed her to step inside, motioned for her to follow him to the unit at the end of the hall, and pushed the door open. She saw a cramped entry that led to a dining room with brick walls. The air was thick with the smell of onion. A set of simple blonde-pine chairs and a table held the center of the room; a napkin, tightly bunched on the surface, and a glistening spoon indicated a recent meal.

The man rounded the table and pulled away a chair. "Elle viendra." *She will come.* He stepped through a doorway into what Gatsby assumed was the kitchen.

She glanced around the room. To her left, a fire burned in a fireplace. There were no photographs or art on the walls, and no rugs on the wood floor, as if the resident had recently moved in or was about to move out.

The figure that stepped from the kitchen brought to mind Panzer tanks and Juden armbands. She was about eighty years old; a cream-colored shift hung almost to her ankles, and a wool scarf floated around her neck. Her pale blue eyes, blonde hair, and fair skin hinted at Scandinavian genes. Creases and rough patches indicated that she worked with her hands, which were crisscrossed with capillaries. She slowly lowered herself into a chair and cleared her throat.

The man reappeared and reached over the table for the tureen. Madame Cambier muttered, "Tristan, apportez du thé, s'il vous plait." He slid back into the kitchen.

She turned toward Gatsby. "Who are you?"

"Dr. Donovan." She summarized the work that led to becoming lead consultant for the Department of Orthography and Translation. With broad strokes, she painted a picture of her conversations with Affiato and the search for the Phaistos Disk that had brought her to Cambier's dining room.

Tristan entered carrying a platter with rye bread, butter, and cups of raspberry tea. He quietly set it on the table. He moved to the doorway between the kitchen and dining room and stood silently, staring into space.

"The Disk at the Heraklion Archeological Museum. The curator ran a TL test three times, and it's a fake. I want to find the original."

"Vraiment?" A frown wrestled across Cambier's face, perhaps from a lifetime of incongruity or regret. "Pour quoi? Perhaps it does not wish to be found."

Gatsby's hands wrestled in her lap. "The Phaistos Disk is a treasure beyond value. It belongs to all humanity, all mankind, and it is lost somewhere on the planet. It must be recovered and preserved, and its purpose must be discovered. In nearly four thousand years, it hasn't been deciphered, and I can't believe that someone would invest that much effort in creating it unless the message was crucial." She felt the hematite pendant under her shirt rub against her sternum.

Cambier rubbed her cheek as if questions flowed through her. She sipped her tea. "Tell me about your family. Your mother."

"My mother? Why?"

"I wish to know. If you want my story, you must offer your own."

Quid pro quo? Fine. "She died when I was eleven. Brain cancer. It was very quick—four months after the diagnosis, she was gone. A visiting professor from NYU presented at a symposium in Seattle. She introduced herself to my father and throttled him with her odious style of charm. In the spring, they were married."

"There is more, I suspect."

Pulling in a long breath, Gatsby said, "Livia Rudden won an Aeon award for her work on mythemes—modern sociological memes cultured from classic mythology. Then her methods were discovered. Plagiarism, extortion, identity theft, even physical threats—that's the short list. The committee revoked the award. It was the ultimate blow. She turned into an inferno of anger and ambition. It taught..."

(Never let go!!)

"Taught me to never give up when you, when you deserve..."

The anger in Cambier's eyes matched the fire in her voice. "You come to me and seek the ROSETTE? The Disk? You think you *deserve* it? You say it belongs to humanity? It does not belong to anyone!" She licked her thin lips. "Not even me."

Gatsby swallowed. "Do *you* have it?"

Cambier struggled to her feet. Pressing a hand to the small of her back, she paced the length of the table and shuffled back. "I was a CAT, a young recruit, full of the passion of the fresh foot soldier and driven to follow those who had power. I wanted to prove my worth. Taking the ROSETTE proved my dedication to the Circle."

"What circle?"

Cambier's eyes widened. "Incroyable. I was sure there were no more PEDESTRIANS. Your ignorance ends now. Imagine every large organization, league, military or intelligence force combined as a unified network."

She shook her head. "*That* is an ambitious proposition."

"It exists. And now imagine that every member of this network is female."

"What?"

"Those outside the Circle know nothing of it. It has its own language, laws, methods of enforcement..."

"But something that widespread could never stay underground."

"And that is the belief that sustains it. We are air— invisible and everywhere."

Gatsby ran her hands through her hair. "*Just* for the sake of argument, let's say that this female-led network exists. Are you telling me that you are part of it?"

Cambier nodded. "I was recruited in the late fifties. When the ROSETTE was discovered in 1908, it was taken to the Pagnorini National Museum for preservation. One of the interns was fascinated by it. Obsessed, je dirais. Ilya Kameroff...she formed a small study group, and their initial goal was translation of the Disk."

"A task that's evaded the best linguistic minds for more than a century."

"Oui. The group evolved into an antiquities society and became more exclusive. Elitist. They deemed themselves as unique and mysterious as the ROSETTE itself, adopted it as the unifying symbol. They created their own language. In 1923, they established ruling positions, like a small government, naming the roles after the symbols— THISTLE, SWORD, HAMMER et comme ça. They gave it an innocuous name: The Circle."

A bead of sweat trickled down Gatsby's neck. The hulking Tristan, the cups of cooling raspberry tea, the shadow of bitterness on Cambier's face—it all felt slightly hallucinogenic.

"It grew at an astounding rate. With great numbers, leadership emerges, naturally or through force. Kameroff was forced out and replaced. By that time, the Disk had been moved from the Pagnorini to the Heraklion. The new HAMMER wanted the Disk. She wanted to possess it, as if possession brought more than status or even monetary value. She devised a plan to take the ROSETTE and replace it with a replica that the Circle members made." She stared toward the hallway as if drowning in her memories. "The order came to me."

Gatsby swallowed. "*You* stole the Disk?"

"A worker at the museum gave me the information I needed—how to avoid the sensors and security systems. If they went off, how to report a false alarm."

"The worker was your—your friend, Doumas, right?"

Cambier raised her chin, frowning. "Qui?"

"Doumas." She fumbled awkwardly. "Your lover."

"Certainly not. It was Mara Dolastanos. She wanted to enter the Circle, so she traded her knowledge for mine."

Gatsby felt her mind spin. "I was told that a man was involved, a Greek named Doumas. I saw a box full of love letters that you sent him. "

"Jamais." Cambier glared at her. "Ca c'est absurde. Someone has told you a ridiculous story."

The lying bastard! "Then how did you do it?"

Cambier turned her back to Gatsby. "There were four systems to bypass: motion, temperature, vibration, and infrared. All extremely sensitive, networked internally and to external servers with redundant backups. Dolastanos gave me instructions and floor plans. She knew how to disable certain systems and bypass others. She knew the day and time when security watches were weakest. She helped me to design diversion tactics to distract the guards and trick the video cameras."

"How?"

"All high-security systems, especially those that protect physical objects, scan for specific critères. Vibration, light, temperature, proximity, moisture, air pressure, even the chemicals of human sweat. The method we used had nothing to do with any of these." She took a breath. "I put the false disk in place. The ROSETTE was stored in a carbon-fiber case. It switched couriers six times as it was moved through crowds and taken out of the museum."

"You did this during the day?" Gatsby tried to imagine Cambier explaining such an elaborate theft from a museum to Clevis.

Cambier nodded.

"Where did you get the replica?"

"The team within the Circle produced it." The old woman shuffled a few steps toward her. "I took the ROSETTE to the safe house in Athens. It was locked in an underground vault. That was when I learned first-hand how the Circle protected its possessions and enforced its rules. Obscene measures. I learned of those who had been killed." She held a trembling hand against the table. "Terrible ways. Some rules carried a death penalty. My Helena..." She dropped her head, muttering as tears swelled. "My daughter, Helena. She was my joy." She took a few ragged breaths. "I could not leave the ROSETTE with such people. I went back to the vault and took it."

She padded back to the far end of the table. "Then I hid from the Circle. Russia, Croatia, Italy, Morocco—until I was too tired to run anymore." She stared into the fire in the fireplace, now burning weakly. "So tired. I came to Marseille, but even with Tristan by my side, I live every day in fear. Coureurs ne survivre pas."

She seemed to notice Gatsby frowning at the stone-like man at the doorway. "Not a member, évidemment. He simply protects me." Her gaze shifted back to the embers in the fireplace and fixed there as if her will to live had sunk into an abyss decades ago.

Gatsby cleared her throat. "The Disk, the real one—do you know where it is?"

A knot in the firewood popped, making them both jump.

Cambier sighed. "I met the man in Zagreb. Ivan Hobart. Un archéologiste. I told him that I had the ROSETTE in my possession. We talked for many hours. He asked me if I planned to return it to the Heraklion. No, I was too afraid." She shook her head. "Hobart told me that he could keep it safe." Her eyes narrowed, and she seemed to be tiptoeing through the shadows of the past. "I gave it to him. He wanted to tell me where he would store it, but I said no. I insisted. Hobart knew nothing about the Circle or the danger he took upon himself, but he said that he felt as I did. The ROSETTE did not belong to anyone. To me, to him, to the Circle."

"This archeologist, Hobart—does he still have it?"

"Je ne sais pas. When I placed the ROSETTE in his hands, it was the last time I saw it or him. I returned to Marseille." Cambier pressed her fingertips together. "Then I was walking home from the supermarket. A man approached me—from the colorful garb, I thought he was a street performer. He grabbed me—he was very strong—and dragged me into an alley. I did not have time to shout. What did he want? My money? My food? I could see from the clothes and gold rings that he was not poor. I was terrified that he would kill me, but he only asked me a question: where is the Disk?"

"That's...how could a random stranger in Marseille know anything about it?" *Colorful garb, gold rings, a performer?* Gatsby's eyes bulged. *Affiato?!*

"Exactement. How *could* he know about the theft? *Multiple* thefts? Someone had breached the Circle. I realized its reach, and I knew that I could never trust anyone again, no matter where I went. I knew too that giving the ROSETTE to Hobart had been a mistake. Catastrophique."

She took a breath. "I could only say to the man 'I don't know.' It was the truth. I should have lied, but I had no more strength to lie or run. Then he put his face close to mine and said, 'It will bring you immortal glory or destruction.'"

(There it is on a clay platter—your immortal glory)

"Did Aff—" Gatsby clamped her lips together. "Did you ever see the man again?"

"Non, jamais." Her mottled hand fluttered. "Come this way."

She led Gatsby down the narrow hallway into a study and walked toward a desk. Her knuckles popped as she opened the top drawer and pulled out a spherical object about ten centimeters wide. The spiral of symbols was so familiar to Gatsby that it regularly appeared in her dreams. She felt her heart pounding.

"The Circle made several more replicas like this one to confound treasure hunters or art collectors. Black market traders." She held it forward. "You must take it."

"Another fake Disk? I don't want it. I just want to find the real one!"

"You will not find the original without this. You must accept it." The intensity in her blue eyes said *this is not a matter of choice.* "To answer your own question."

Gatsby felt her jaw tighten. "What question?"

"What *you* will risk for glory. What *you* will destroy." She curled a claw-like hand around Gatsby's forearm and herded her back to the kitchen.

Pulling the chairs away from the table and toward the fireplace, Cambier motioned for Gatsby to sit with her. She set the replica on the table, leaned toward the fireplace, and stirred the coals with an iron poker, throwing out a wave of sparks.

"Madame Cambier, I am grateful for…"

"Save your gratitude."

Gatsby felt her cheeks flush from the heat of the fire. As she tugged off her sweater, the hematite pendant popped out from the V of her shirt.

When Cambier's gaze shifted to it, her mouth popped open. For a long moment, she took deep, rapid breaths. "How did you get that?"

Gatsby leaned back out of the woman's vehemence and stammered, "It was sent to me in an unmarked package. I was seventeen."

Cambier's eyes bulged as if the pendant might explode. "Donnez le moi." *Give it to me.*

Gatsby pulled the gold chain over her head and held it out. Her fingers locked as if they had been encased in cement.

Dishes, books, baskets, light bulbs, picture frames...

(Don't let go!! If it touches the floor, you will regret...)

Livia's neurotic tortures! Fuck! A gasp burst from her lips when her hand snapped open.

Cambier reached out to take it, brought it up almost to her nose, and examined the rune-like markings. "Conservez-le soigneusement." *Guard it carefully.*

"Why? Cambier, why are you telling me all this? You said that you would not talk to anyone about the Disk."

The flames of the dying fire reflected in Cambier's eyes. Her chin dropped to her chest. She whispered, "For the sake of my Helena. Because of what I have told you, the Circle will find me."

"Cambier, no, I swear I won't..."

"They will take my life. I have wanted to die for a long time but have not had the courage to do it." She grabbed a teacup and flung it into the fireplace. It shattered against the brick; the liquid doused the coals into blackness. "Now I am ready."

The TGV flew through the darkness. Gatsby anchored her hands against the padded armrests, trying to relax but gripping them so hard that her knuckles cracked. The replica was securely stowed in the padded book bag on her lap. She stared down at it, swimming in questions. *Why the hell did she insist on giving me this? Another fake Disk?*

The feeling that wormed through her was forecasting nausea.

She retraced Affiato's trail of deceit and closed her eyes, willing the darkness to drown the fire in her gut, the voices that whispered like phantoms.

There it is on a clay platter—your immortal glory...

It will bring you immortal glory or destruction...

After a light breakfast, she paced her office, a full mug of Sumatran coffee in one hand and her smartphone in the other.

She said to guard the pendant carefully. Why? What did she really mean? She dialed Cambier's number.

"Oui?" The voice was that of an old man—impatient and stuffy. She remembered Tristan speaking with the subdued tones of a servant.

"Oui? Hello??"

"I'm sorry, yes, bonjour monsieur. I visited yesterday, um, I came to speak with Madam Cambier. Is she there?"

She heard him clear his throat and spit explosively. "Vous avez le nombre mauvais. Il n'y a pas un Cambier ici."

"I just...what? I saw her yesterday, and we talked for over an hour. 35 Rue de Cazes, right?"

"Je vous *dis*!" He paused. "Ohhhh, moment, vous avez dit Cambier?"

What the hell is this? "Yes, Eloise Cambier."

"Peut-être je me souviens maintenant. Je pense qu'elle a vécu ici il y a tres longtemps. Elle aurait pu mourir maintenant." *Perhaps I remember now. I think she lived here a long time ago. She may have died by now.*

"No, you...but I just..."

(Because of what I have told you, the Circle will find me)

"Vous m'entendez? Pah! Au revoir."

A click. The silence made her knees buckle.

CHAPTER 16

Gatsby maneuvered into an empty spot and pulled up the parking brake. Shoppers ambled past the driver's side window.

What bizarre joke this time? What new lie? There was no Doumas, or so she said. The man on the phone could have been lying, but the woman I met HAS to be Cambier. Why would someone of her age and experience give me a mountain of detailed information AND a performance that believable? She said she was part of this organization called the Circle and that SHE stole the Disk and gave it to someone named Hobart. Maybe the secret lover was actually Affiato. Who is telling the fucking truth?

(The scribe is a liar)

(The world has been deceived)

Groaning, she tipped her head back against the seat.

Volunteer any of it, or wait to see what he tells me? Just walk away from this insanity? She smacked a fist against the steering wheel. I can't. He's the ticket to finding the Disk.

Inside The Sorcerer's Apprentice, she found Affiato in THE ATHENAEUM.

He stepped from a dark corner of the room and strolled toward her. "There you are, delicious as ever! What is the report? Did you find Eloise Cambier? Speak to her?"

"Yes. Eighty years old or close to it."

"Eureka! The first piece of the puzzle has been found. What does she know about the Disk?"

Don't reveal everything. First find out what else he *knows.* "She said that she never knew Doumas and that he didn't take it from the Heraklion. Someone else did."

His hands flew up in a *how?* gesture. "Impossible. Kyro Doumas took it. He was adamant, and you saw all those love letters she sent him!"

He never stops! "Maybe Doumas knew who took it but decided to lie to you."

Affiato fingered his goatee, leveled a stare at her, and walked to the far side of the room. Once behind the bar, he pulled a bottle of Campari from under the counter, reached up to a shelf of glassware, selected a glass, and poured. His face clouded; the four fingers of his left hand undulated.

She leaned against the back of an armchair and swallowed; her mouth tasted coppery. *Do I believe an old woman who is terrified and hunted by some sort of shadow organization, whose memory may be muddy or completely ruined, assuming that anything she said is actually the truth? Or believe the pathological liar in front of me?*

Affiato sipped the liqueur. "Someone else, she said? Then who?"

"She didn't know."

"If she never met Doumas, and he never told her about his plans to steal the disk, how would she know anything about who took it?"

"Affiato, do you expect me to know every action that every person on this planet has taken for the last thirty years and the full extent of their motivations? I'm not omniscient! Christ."

He banged the glass down on the counter. "She must be lying. Or she is remembering incorrectly or misinformed. Talk to her again."

"I can't."

"You can't or you won't?"

She walked to the corner of the room and toward the Egyptian sarcophagus. "Both. Cambier..."

May or may not be the woman I just talked to. She may not even be alive.

"...is a dead end. Are you out of ideas?"

His eyes narrowed. "For the moment, but this is why I have called on you. Whatever information Madame Cambier may be able to provide is still valuable, and she was my suggestion. What is yours?"

Running her hand over the lid, carved to resemble an epicene face, she took a long breath. "We take a step back. We could be overlooking something that's hidden in plain sight. Maybe the Disk itself provides some clues. Whoever has it, maybe they pulled some esoteric meaning from the symbols and used it to select a hiding place, like designing a treasure map. I need to look at the symbols again." She shrugged. "And think."

Affiato rotated the gold rings luxuriously as if falling in love with them. A muscle twitched at the corner of his lip. "A fine idea. With your prowess over ancient languages, you may well be the virtuoso who ultimately deciphers the Disk. I will have it soon, and you will have your fingers on the throbbing jugular of posterity."

"God. I just want to find it. Don't you? If that's not your objective, tell me now, and we can jump off this crazy merry-go-round."

"Of course it is, more than ever." A greasy smile spread over his face as he edged toward her. "We both know that enterprises of great merit require great investment. Think of the investment I have made in you. You realize what you will owe to me in this venture, don't you? When the real Disk is found, it will be because I sought *you*."

He moved in until the hem of his cape swirled against her thighs. "Let us not forget the price of *your* impending glory, because there's something very desirable in it for me." His expression hinted at options for where his tongue might fit. "Something that you will offer quite willingly." His hand crept up and nestled on her breast.

She smacked it away as blood flushed her cheeks. "Fuck you!"

"Effettivamente." He chuckled.

CHAPTER 17

"I know, I know. He's a lunatic." She heard a drawn-out sigh, then silence. "Roman?"

"What do you want me to say?" He sounded as if he was trying to clear his throat and not succeeding. "The more reasons you have to stay away from him, the more you ignore them. This isn't like you. I've never known you to…" He paused. "Good god, Gatsby, we both know that scholarship can produce monumental discoveries, but each time you go near this man, you're begging for disaster. Is it *really* about the Disk?"

Leaning against the arm of the loveseat, she let the question submerge in her subconscious and glanced at the television at the other side of the living room.

"Are you there?"

"Yes."

"I can't stand by while you deliberately plant yourself in harm's way. It pains me to read obituaries!"

Gatsby squeezed her eyes shut. "Don't worry, Roman, you won't be reading mine. You know the mantra of academics and archeologists: great deeds require great daring."

An icon pulsed at the bottom of the phone's screen, and she heard a beep. "I have another call, Roman, I'll get back to you."

"But GM, don't y—"

She pressed the icon.

"Gatsby?"

A whirlwind blasted over her. The beige walls and artichoke-green furniture faded as heat bloomed in her chest. *No!*

"Are you there? Can you hear me?"

She pressed the phone against her temple hard enough to bruise the skin but didn't feel it. "What…*why* the hell are you calling me?"

"I need to know that you're all right."

"All right?" As she slumped into the loveseat, the anger erupted as staccato laughter. "That's light years from the truth, Livia. We haven't talked in eighteen years, and that's the best you can do?"

A sigh floated over the line. "Believe what you want. You always have." A pause. "I want to know if anything strange has happened to you lately."

"What, stranger than *this*? How the hell did you get my number?"

"Any strange people…"

"You have no business contacting me at any time for any reason. I don't…"

"Gatsby, stop." Rapid breathing. "I don't want a brawl. That's not my intention. I know that we haven't talked for a long time, and you had no reason to expect to hear from me."

(Never stop! Never give up!)

(NO MATTER WHAT IT TAKES, you little stoat!)

She pressed a hand against her belly, gritting her teeth. "Then what do you want?"

The silence dragged on. Five seconds, ten, fifteen. "To make sure you're all right."

The laugh hurt her throat. "Oh wait, let me check out the window for the horsemen and the rain of fire and the end of days. This is a joke, right? Did my father dare you to reach out and touch…are you stalking me?"

Blips and static crackled over the Atlantic-Pacific line.

Livia's voice was a rough whisper. "Tzadok, Nassarim, Bianchi. There will be many more. That's why I'm calling. Every turn of the wheel means sacrifice, Gatsby, and you are in the crosshairs."

"What are you talking about?"

"I can't give any more details." She paused. "Gatsby, ter-mot oh-pan-ker…"

"Go to hell!"

She ended the call and collapsed against the cushions. Outside her awareness, her hand rose and rippled over the pendant.

She stumbled toward the kitchen. Eighteen years, and she calls out of the blue? Every turn of the wheel means sacrifice—what the fuck does that mean?

In a few minutes, she returned to the loveseat, a White Russian clinking in one hand, and picked up the remote control. The television flared to life as she downed the drink in one gulp. She curled sideways, pulled the wool throw over her, and felt herself drifting off as the BBC news started.

"…when the body was pulled from a reservoir at the El Saad-el Aali, the Aswan High Dam. He appears to have drowned, but police are conducting a full investigation to determine whether this was a homicide or suicide. Abdul ben Nassarim was a top general in Hesh al-Dalah, the Egyptian network of Hamas. We go now to the United States and the disturbing story of Rico Bianchi, the son of Antone Bianchi and the Don of one of the most powerful Mafia families. This morning, he was found dead in his room at the Hotel Palomar in Chicago…"

CHAPTER 18

Livia gunned the engine of the Lexus, waiting for the traffic light at Sand Point Way and NE 70th to turn green. She glanced at the dashboard clock. *Fifteen minutes to get to the U District. Why didn't I take the freeway?*

"Come on, come on, let's GO!" Tapping her nails on the steering wheel had no effect on the light. The passenger seat was piled with academic detritus: a collection of parking tickets, the origami of wax paper that once held a cheeseburger, a dripping umbrella, and a leather briefcase packed with paperwork. She spotted the slip of paper, hastily read and then folded. See you Saturday—Thomas.

Maybe, Thomas.

Rendezvous with her husband were becoming rare. The hours at the computer, the guest lectures, readings, and conferences, the full teaching schedule—she was married to all of them in a type of intellectual polygamy.

She drifted back to their heated discussion, two days ago, about his daughter.

(There's no mystery here, Liv. Why should she call? When she does, you start the yelling and insulting, and I'm forced—AGAIN—to play referee)

(There's not one grain of sense in her and you know it. I've done everything I can to...)

(To what? Crucify her because she doesn't worship at the altar of YOUR achievements?)

(Thomas, for chrissake, how can you think...)

The light turned green. She floored the pedal, but the car ahead of her stopped suddenly.

BANG!! The impact threw her forward. The seatbelt caught, snapping hard against her chest. The horn sputtered and then stuck, blaring a continuous scream. The emergency lights of the car in front of her began flashing as the driver's door flew open, and a red-haired woman in a Mariners sweatshirt and Levi's barreled toward her.

"What do you think you are DOING, you crazy..."

Pulling in a breath to focus, Livia unbuckled her seatbelt and pushed the door open. Ignoring the woman's made-for-TV tirade, she checked the front fender of her own car and the rear bumper of the woman's Accord, relieved to see that the damage was superficial. She walked back to the driver's side of her Lexus and leaned in to pull her bag from the front seat.

"LEARN HOW TO DRIVE, BITCH!? BEFORE YOU FUCKING…"

"Shut up before I rip out your ovaries and serve them with coq au vin."

The woman froze, mouth open. She took a halting step back.

An SPD squad car pulled up behind the Lexus, and the door popped open. A burly Hispanic policewoman moved toward them, looking Livia up and down and then eyeing the redhead. "Anyone injured?"

The cop looks familiar. Where have I seen her? An image popped into her mind, and the association clicked. Ram2 in Vancouver, BC. "Dan-ruz?"

The officer stared for a moment, face blank, and then nodded. "Mil-ser oh tan-wuz."

The redhead's expression melted into tepid neutrality. She pushed her hands into her pockets and shifted her weight from one foot to another. "Man ruz-in-dan sil oh suz-mer."

The policewoman knelt on one knee to examine the paint scratches on the fenders. "Per wil-un der, kan un."

Livia moved toward the redhead, close enough to speak in a whisper. "Mer oh-ser? Ensh pan oh. San Ivy9?"

Eyes wide, the redhead shook her head.

With furtive backward glances, the women wandered back to their cars. They slid into their driver's seats and began to creep back into the bumper-to-bumper traffic.

CHAPTER 19

In her office, Gatsby turned her chair as if the pendulum-like motion might jostle ideas. She glanced at the bottom-right corner of the computer screen. It was almost midnight. The only sounds in the flat were the ticks of the radiator and an occasional honk on King's Road.

The deep silence, solitude, reminds me...

She was back in the bedroom of her childhood: ecru-colored walls covered with posters of Kenya and Einstein, the door painted with swirls of letters, glyphs, and symbols, the bookcase stuffed with her own books and titles from the Seattle Public Library, the cloying smell of lavender air freshener that instantly made her think of Livia.

RUZ WER DAN.

Over the years, she had played amateur cryptographer and researched the basics of encryption, finding it a mind-numbing labyrinth of mathematics and esoteric strategies. Efforts to conceal the meaning of messages went back as far as the Caesar Cipher, devised during the reign of Julius Caesar, and since the 1700s, dozens of methods had been invented. She found that a key feature of encrypted text was the frequency of symbols or letters in the ciphertext. She scoured websites to learn about the Polybius Checkerboard, the Cardano Grille, the quadrilateral alphabet, and Alberti's Disk.

She traded volumes of instant messages, late at night, with a "Hash-Diff" who introduced her to ciphers: wheel, polyalphabetic, Talmadge, Freemason, Rosicrucian, and Playfair. Hash-Diff gave her the ciphertext GPZE IBURW PJOF to decrypt, quietly logged out of the conversation, and went dark.

She warned me not to look for you. Why can't I let this go?

Gatsby ran her fingers through her hair.

(NEVER LET GO!)

Because I was well trained...

"Stop!" The outburst echoed off the walls and barreled back at her like gunfire. "Put it aside. For fuck's sake…"

She saw the etched canvas of Cambier's face: *You will not find the original without this…guard it carefully.*

Spinning harder in the chair caused the hematite pendant to bump against her breastbone.

A circle with seven dots, flower with eight petals. She tugged the pendant from around her neck and studied the markings with laser intensity. The images and sounds of academia rose in her mind: a wide auditorium, dimmed lights, the podium, slides projected on the enormous overhead screen, polite coughs from the audience.

When was that, three years ago? Four? The lecture series at University of Bristol, right. A study of the symbols that are clearly pictographic in both Linear B and proto-Minoan.

The details were as fresh as the almond biscotti she had that morning at Panerie SW3. She saw the curious faces of the students and faculty members, remembering that Roman not only attended but provided a lengthy, handwritten critique of the presentations. She remembered the scream of feedback from the microphone, then her voice echoing.

"Attempts to assign meaning to the images are plentiful, but it's critical to look at the anomalies and to evaluate which symbols are unique. For example, a number of them appear only once. As you can see, here on the A side, one unique image is the labrys or axe. It represents the slaughter of enemies, so it's thought to be a symbol of death, of destruction. On the B side, the symbol of the lily correlates to the olive branch that was given to the victor of a battle, alluding to praise or glory…"

The chair squeaked like a small animal as she pivoted. *But are they a proper language or arbitrary? A game? A poem? A mathematical equation? A recipe for bloody souvlaki? What would make sense to whoever created them in 1850 BC?*

She swiveled toward the computer and clicked on a folder containing the bulk of her research notes on Linear B.

The primary use for Linear B was measurement—how many oxen, casks of rice, bundles of wheat—but the Phaistos Disk has a clear relation to time. Thirty-one word sets on Side A, thirty on B—the number of days in the months of the Gregorian calendar. Then there's the spiral shape. For the movements of the planets? Unending cycles? And the symbols appearing on both sides, perhaps for yin and yang? Dark and light? Underscoring how all cycles have a season of growth and a season of death?

She tucked the pendant back under her t-shirt while rapidly tapping her foot on the caster of the chair. *Decipherment isn't the burning question right now, Donovan. Finding the Disk is.*

The long-buried desire to know who sent her the pendant flared. *These symbols—the axe, the slaughter of enemies. The lily, the victor of a battle. When this damn thing arrived in the mail, I was still in high school. Decades ago. How could this help, in any conceivable way, to find the Disk now?*

She gripped it tighter. Questions emerged vividly in her mind, almost as though she were drawing them on a whiteboard.

What is the hidden message of the Phaistos Disk?

Where is the Disk hidden?

Who sent me this pendant and why?

What is the element that links all the pieces?

One piece is undeniable: Affiato. The next thought crept into her mind on spider legs. *Cambier said "it will bring you immortal glory or destruction."*

Outside her awareness, her hand rippled over the pendant.

She heard Cambier's voice again, dry as eggshells: *You will not find the original without this. You must accept it to answer your own question: what you will risk for glory. What you will destroy.*

(NO MATTER WHAT IT TAKES, you little stoat!)

The steam radiator blared to life, making her jump. Her fingers tensed, gripping the pendant through the fabric of her shirt.

Ten minutes later, she returned to her office and logged into her email program. A message had arrived in the inbox fifteen minutes ago. As she opened it and read, her eyes widened.

```
THE INFINITE CHAKRA
SERVES THE GUARDIAN
THE GUARDIAN DECAYS
IN THE CAGE OF TIME
```

Her eyes darted to the sender's address.

```
tsvk249@blicko.uk
```

She opened Google and did a search for the domain name. The error message popped up.

```
Can't find the Web site
(500 unknown Host)
The site may no longer exist
or it may have moved
```

A phony address. It was probably sent through a remailer, a no-name server. I think that tracking down an anonymous user is doable but takes time.

She went back to the message. *Chakra again. Wheel. Like the earlier message, 'The ancient chakra did align.' What Guardian? What cage of time??*

She combed sweaty hands through her hair. *It HAS to be Affiato. He has new information, and this is his sadistic way of providing a lead.*

(Every turn of the wheel means sacrifice)

Bits of the BBC evening news, half-heard as she had dozed, trickled into her mind and tripped a vague association. *The story about two men who were killed. Did one of the names sound Arabic? Where were they? One was somewhere in the Middle East. One was...some kind of*

Mafia connection, I think. Livia mentioned three names, and there was a...Bellini? No, Bianchi, that was it.

Her heart began pounding in her ears.

She must have heard this news story and then called me? She swallowed hard. Did Livia Rudden know these people were about to die?

(There will be many more. That's why I'm calling. Every turn of the wheel means sacrifice, Gatsby.)

Wheel, the infinite chakra, the Phaistos Disk.

Sacrifice sounded like a ticking bomb.

(And you are in the crosshairs)

Fear knotted her stomach.

CHAPTER 20

"You love to take the blame for things you haven't done wrong, Aria. Don't be eblan." *A dumbass.* Miranovski sat back in the executive chair, her face tight. Hoda and Dhar glanced at each other across the conference table.

Vlahos leaned against the doorjamb, arms crossed over her chest. "Tell me why then. I deliver the reports, and the next day, she leaves for London." She walked across the room, staring down at the carpet and muttering. "I screwed up the delivery. I missed something, or the CAT wasn't..."

"For fuck's sake. Sit down, Vlahos. If you're going to have a meltdown every time the SWORD gets on a plane or takes a shit, I swear I'll call the dog." Dhar sprawled across the table, whimpering and pounding her fists in a mock tantrum, before she sat back and shot Vlahos a look.

A breeze wafted in through the window, making Miranovski's hair flutter. On Ippokratous Street, two men were engaged in a passionate argument about the Greek economy. A dog barked until someone shouted, "Kane isychia!" *Be quiet!*

With a sigh, Vlahos dropped into a chair at the far end of the table.

The hard set of Miranovski's face showed her wariness. "It feels odd to convene without the SWORD."

Dhar spun her STAR SEED in circles on the table top, still yawning to pop her ears after the four-hour flight from Reggio Calabria Airport to Athens International Airport. "Forget how it feels. When we need to know why she went to London, she'll tell us. Miranovski, you were doing the post mortem, so can we get on with it?"

"All BOOMERANG operations were successful but with mistakes. Tamar Tzadok breeched confidentiality. It almost required intervention, but she managed to complete the operation. Musgrove fucked up placement."

Tess frowned. "How?"

"She attached the DOLIUM at the neck instead of the groin." Dhar scoffed contemptuously. "Inexcusable, especially for a fucking MAIZE."

"What's your AXE recommendation?" Miranovski said.

"You'll have it in the morning."

Tess pressed her palms together. "Let's move on. WHITE BIRD is seventy-two hours. Your status reports—Hoda?"

"Code for the container chip needs to be refreshed," Hoda said. "Completion expected this evening. I almost put the CAT from Palo Alto on this. She's a machine—I'm not convinced that she has a pulse." She shook her head. "But she doesn't have the experience for this operation. I installed three sets of TOR socks. Tonight I'll finalize the TRAN packet filters and proxy load tests."

"Who is your team lead?" Miranovski asked.

"Crowley."

"Noted. Dhar?"

Dhar recited the names in one fast breath as if repeating an incantation. "Amira Jazazi, Rachel Moskowitz, Sabeen al-Najdi, Farida Sharraf, Ishtar Wahid, Carol Young, Devin Blaine, Maria del Scorro, Franca Volante, Marta Obsanje, Jun Tokada, Rose Perrin. All checked in at 0700, all operational. Perrin reports arrests and shootings in her region around the presidential convention. The Americans are in the middle of a clusterfuck."

"Is it a blocker?"

"Not until it turns into riots." She entwined her fingers and tucked her hands behind her head. "I'll add Orion."

Miranovski grabbed the weight of her blond curls and pushed it over her shoulder. Her eternally serious expression made the other BOAT members joke that she looked like a ship captain navigating rough seas. "Noted. We need to assess the threat of SHIP-1 and SHIP-2. The American has a history of studying the ROSETTE. Writing, teaching, conferences, and the like. Academic types are usually benign."

"Not always," Hoda said. "They're walking databases. Every so often, one gets tired of scrambling to survive on a teacher's salary and looks for a financial shortcut."

Dhar cut in. "Forget her profession, did you see who raised her? A RAM, the one that received some kind of high-profile award!"

"And then had it yanked," Miranovski said. "An Aeon Award. Dolastanos tells me it's the equivalent of a Nobel Prize in the field of antiquities. More important, she's a RAM who chalked up five Level 3 violations. How likely is it that she *didn't* pass on her tendencies to a stepdaughter?"

"It's inevitable," Vlahos muttered.

The BOAT members turned toward her with surprised looks.

"Agree," Miranovski said. "We don't know what she picked up from her notorious stepmother. We don't know exactly what her association or business is with SHIP-2. We do know that decades of her life have been devoted to the ROSETTE, enough to border on obsession. Who is on surveillance?"

"Bashir," Dhar said. "CAT46 as backup." She began fiddling with the pouch of her waistpack.

"Keep me updated. For SHIP-2, the obvious bug is gender." Miranovski's eyebrows curled over her deep-set eyes. "We've handled plenty of infiltration attempts before, but this raises a red flag: an association with SHIP-1 that is both close and fresh."

"And the lack of records prior to opening the retail business in London," Hoda said. "Criminal background. There have to be records with law enforcement or INTERPOL. He travels everywhere and has lived in at least five countries, not including the UK."

"Who do you have running down leads?"

"Kosek. She's the best."

Dhar stood, walked to the other side of the table, hands pressed on her hips, and started moving toward the door.

"Where are you going?"

Her tone was belligerent. "I'm bored. Are we done here?"

"No, so sit down." Miranovski shot her a stern look. "One thing keeps bothering me. The message that...Dhar?"

Standing by the doorway, Dhar leaned against the wall. She shrugged, a "what are you going to do about it" expression on her face. Hoda and Vlahos looked her up and down and then turned back to Miranovski. They knew Dhar to be an active agent, not a passive listener. Her inability to stay in one place for long proved to be an asset—a trait that made her nearly as fierce an assassin as the SWORD.

Miranovski continued. "The message that we received from the HAMMER. The infinite chakra, the guardian, all that der'mo. That crazy challenge is so old it's practically mythic. The SWORD said that it may seem innocuous or arbitrary but doesn't think it is. I believe her. Hoda, when did it start circling the BEEHIVE? Do you remember?"

Hoda shook her head. "Before my time. A FORK brought it up during my training, recited it word for word and never mentioned it again."

"It means something important to someone. Pranks disappear and are forgotten, but this is a zombie message. It won't die."

"Sure it will." Dhar pushed her hand into the waistpack pouch, pulled out a TIARA, turned toward the screen mounted on the side wall, and took aim. Miranovski and Hoda kicked their chairs over and bolted, scattering to the corners of the room. Vlahos squealed and smacked her forearm against a leg of the table as she scrambled under it.

"Tchyo za ga'lima! What is this??"

Dhar pointed the barrel of the TIARA at each of three framed art pieces on the wall and then lowered her hand. She stowed the TIARA back in its pouch and shrugged. "Zombies are easy to kill when you have the right ammunition."

Trishna Banerjee rubbed her eyes until dots sparkled in her vision. She glanced at the clock on the far wall of the lab. *0400. God. The third time Leesha has missed her shift because of illness, and the last bloody time I cover for her.*

A flu going around in Prabhadevi? No way. HORN. She's probably pregnant again.

As she folded the top flaps and sealed the box with packing tape, fatigue blurred her vision; she shook her head and took a deep breath to refocus.

The address label…where is it?

She reached across the counter and grabbed the shipping label that had printed a few minutes earlier. With a quick motion, she pulled off the self-adhesive backing and smoothed the label over the top of the package.

One last tracking step.

She rolled her stool toward the far end of the counter and pulled a keyboard toward her. The monitor showed a time-tracking and project management program. Banerjee moved the cursor to a box at the bottom of the screen and clicked. A small checkmark appeared as *Complete* flashed.

Shipment on its way to Palermo—done! I'm outta here.

A huge yawn moved through her, and the sleep-deprivation headache throbbed insistently. She walked around the room, making sure that all the containers and shelving units were locked. After she powered down all six computers, she grabbed her jacket and walked toward the entrance, too quickly and too buzzy to notice that the shipping label read "313 King's Road, Chelsea SW3 London UK."

CHAPTER 21

She dried her hands on the seat of her jeans as she walked down the hallway to her office.

(He said that he could take it to a place where it would be safe...I gave him the Disk...he knew nothing about the Circle or the danger he took upon himself)

I have to find this archeologist, Ivan Hobart, but if he still has the Disk—or ever had it—would he admit it? How remote are the chances that he will talk to me?

The doubts made her head hurt, and while more questions piled up, she sat before her computer, opened Google, and typed "Ivan Hobart" in the search field. Links and photos filled the screen: a modern artist, a high school teacher in Perth, a microbiologist, a German restauranteur, a professor of archeology...

Bingo! She zeroed in on the last link and clicked.

**Barcelona Prof Receives ICFP Grant for
Funerary Site Research**
The recipient of the ICFP grant for academic research is Dr. Ivan Hobart at the University of Barcelona. Along with Pascal Broussard, Université Paris-Sud, Hobart was instrumental in excavation and findings at the Gobero burial site in Niger. He will head three projects to study the convergence of commemorative practices, ecology, and hominid culture. The focus of the work is genetic relationships based on morphological traits in the skeletons of...

As if an afterthought, a short biography followed the article.

Hobart received a doctor of philosophy in archeology at the University of Exeter and led the osteoarchaeology programme at University of Barcelona. He is the coauthor of Songs of Burial: Archaeology of Graves of Tontan (Welles-Ryder

Press) and a regular contributor to Social
Archaeology. Dr. Hobart lives in Sabadel, Spain.

She scanned for a date and spotted it. *From five years ago, but he may still be there.* Clicking back to Google, she scrolled, and a second link caught her eye.

**Egyptian Artifacts Recovered,
Archeologist Arrested**
MADRID—A collection of funerary artifacts, recently discovered in Minya, Egypt, was stolen during transport to the Cairo Museum of Egyptian Antiquities. Through the cooperative efforts of the Policia Nacional, INTERPOL, and the International Council for Museum Security, the artifacts were located and confiscated from Ivan Hobart. He was sentenced to a term of 15 years at Bajestaros Penitenciario. Dr. Hobart taught at the University of Barcelona until 2005.

He's arrested for stealing artifacts and now serving time in a Spanish prison. Cambier said she met him in Zagreb, and this is who she entrusted with the Disk? If there was no Doumas, maybe there is no Hobart. She shook her head. *Maybe there is no Cambier.*

Her next search took her to the Bajestaros Penitenciario website. The prison was in Vicalvaro; a map showed that it was a district southeast of Madrid.

I've never been inside a penitentiary. How do you do this? She located the FAQ page and read the top paragraph.

VISITING / APPOINTMENTS

If you wish to visit an inmate, call the Services Office and leave a message. The Services Office will schedule your visit and contact you within three business days.

She picked up her phone and dialed. *Exit code, country code, city...00 34 91 375 9079...here goes nothing.* The line connected.

After waiting for the recorded message to end, she cleared her throat. "This is Dr. Gatsby Donovan. I work with

the British Museum, and I need to schedule a meeting with
Ivan Hobart as soon as possible."

CHAPTER 22

The call from the Oficina de Servicios came the next day. Huddled at the computer in her office, Gatsby jotted notes on a scrap of paper as she replayed the voicemail message.

Your request for a visit has been processed and is scheduled for Friday 3 June at 1:00 p.m. Please read the Visitations page. Sign the acknowledgment form where indicated. Then click the box below.

While she read, something banged in the hallway hard enough to make the monitor shake.

What the hell was that?

She walked to her entry and opened the door. A package the size of a shoe box, wrapped in brown paper, sat on the blue carpet. As she picked it up, she was instantly seventeen years old, rooted on the landing of her house in West Seattle, staring at a package wrapped in coarse brown paper with no name or return address.

With each step between the entry and the living room, she felt her heart beat faster. She slid into the loveseat, mind whirling, and tore open the paper. It was a squarish container of molded, light-grey plastic.

Medical supplies? Or some kind of hazardous waste?

The lid was attached with a small clasp. She pushed on the underside, and the lid snapped with a POP, making her jump. She gripped the edge and raised it to find that the container was filled with packing foam that looked like grey cotton candy. It held a second container about the dimensions and thickness of a CD jewel case, the edge secured by a hinged bracket.

As she wrangled the bracket open and raised the lid, she saw a flesh-colored square that resembled a transdermal nicotine patch. She carefully pulled off the backing to see a thin sheet of spongy material.

This has *to be a medical shipment that went to the wrong address. Why all the tedious packing?*

She meandered to the kitchen, went to the metal waste bin in the corner, and tossed the patch in. As she walked toward the hall closet where she kept a larger recycling tub, she thought, *Any delivery from a legit medical lab or clinic would have a return address. And why hand delivery?*

In the kitchen, the waste bin was spasming.

She turned and ran. By the time she got to the kitchen, the container was shuddering with thuds and high-pitched screams. Empty soup cans and microwave boxes were hurriedly tossed from the bin. At the bottom, a brown mouse lay on its side. When it nosed at the spongy surface, the patch had adhered to its face. Its arms and legs clawed, it tail went rigid. A blood bubble popped from its open mouth, and it collapsed, eyes fixed.

Christ! Who sent this? What if I had touched it?!

CHAPTER 23

The voice on the PA informed the passengers that the plane was landing at Madrid-Barajas International Airport in fifteen minutes.

Gatsby saved her notes, powered down her laptop, and stowed it away in its case.

She wandered the halls of the concourse, looking for signs that directed travelers to the taxi bays. She found the pickup zone, and in a few minutes, a red-and-black cab pulled over to the curb.

She climbed into the back seat, digging the city map out of her shoulder bag. "Vicálvaro, Calle San Carrera 10."

"Muy bien." The driver's voice was deep and cigarette-dry. He gunned the engine and started down the exit ramp toward the highway.

During the half-hour ride, she was struck by the vibrancy of the city. The azure sky was reflected in the lakes of the plentiful city parks, many with running waterfalls. She saw Old World architecture with Catholic statuary and frescos, a bustling if dilapidated downtown, and lavish churches flanked with spires. Down every cobblestone street and alley, she saw shops overflowing with glass art, fabrics, jewelry, and clothing. Classic and modern artwork graced the windows. Rustic housing with dusty-rose facades was juxtaposed with hotels that resembled the castles of Moorish invaders.

The cab slowed in front of Bajestaros Penitenciario until it stopped, and the driver turned around to glare at her. "You sure this is where you want to go?"

She nodded, handed him €25, and climbed out of the cab.

"Gracias." He muttered and began whistling as the cab pulled away.

The angular avant-garde architecture did nothing to soften the building's despotic presence. The concrete and glass brought to mind the song "Hotel California," but with a deep breath, she started down the cement path and the stairs leading to the entry.

The lobby resembled an airport security checkpoint. She loaded her shoulder bag and laptop onto a conveyor belt, emptied her pockets of keys and coins, stepped through an x-ray scanner, and retrieved her items. As she walked toward the information counter, she spotted black-uniformed officers working in front of monitors. One looked up at her. "Yes?"

"I scheduled a meeting with Ivan Hobart."

He typed quickly on the keyboard, eyes zipping across the monitor. "7922, Donovan. There it is. I need to see your photo ID."

She dug in her shoulder bag, pulled out her passport, and held it forward. After looking at the photo, he typed rapidly. "It will be a few minutes. Please have a seat."

She moved to a huddle of padded chairs and sat. *The article wafted through her mind: The artifacts were confiscated from Dr. Ivan Hobart, a professor of archeology. He was arrested and received a sentence of 15 years at Bajestaros Penitenciario. He taught at the University of Barcelona until 2005...*

Fifteen years in this place? I can't imagine what sort of...

A lanky officer with a surly expression hovered over her. His nametag said NGEMA.

"Dr. Donovan? Come with me."

He escorted her down a narrow hallway, stopped before an office door, opened it, and gestured for her to enter. An officer sat behind a desk strewn with paperwork. The nameplate precariously close to the edge read LEAH CABRERA / OFICINA DE SERVICIOS. She raised her eyes to meet Gatsby's and waved her toward the chair on the other side of the desk. "Please."

Ngema remained at the doorway. Gatsby frowned over her shoulder at him. "I'm here to see Dr. Ivan Hobart. What is..."

"I know that," Cabrera said in a stress-ragged voice. A scar, lighter than her dark skin, trickled from one temple toward her ear. "I want to know why. Please sit."

Gatsby felt her neck muscles cramp. *Called for questioning in a private office in a Spanish prison. Some of these institutions are notorious. Make one wrong move, look at the wrong person the wrong way, and they can hold you for any bloody reason and for as long as they want. Play it cool.* She coughed lightly. "He worked in an esoteric field, funerary osteoarchaeology. He's the top expert on the subject, and I need to talk to him. I'm writing a monogram."

"A monogram." Cabrera tapped the eraser of a pencil on her desktop. "Hobart was convicted of stealing a cache of very valuable pieces. You are aware of this, Señora?"

Gatsby tried for a placid expression. "I read an article about it on the web, but that's all I know."

"How do you know him?"

"I don't. I've never met him personally."

"What else do you know about Dolly?"

"Dolly? What do you mean?"

The officer raised her chin. "I mean Señor Hobart."

She closed her eyes, trying to remember the details of the article. "He was given some kind of award from his institution. University of Barcelona, I think. And INTERPOL tracked him down to recover the stolen Iranian artifacts." She pulled in a deep breath.

"Egyptian." Cabrera stared at her with amphibious eyes. "You've never spoken by phone? Written correspondence? Email?"

"No, never."

"Tell me about the paper you are writing."

"It focuses on links between funerary relics and my field project, the Phaistos Disk."

"Who are you writing for?"

"It will be released through the publishing department of the British Museum."

Cabrera looked past Gatsby, caught Ngema's eye, and nodded. "Okay, bueno."

"This way." Ngema slid to her side and turned to usher her into the hallway.

Gatsby followed behind him and heard beeps as Cabrera dialed a phone. She spoke in a muted voice. "Kan-ser-ruz. Oh mer-kot-tuz dan..."

Ngema led her down the hallway, reciting institution policies. "Smoking is prohibited in all areas in the facility. You may be observed or video-recorded. You have thirty minutes. Room D." He stopped before a grey door and unlocked it. A cynical grin moved over his face. "Good luck with Dolly."

"Dolly? What is that about?"

"Oh, a nickname. They call him dolly because he draws these crazy pictures like the artist, Salvador Dali."

She nodded. "All right."

"Thirty minutes." He pushed on the door and motioned inside.

She stepped into the room to find two padded chairs sitting at a plain conference table. The walls were bare except for light switches, an intercom panel, and an oblong mirror with no frame. *For two-way viewing? No doubt.*

The door squeaked, and a lanky man in prison uniform— dark blue shirt, loose pants—ambled toward her. His weary smile accentuated the web of creases around his eyes. "Gatsby Donovan, well-ummm." He shuffled toward the empty chair and sank into it, grimacing as if his joints hurt.

"Hello, Dr. Hobart. I'm honored to..."

"Cut the shit." He tipped his head back, squeezing his eyes shut for a moment. "Sorry. I don't mean to be rude, but, well, as you might imagine, I am out of practice." His gaze drifted over the grey concrete walls. "We can skip the erstwhile niceties, sparrow. And the preliminaries."

She sat forward in the chair. *Sparrow?* "Fine with me."

"You're with the, um, British Museum, yes? Ha ha ha, well, so good for you. I've read some things, many things, about you." He cleared his throat. "I would hazard a guess, but ha ha, you grace me with your esteemed presence, and I have so few visitors. Well, none. Why are you here?"

"I need to talk to you about the Phaistos Disk."

His expression was flat, but she saw his chest undulate. He spoke breathlessly as if being chased. "The Phaistos Disk, well. Ha ha. Yes, it's good, good to have a disk, always better than a whisk. The artifact at the Heraklion Museum, Crete, I believe, Minoan, yes? Most say it is a hoax. Why talk about that?"

"The French woman, Cambier. I met her, and she says that she knows you."

"Hmm." He pulled in a breath, exhaled slowly. "Eloise. Lady fair, well, yes yes yes. Effusive, all the many details."

What will he reveal? Or deny?

"Her daughter knew Paolo, one of my top students, lazy hearsay, so she knew where I was teaching, of course. Ah well. She came to me to discuss a stupendous proposition."

"She said she met you in Zagreb."

"Well, ha ha! Zagreb. No, no, I met Eloise in Marseille."

Unbelievable. "What was the proposition?"

"She was joking, yes? She had to be. Her own salvo haptic covers, yes? No? Of course! That she could possibly have in her possession the world-famous Phaistos Disk? How? And moreover why? No, it was behind bullet-proof glass in Crete. Oh well, a dispossessing game. I didn't believe it, couldn't. I brushed it off. I laughed."

"And?"

His eyes narrowed. "When she placed it in my hands, I almost collapsed. Insensitive, hmm, tinsel sad, sadly, badly…"

What the hell did these people do to him? Psychotropic drugs? Electroshock?

She spread her hands across the table top as if it might levitate. "Eloise Cambier. I went to her home in Marseille and talked with her for several hours. She has an astounding story, and she gave me a lot of information about the Disk, but not everything. I'm not sure whether or not to believe any of it. She's an old woman, and her memory may be fuzzy. It's entirely possible that everything she said is imagined."

(Je pense qu'elle a vécu ici il y a tres longtemps. Elle aurait pu mourir maintenant)

"Hobart, did she tell you how she acquired it?"

"No. I didn't want to know. Better for both of us and the best of us, all of us. I didn't know, um, that by taking it, I sealed my fate in the delicate flight. The deep prefix of science. The educator, ha ha, the respectable professor of archeology, Barcelona, soon to turn to black market trading, reputable hater of agents, but, well, um, you know that hunger can turn even the upstanding man to crime. Several delicious markets." He gave her a hard look over the top of his battered eyeglasses. "Or the upstanding woman."

"I haven't broken any laws. That I know of. So you're saying she did give you the Disk. What did you do with it?"

"I wanted to donate it to the Louvre, anonymously, no name, no fame, the ghost in the workable caster, no? Ha ha, let them deal with it. Well, I kept it for six months, um, all ergo bravado, but life turned upside down." He gave a morose sigh while scratching vigorously at his chin. "No job, no money, working savvy, all for some dystopian morsels, and then no food. I was desperate, crazy, to go to the big top mill and the trader. I finally decided to meet with the trader."

"Who is the trader?"

He raised his chin. "You don't need to know *that*, sparrow. He learned that I was an archeologist go-dig-go-dig and that I needed money. I learned a lot from him, um, quickly, ha ha, about the arts of buying and selling antiquities. Highly profitable, prescription processes demonstrandum!" He coughed. "All completely illegal, of course. Malevolent, regency or Socratic diversity. He knew that a cache of artifacts had been discovered in Minya and was being delivered, yes, to the museum, all preparatory conservation and talented, in Cairo la la, high-energy salutation, so he hijacked the shipment."

"Wait—*he* took the artifacts but you were caught?"

"Yes. All funerary items. Statuary, masks, a lot of gold jewelry, ah lustrous, golden treasure, and at first he wanted me to store everything. Then he offered to sell them, solution classification beatitude, to me, ha ha, free speech for venerable Signore Dali." He glanced up at the frameless window, winked, and crossed his arms; his fingers wriggled like flukes. "Reselling that cache would be the transaction of a lifetime, go get the gold, my indifference, the end of poverty, um, but, well, hard times, the crack in the tovarich, but I screwed up, and once I had them, I broke the terms of our contract, international indoctrinated flippant." He shook his head. "The trader was not the type of man you want to anger. Ingratia inconsistent! I knew I would pay, eventually, dearly, medieval valley, sad sad sad. He told the International Antiquities Recovery Agency that the missing artifacts were with the, um, guilty party, diagnostic artifact, and the next thing I know, I am rudely awakened, lithic skeletons, and the agents are knocking at the door of my villa. Storming the test pits!"

As he curled sideways in the chair, he gave a weak laugh. "We all got what we deserved. Yes? Ha, maybe forever delusionary. Or clarity. The artifacts are imprisoned in Cairo. I am imprisoned here, sparrow. World aesthetics, ta da, ta da, site debitage, all datum, the rate for this average rubble."

Has he gone insane? She spoke deliberately, slowly. "Tell me what happened to the Phaistos Disk. It's not at the Heraklion. I contacted Stephanos Alexiou, the curator, and pressed him to conduct a TL test. The disk he's storing is a forgery, about thirty years old. I have to find the real one, and if Cambier gave it to you, you're the only person who knows its location. Where is it?"

Hobart leveled a stare at her, fingertips pressed deep into his cheeks. His eyes shifted rapidly between the wall, the floor, the table, and Gatsby's face. "Well well well. A forgery. Fascination, clever arrow, bilingual discoveries in Crete." He pulled in a breath, leaned forward, and whispered. "The day before I was sentenced, in situ dogs, I hid it. Hiding abiding. It is quite safe, spatial local. All decadence in a sober cage."

Cage…decays in the cage of time? A bolt shot through her. "Hobart, I got an anonymous email with a strange message, a sort of riddle, and if it has anything to do with the Disk, I can't figure it out. The infinite chakra serves the Guardian, the Guardian decays in the cage of time."

He turned away, eyes shuttered. His hands splayed over his thighs, fingers rippling as if playing a keyboard instrument.

"Hobart, look at me. Focus! Does this mean anything to you?"

He sighed, seeming to ponder cosmic questions. "Paenitet me, sparrow. Sorry."

She studied the grizzled face, darting eyes, and frantic hands. "I wasn't sure you would be willing to talk with me about any of this. Convinced you wouldn't, actually. You just met me and have no reason to trust me. Why tell all?"

"All? Ha ha." Hobart stood abruptly, rubbing the small of his back. "We both know that the Phaistos Disk is a one of a kind, settle mettle, you know, kettle. After four thousand years, it remains the mystery of the ages, apathetic monologue, the enduring puzzle that, um, no one can crack ha ha ha! Bronze goddess facet! Enigma baby! We—you and I—are not the only ones who want it, sparrow, ever leftist anonymous, and since the day I lay hands on it, I have received more death threats than I can count. Temporal components crash!" He sputtered with anger, jammed his hands into his pockets, and glared at her with bulging eyes. "Other than our dear Eloise, who the hell could know that I had it? Mortui non mordent! I want the fucking thing out of my life!" He tipped back against the wall, panting.

She spoke quietly. "Are you going to tell me where it is?"

He stared at the floor for a long beat, then nodded.

"A trader will not give away information, especially information this important. Aside from the historic value, the Disk has to be worth millions on the black market. You wouldn't tell me all this without wanting something in return."

"Of course I do. I want my fucking life back. My peace of mind, all pieces of mine, my ethnographic shards. Copious accomplishment! Take the bloody Phaistos Disk, and you will give me that. Take it away, take it to hell!" He leveled a chary look at her. "But knowing what you know, why do *you* want it, sparrow?"

She frowned. "Why do you keep calling me sparrow?"

He threw his arms out, palms pressed against the concrete walls as if pleading with the ceiling. "Dum spiro spero, of course. Use those famous brains, girl."

"While I breathe, I hope." She stared down at the polyethylene table, poked at something nonexistent on the surface, and looked back up at him. "Okay. Where is it?"

He shuffled back to the table and sat, then reached into his shirt pocket, withdrew a scrap of yellow paper and a pen, and began to draw. Gatsby tipped her head, trying to read the squiggles upside down.

The door squealed. Officer Ngema stepped into the doorway. "Time. Dr. Donovan, please come with me."

Hobart drew faster, but Ngema lurched forward, grabbed him by the elbow, and yanked him to his feet. "Now, dolly."

Hobart scribbled furiously and then shoved the scrap of paper into Gatsby's face. "Typical time! Volcanoes topple rapid transition, months belong in severe anecdotes! Emphatic victory owed to the elitists! Regiment numeric requirements alumnae! Valor is short, sparrow!!" Saliva glistened on his lower lip.

Ngema frowned at the crazy doodles that Prisoner 7922 drew every day on napkins, sheets, even across his skin. He turned to Gatsby with a look of bored permission. She tugged the paper from Hobart's twitching fingers.

"Capital warning, seculorum omitted memoranda! Strata! Kato apo choma rie! Ecstasy galaxy!!"

Kato apo? That's Greek... The words danced in her mind and then ebbed into the past.

Cabrera hovered in the doorway. "This way, Señora." She pointed in the direction of the lobby.

Ngema ushered the prisoner down the hall toward the low-security cells. Hobart raved, howling word salad.

CHAPTER 24

"This is your first time, right?" Trishna Banerjee scrutinized the young woman standing next to her. *Rhetorical question.* The anxiety on the woman's face gave the answer.

She thought about the dark faces of the security guards and the intricate screening process required to enter the building. Just getting to the campus meant the nightmare of the commuter train and voice-recognition ID to access the parking lot. The campus of the Internet security corporation had a cafeteria with an elevator; she had to take the elevator to a basement network of corridors and then ride another elevator to the top floor of a separate building. The lab was there.

Raavi Dhawan forced a smile. "It is, but I got one hundred on my tests. Leesha prepped me very well."

We'll see.

Banerjee entered a code on the wall-mounted keypad, waited for a green light, and then swiped her passcard through the authorization scanner. When the green light blinked, a click told her that the door was unlocked.

"Let's go." She pushed the door open, and both women stepped into the air shower: a narrow, claustrophobic room with shiny steel walls dotted with wide air gates and nozzles. "Are you ready?"

"Yes." Dhawan nodded again.

Banerjee closed the door behind them. A loud click confirmed that it was sealed. She reached toward the lever at eye level on the wall. "Close your eyes."

As soon as she depressed the lever, air blasted from the gates, cleaning them from head to foot of impurities and dust. Their hair fluttered like escaping birds and settled on their shoulders as the blast subsided.

"This way." Banerjee herded Dhawan toward the exit. They waited for the panel on the wall to flash the green light; when it did, Banerjee pushed against the door, and they stepped inside.

The lab was only 10 meters square, but it had all the materials and equipment needed for making the DOLIUM. Two islands with black granite countertops held the center of the room. A desk packed with computers sat against one wall, and in another corner, a sturdy table held a JERN mass spectrometer and a Cole-Eppen microcentrifuge. Dehumidifiers ran around the clock to clean and desiccate the air. All the wall space was given to shelving. Four of the gun metal-grey shelves were loaded with orange-capped Kimax media bottles. Most of them held solvents such as acetone, ethyl alcohol, and ethyl acetate.

They strode to the other side of the room where nylon pants, jackets, and hoods hung like corpses, took down two sets, and wriggled into them. With pairs of nitrile gloves and clear goggles from a nearby shelf, they were fully protected.

Dhawan looked around the windowless room at the long tables and countertops. All around her, she saw uniform arrangements of microscopes, condensers, test tube holders, beakers, graduated cylinders, and Erlenmeyer flasks. She pointed to a wire rack that held a phalanx of glass test tubes. "Where's..."

"Come on. Follow me." Banerjee walked to the nearest shelf and began gathering her supplies: a pipette with a custom-made tip resembling a tiny toothbrush, a locking waste receptacle, and the three primary materials: the front layer, the carrier, and the back layer.

She grabbed a box that held a dozen flat, plastic containers, sat everything on the island in front of her, and pulled in a deep breath. "That's everything. I'm ready to start. You?"

Dhawan frowned. "Just a minute." She walked to the back of the room, stepped toward the corner, and stood next to a squarish cabinet. She looked down at the clear tube that ran up the side of the cabinet and was secured at the top. Dhawan drew the tube toward her and plugged the end piece into a similar tube that was coiled and clamped against her hip. Light-yellow fluid flowed from one tube to the other. After a minute, she sterilized the end pieces, moved the equipment back into place, and walked back to the island.

"Okay." She gave Banerjee a quizzical look. "Have you ever used the DOLIUM?"

"No, but I know someone who has. She lived in Bangkok with her movie director boyfriend. He kept casting her as a prostitute in his films and then told her she had to become one. He got violent," Banerjee shrugged, "and she got fed up with it. That was a year ago. Let's move. We have to get this done quickly."

While they focused on their work, the chaos of Mumbai, eighteen million residents and growing, flowed like the ceaseless currents of the Arabian Sea.

Banerjee reached a gloved hand to a plastic container sitting on the shelf and pulled from it a glass container that was secured by an orange lid. "This is the compound. I'll take it to the holding chamber. You bring everything else."

Holding the glass container at eye level, Banerjee walked to the second island and stood in front of a wide glove box—a clear acrylic chamber made for handling caustic or hazardous materials. On the face of the box, two round openings provided access to the interior. As a technician put her gloved hands through the openings, they were automatically covered with heavier, black gloves so that no part of her body touched anything inside the box, even the air.

Banerjee reached toward the holding chamber that protruded from the side of the glove box and tugged on the front panel. It opened outward. She moved all the supplies into the holding chamber, closed it, and secured the panel.

"The vacuum pump," she whispered. The lights on a boxy machine behind the holding chamber were dark. As soon as she pressed a button on the top surface, the lights glowed, and the machine and chamber began to hum.

Dhawan chewed at her lower lip. "What's it doing?"

"Pumping out ambient air and replacing it with argon. That removes any particles that may have contaminated the equipment."

The pump completed, and Banerjee repeated the process two more times. The pump finished, and with a beep, the lights on the machine went dark.

Banerjee stood before the right opening of the glove box. Now covered with both a light-blue glove and a heavier, black glove, her hand slipped into the holding chamber, and she moved the purified materials into the larger staging area of the box. She slipped her other arm into the second black glove and stopped, her eyes darting, to make sure that she had everything. She unscrewed the lid of the orange-capped container, sat it on the floor of the box, reached for the primary materials of the patch—the front layer, the carrier, and the back layer—and lay all the pieces on the floor in a neat row.

She began assembling the patch: a precut square of polymer became the backing, and a translucent slice of sea sponge, 2 millimeters thick, was used as the carrier. When the sticky side of the polymer was pressed to the carrier, the patch was ready to be loaded.

"This is the tricky part," she whispered.

Standing beside her, Dhawan pulled in a breath. Her eyes widened.

Banerjee lowered the pipette into the glass container and drew up thirty milliliters of the toxin. While depressing the slider, she slowly pulled the operating end of the pipette across the carrier. After the surface was fully coated, she waited thirty seconds to allow the acidic solvents to dry.

"Step one complete."

She turned the carrier over, picked up a second precut square—this one a translucent sheet of polyethylene paper—and pressed it against the carrier, creating a sandwich. The front and back sides were protected, and the carrier in the middle was now "loaded."

Banerjee let out a lungful of air and reached toward the remaining item in the corner of the glove box. She picked up the hard plastic container, the size and thickness of a CD jewel case, popped it open, and placed the loaded patch inside. She closed the lid and slid it into the holding chamber.

"Step two complete." She turned to Dhawan; they eyed each other through the goggles. "Put it in the preshipping case. You have to get used to handling them."

"Do we need to run the pump again?"

Banerjee took a half step back from the counter. "No, but it's good that you ask. In this lab, a mistake will kill you."

Dhawan pulled the front panel of the holding chamber open and brought out the finished patch and the used pipette tip. "Where do these go?"

Banerjee glanced over her shoulder toward a table near the computers. "Over there. The locking waste receptacle— the tip goes there. See the red bin with secure pins? The DOLIUM goes in that, and it's ready for transport. Leesha is the lead in charge of shipping."

Dhawan walked to the table and dropped the pipette tip into the waste receptacle. After she placed the patch into the red bin and secured the pins, she said, "What's the potency of this batch?"

Banerjee stepped to the computer on the desk, her eyes moving over the screen. She reached a glove toward it and pressed a black button. The data on the screen refreshed.

"Nine point six."

"Chod!" *Fuck!* Dhawan laughed. "I'd like to see the Bolivian division beat that."

They both leaned back against the island, taking a few deep breaths.

"Where did you say you worked?" Dhawan asked.

"Pune. The National Chemical Laboratory."

"Me too. Was Musuri Rashan still the director?"

"I don't think so."

Dhawan looked down at the tile floor as if wrestling with a question and then focused back on Banerjee. "Have you ever seen her?"

Banerjee scowled. "The SWORD? No one sees the SWORD. You know that."

"My cousin in Bangalore, she thinks she knows who the SWORD is. She says that she saw her."

Always happens with new recruits. "No, she didn't. You won't see the SWORD and know that it's her, ever. Just get used to it."

"Aren't you curious? Any woman you pass on the street could be her."

"What makes you think she lives in Mumbai?"

Dhawan was silent for a moment. "I assumed that…"

"That's a mistake. Don't make any assumptions about the BEEHIVE."

Dhawan tipped her head toward her right shoulder, then her left, and they both heard her vertebrae pop loudly. "Can we go? I need to get something to eat."

"Not until we make eleven more."

She groaned, glancing at the clock on the computer monitor. "Eleven? Why?"

"All locations were fully stocked but…"

Seeing Banerjee's face clouding, Dhawan pressed. "But what?"

"We have to keep ten loaded DOLIUM at this lab, so we need to make a replacement. Two days ago, a shipment went to the wrong address. It was supposed to go to Palermo, but somehow it was delivered in London."

"*Somehow*? Didn't you say that in this lab a mistake will kill you?"

"Stop asking so many fucking questions and get busy, Dhawan. We have work to do."

CHAPTER 25

The Airbus A380 cruised at eleven kilometers, headed for Paris and the connecting flight to London. Dacea swallowed a mouthful of yogurt-covered pretzels, crumpled the package, and tossed it on the seatback tray. Her thoughts spiraled around the misdirected package.

What a colossal fuck up! The Mumbai division sent SHIP-1 the DOLIUM by accident?! Does Banerjee have any idea of AXE she faces from the HAMMER, or if a simple delivery killed a SHIP or anyone unauthorized?

She tried to collect herself by reviewing the day's communications. The first was her message to Browning in London.

ARROW ARRIVES TODAY
INSTRUCTIONS FROM CAT7

Bashir sent the report about the mishandled package. Six hours later, a return message marked URGENT was received from Browning.

SHIP-1: LHR to MAD
British Airways

A sudden trip out of the country. What is so important in Madrid? She looked out the window, watching the speeding canvas of rain-heavy clouds.

Her last message had gone to Dhar.

IF SHIP-1 ACQUIRES ROSETTE AND MOVES
TOWARD CRETE: ALERT SWORD

Adrenaline pulsed through her. *If by some miracle of genius she locates the real ROSETTE, her instinct will be to return it to the Heraklion. World-class museums are proprietary; art and artifacts are valuable. Dolastanos is retired, but she can be put on surveillance.* She rubbed her chin. *If the American can do this, if she achieves what the*

Circle has failed to accomplish for decades, all the better. Let her. If the real ROSETTE is returned to the BEEHIVE, the HAMMER will add a name to WHITE BIRD, and there will be plenty of GRASS for the living.

She allowed her head to settle against the headrest and closed her eyes. The roar of the engines grated on taut nerves. She snuggled headphone earpieces over her ears, adjusted the qunae over her mutilated face, and looked away when passengers stared at her. She felt her teeth grinding, unable to stop it and unable to drown out the old ghosts.

...you were wrapped in a fabric bearing the image of the ROSETTE

...Someone wanted you in the Circle

The ache in her jawbone throbbed. *When they found the screaming infant, why didn't they kill it?!*

She shook her head. *No time for that.* The word *time* floated a memory to the surface. *Perhaps it will be useful, perhaps dangerous. It may uncover nothing at all, but it was a risk I had to take.* In her mind, she replayed the message that she sent to Bashir three days ago.

ROUTE MESSAGE TO SHIP-1:

    THE INFINITE CHAKRA
    SERVES THE GUARDIAN
    THE GUARDIAN DECAYS
    IN THE CAGE OF TIME

CHAPTER 26

In the Bajestaros Penitenciario lobby, the guard sitting at the counter scowled at her and motioned to the electronic signature tablet. Gatsby scrawled her name and walked away quickly, avoiding eye contact, headed toward the glass doors.

Her thoughts spun. *It is quite safe, he said. Safe enough to elude Spanish police? INTERPOL? Other black market dealers? What did he scribble on that paper, and what was he shouting when Ngema hauled him away? Was it Greek?*

She walked across the street and traversed a tourist-filled plaza, heading to the adjacent boulevard. Store fronts came into view—bakeries, clothing boutiques, jewelers, florists. On San Andres Street, she spied a sign that read Cafe del Foro and slipped inside.

Armed with lethally strong coffee, she opened her shoulder bag, pulled out the scrap of yellow paper from Hobart, and spread it on the table. Her eyes darted over it.

Symbols. The only way Hobart could pass a message that the guards wouldn't confiscate. His field is osteoarchaeology—what symbolic languages would he be likely to know?

She pressed a fist against her chin. As she stared, she recognized it. The crude scribbles began to unfold with meaning. *WOW. Linear B.*

Ma-ri-so-pa...

— ||||

Fourteen...

⊕ Ŧ Ƭ Ꮗ Ϙ Ӿ

Ka-to-ai-po-ko-ma...

Her pulse raced. *That's what he shouted—"under" and "ground" in Modern Greek.*

He didn't get to finish the last one—RO or RI?

She glanced at the first four symbols. Marisopa. Sounds Spanish. She dug her map of Madrid from her shoulder bag, spread it across the table, and searched for anything resembling "marisopa."

School, church, museum, library? Santo Domingo, Ruben Dario, Aveda de America, Cuidad Universitaria...

Caffeine rocketed through her veins. She curled forward until her nose almost touched the map, trying to scan hundreds of names—streets, landmarks, parks, government offices, restaurants, businesses—all printed in miniscule type. A tiny line was labeled Calle Marisopa.

There. Looks like a residential area. Which district? She pulled out the Metro map and schedule. *La Latina. Fourteen Metro stops and then a few blocks on foot.*

Turning back to Hobart's scribbled note, she took a draw of coffee and stared at the last symbol. *RO or RI—what is he trying to say? Right? River? Rose? Rope? Is it really Linear B? Spanish? English? Greek? He's obviously gone off the deep end. His mental state is far from stable, and all this could be a big joke or pure insanity.*

She finished the coffee in one gulp. Tucking €2 under the cup, she rose and headed for the door.

As she walked down the street, a Metro station rose into view. She descended the stairs; the walls of the underground concourses, covered with advertising, were new, almost sparkling. A glowing screen above the platform offered arrival times, and riders wandered around her, fractious and noisy, as she found a kiosk and bought a day pass.

The forty-minute ride was a barrage of mental havoc. *He said, "Take the bloody Phaistos Disk, take it away." When I asked him directly where it is, he drew these ten symbols. Is it possible that he's given me the location? Christ, what if I actually found it??*

A shudder, almost painful in its intensity, gripped her.

At the San Andrassi station, she got off, followed the exit signs and stairs, and stepped out onto a sunny sidewalk. Within minutes, she was on a wide boulevard, lined with Spanish fir and a mix of apartments and row houses.

Volkswagens, Renaults, and Smart cars were parked by the sidewalks. A gaggle of women, paper coffee cups in hand, crossed the street and headed for a bus stop; a girl on a Vespa buzzed by, her onyx hair flying.

Gatsby walked toward the nearest intersection. She pulled out the city map again, ran her finger over the street names and numbers, and walked south. Numbers came into view as she passed each residence.

24, 22, 20, 18, 16...

She stopped before a series of tall, narrow row houses; the weathered bricks were covered with English ivy. Short sets of white stairs led from the street to separate side-by-side entrances.

Right door, fourteen. She looked up and down the street, and other than a calico cat padding across the street, the neighborhood seemed deserted. *Now what?*

Stowing the map in her shoulder bag, she walked to the north end of the house and followed a narrow gravel path between the row of buildings and the adjacent row. It ended at an alley—wide enough for pedestrians but not cars— where residents stored bicycles and trash bins. On the back side of each home, she saw a tiny porch with stairs that lead down to the alley.

She glanced up at the back entrance to 14. *What if there's a security system? What if this isn't even the right house?!*

The symbols tumbled through her mind.

ma ri so pa

14
kato apo choma
ro / ri

Heart hammering, she walked up the stairs to the porch, stood at the door and took a deep breath. She turned the knob and pushed, astounded when the hasp retracted and the door swung. It opened to a cramped kitchen where she saw a sink, refrigerator, cupboards, and cookware hanging from wire shelving. There were no bowls on the table, no rumpled dishcloth, no indication that anyone had recently been there.

Whoever lives here could come through that door at any second. What the hell am I doing? Panic pushed her through the nearest doorway and into a living room. The couches and tables pointed to a middle-class income, but the upright piano was a high-value antique. A floor-to-ceiling cherry bookcase offered three niches like Greek porticos, and the shelves overflowed with texts, framed photographs, and polished figurines from around the world.

Her gaze zipped to the photo at eye level that showed a lean, bespectacled man; he was smiling and shaking hands with a taller man wearing a crimson robe. A caption below the photo read UNIVERSITY OF BARCELONA.

Could it be? She let her eyes race over the spines of the books. At the right end of the middle shelf, she saw five copies of *Songs of Burial: Archaeology of Graves of Towtan.*

Her mental alarms were screaming. *Hobart sent me to his own house? Is it a setup? Get out!*

She dashed back to the kitchen. Hand gripping the handle of the back door, she felt the thoughts flurry.

…The ROSETTE does not belong to anyone
…It is quite safe
…Kato apo choma

She spotted a door at the right side of the room, tried the handle, and opened it. *Underground.* A steep staircase loomed in the dark before her. She saw a switch on the wall to her right, flicked the light on, and felt her mouth go dry as she began the descent. *Exactly where I'll be after the autopsy.*

At the bottom of the stairs, a square room held what could have been remainders from an estate sale: antique furniture, rugs rolled into long tubes, racks of clothing, picture frames, and old books, stacked into leaning towers. The walls were lined with wood shelves that held dozens of banker's boxes. In the far left corner, she spotted something that looked out of place: a rectangular box made of plywood. The stone containers placed inside it, each about a meter tall, made her think of headstones.

(It is quite safe)

Moving closer, she saw that the stone containers were filled with a type of tiny white beads.

Ro / ri...could RI be for rice?

She plunged her hands into the first container, swept them back and forth, and did the same in the second container but felt only dry, undulating grains of rice.

Rice is hygroscopic, a desiccant that attracts and absorbs water. The British Museum maintained strict controls over humidity, sometimes employing a tub-like hammered metal box filled with rice, called a "boat," for short-term storage before eventually taking an artifact to a lab.

In the third container, her finger collided with something hard, and she gripped the object and pulled on it. The rice rippled like water, making a *shhhhhh* whisper, as she brought the object to eye level. It was a steel box about 15 centimeters square; the lid was hinged but not locked. She opened it to find a pouch fashioned from cerulean velvet. Gatsby tugged the drawstring mouth open.

Impossible...it can't be...

As she slowly pulled it off the plate-shaped object, the world froze.

Four thousand years trembled in her hands.

The adrenaline sizzle made it hard to grip the Disk without crushing it. Her mind was a hurricane of terror and amazement, crushing reason and words, ephemera, death, creation, eternity. Each pulse of her heart was a sledgehammer against her ribs.

*Dog...flower...runner...bird...baby...ivy...ship...pyram
id...wave. My god!!*

She ached to run a finger across the symbols but knew
that nothing could touch the surface until it was moved to a
lab. *How do I get it to a lab?* She glanced at the velvet pouch
and the metal box, resting on top of the second stone
container, and then around the room. The hanging rack of
clothing caught her eye. She carefully nestled the Disk into
the rice and walked toward the clothes rack. Her eyes raced
over the items; a white blouse appeared to be lightweight,
undyed silk. She tugged it from the hanger and went back to
the stone container. She sat on the edge of the plywood box
and wrapped the silk blouse around the Disk twice.

*Not nearly museum-quality packaging, but it will have to
do. Now to get it inside the pouch. Like putting a million-
dollar pillow inside a pillow case.*

As she began to tuck the Disk back into the pouch, her
hand locked—

(Never give up! Never settle for...)

—paralyzed.

(PUSH HARDER, then push some more!)

(Grab them before someone else does, hear me?)

(NO MATTER WHAT IT TAKES, you little stoat!)

SHUT UP!!

As if electricity screamed through them, her fingers
straightened.

The Disk dropped a few centimeters before she caught
it.

"Jesus!!"

Sucking in air, sweat coursing down her neck, she
maneuvered the Disk—with extreme slowness and
delicacy—all the way into the pouch. She pulled the
drawstring opening tight, placed the pouch back inside the
metal box, and closed the lid.

How to get this to London? I need experts.

She walked back to the staircase and climbed the steps
to the kitchen. *Affiato, Cambier, Hobart—they all may have
lied, may be imposters, may even be insane, but it is* possible
that this box is holding the real Phaistos Disk.

She remembered the impenetrable look in Cambier's eyes, her morose voice: You must accept it to answer your own question: what you will risk for glory. What you will destroy.

Every muscle contracted. She was dizzy, almost stumbling. Her limbs felt leaden as she crept through the back door and toward the street. She hugged the box as if it held a bomb.

Another twenty-minute Metro ride, and she was at Cafe del Foro. The barista gave her a "you again?" frown, but she huddled in a corner and pulled her phone from her shoulder bag.

"Gatsby! Hello! What's..."

"Gruedin, listen carefully. Call Talbot-Wei right now. I have an artifact to transport to London. I'll give you the details when I get back."

"Talbot-Wei? What do you mean, when you get back? Where are you?"

"Have a rep sent to Calle del Moscatelar 22, Madrid."

"Is this a joke?"

She smashed the phone against her ear. "No, Clive! Just do it!"

A midsize SUV turned onto the boulevard; Gatsby looked up at the rumble of the engine. Two men—one uniformed, one in a crisp business suit—slid from the cab and strode toward the café.

Gatsby rose, eyeing the man in the grey suit as he approached. "You're with Talbot-Wei?"

He nodded. "Yes. Edward Chiang."

She introduced herself and shook hands. As they sat at a rear booth, Gatsby placed the metal box on the table and opened it. She glanced around the room, checking out the other customers, to assess where and how they were seated. She pulled the plate-shaped object from the pouch, unwrapped the silk blouse and arranged it in a pillowy mound, and placed the Disk in the middle.

"This looks familiar." He frowned but made no attempt to touch the disk. "Isn't it..."

She shook her head, her eyes telling him to not ask questions. "I'll give the details to the curator and the conservation team at the British Museum."

He rubbed a cleft chin, eyes darting, opened his briefcase, and dropped a stack of forms on the table. "Very well. Submit these at that time."

She closed the box. "I understand."

Chiang handed the box to the guard, and both men rose and walked back to the front door. As they stopped before the van and opened the back compartment, Gatsby caught a glimpse of the safe constructed with steel and high-pressure concrete. The guard keyed in a code, and the door of the safe eased open. They loaded the box inside and closed the door of the safe. The guard pulled out a tracking device to note the location, date, and time that Talbot-Wei took possession.

Her eyes darted between them and her phone. While watching their every move, she called a cab and scanned the map on her smartphone, searching for the fastest route to Madrid-Barajas International Airport.

CHAPTER 27

The grandeur of the British Museum's entrance beckoned. In a camel hair Gucci suit, Affiato leaned against one of the Roman columns, casually examining his fingernails. He pushed his hands into his pockets, and a grin opened on his face. "Bellissima!"

The heels of her boots banged like exclamation marks on the stone plaza as she drove toward him. "A box full of love letters, but she's never heard of Doumas?"

Affiato jogged by her side. "What? Slow down."

"Why were you *really* so intent on finding the Disk?"

"For the same reason you..."

"And why send me that stupid cryptic email?"

He skidded to a stop. "Email?"

"Jesus, Affiato! The chakra? The guardian, the cage of time? What kind of fatuous ploy was that?!"

He shook his head like a terrier. "I did no such thing!"

She turned a glare on him. "Your acting skills are stupendous. Your mantle must be sagging with awards!"

He countered her anger with a haughty smile. "Cherie, do not forget what my skills have meant to you. Ask yourself what it matters when the tale puts what you have dreamed of your entire life into your hands, when the illusion brings you what you must have. Not only will you thank me, but—"

They stepped through the doors and into the Great Court. "But what?"

"The acquisition of the Phaistos Disk is only the beginning. You can expect your amazement to blossom a thousand fold."

Gatsby pushed by him and pointed toward the lift. "There's no guarantee that *this* is the real one, and that's why we're here, so shut up and hurry up."

After exiting at the third floor, they hustled down a corridor toward Test Lab 2. Affiato stepped up his pace to stay beside her.

Inside the main room of the lab, four men and a woman, all in rumpled sweatshirts and jeans, milled around. They looked up in curiosity as Affiato and Gatsby entered.

"Gruedin, Koberski. Hello Haversham." Gatsby peered at the fourth man and the woman just behind him. "I don't think we've met."

The man approached and pumped her hand. "Jon Nguyen, Conservation."

Gatsby assessed the petite, dark-haired woman who stepped forward, her hand extended and covered by the pale-blue latex gloves used for lab work. She glanced at the glove and laughed. "Oh, sorry. Ruth Browning, Forensics."

"Good to meet you." Gatsby shook her gloved hand and turned to Gruedin. "Let's go."

"Wait, hold on. First, how the *hell* did you acquire it?"

"A long string of clues, most of which I can't discuss, so don't ask." She ignored his frown. "I learned that the disk at the Heraklion might be a fake, so I had Alexiou do TL testing. Then I got a tip that the real Disk could be in Madrid. I did some bartering." She waved a hand. "Hic est."

Haversham glowered at Affiato. "Who are *you*?"

"Partner in crime, so to speak." Affiato said. They all waited, expecting more, but he shrugged and rubbed his goatee, eyes sparkling.

Gatsby pointed toward the authentication lab. "Come on. Let's put the equipment through its paces."

The group moved down a hallway and into a glass-walled room packed with electronics and testing equipment. As they filed in and found places to stand, Gruedin handed out face masks. "I remind all of you." He gave Affiato a warning look. "Don't touch anything. Don't *breathe* on anything. The slightest contact can contaminate a sample."

Gatsby walked to the table at the middle of the room. A case sat on a table, and she spotted Chiang's business card tucked in the side panel. The technicians spread around the table, leaning forward to get a better view, and strapped their masks in place. As Gatsby opened the case and pulled back the protective padding, soft moans rose. Koberski let out a long, low whistle.

"Incredible," Gruedin whispered.

Haversham shook his head. "My god. This took insane precision to draw each symbol, even more so doing it in a spiral."

Affiato cleared his throat, and six pairs of eyes turned on him. "The symbols weren't drawn, they were stamped."

Gatsby said, "He's right. The division lines that demarcate the fields were drawn, but each symbol was impressed into the clay with a stamp, probably carved from ivory or wood."

Gruedin pointed to the door at the left side of the room. "Gatsby, would you bring it in here?"

She carefully picked up the case and followed him; the techs flowed behind her. While settling in the chair before to a low counter packed with computers and sensors, Gruedin said, "First we need a sample."

"Please don't tell me you have to drill."

"Other labs do, but since 1998, we've used the laser from the Tokyo Institute for Laser Science. We just have to adjust for the radiation of x-rays."

"What is this test for?" Affiato asked.

"Thermoluminescence or TL test," Gruedin said. "It measures how much time has elapsed since an object containing crystalline minerals was heated or fired. Like a pot fired in a kiln. We heat a sample of the object to a specific temperature, which causes reexcited electrons to release light. We measure the number of electrons and the intensity of the emission. It's the best method for dating pottery."

After pulling on a pair of latex gloves, Gruedin moved the Disk from the case to a thick glass tray; the raised edges kept it in place. He took the tray toward a laser bay, a device that vaguely resembled a microwave oven, put the tray inside it, and adjusted the dials. "I pinpoint a location on the edge," he said, meticulously typing in the algorithm that aimed the laser, "and..."

He closed the bay to secure it and prevent eye damage as the laser worked. After he flipped the switch, they heard a deep hum followed by a high-pitched whir. The techs goggled with curiosity. Gatsby leaned toward the bay. "What happened?"

Gruedin removed the security locks. "We have our sample from the edge—about a hundred milligrams, four to twelve microns wide. They're in a reservoir that is pushed to the TL bay. It's happening as we speak."

They all moved in to watch as Gruedin opened the laser bay, removed the Disk, sat the glass tray on the counter, and carefully placed the Disk back in the case. He wheeled his chair to the opposite side of the room and nodded toward a dangerous-looking console.

"The microns are moved over here," he pointed to the TL bay, a rectangular device connected to the laser bay by metal tubing. "They're heated to 400 Celsius, and the degree to which the sample emits light indicates the age." He took a deep breath. "It looks like it's ready."

They all stared at the box. On the right side of the bay, a beep sounded. A light blinked on a printer, and a sheet of paper began rolling from it.

Gruedin looked up at Gatsby. "Will you do the honors, Dr. Donovan?"

She remembered what Affiato said at their first meeting: *There it is on a clay platter. Your immortal glory.* She took a deep breath, walked to the printer, and tore the sheet off at the perforation. Her eyes zipped over the lines of print. She smacked the paper with her fist. "Thirty-three to thirty-eight hundred! Holy shit!!"

"Yeah!" "Damn!" "Unbelievable!" The techs burst into shouts and high fives, breathless, their faces glowing with astonishment.

Affiato gave Gatsby a slow nod as if to underscore his omniscience. "There we have it, as I said from the start." He slid over next to her and raised his hands to eye level, palms up. "Gentlemen, ladies? Grazie mille."

A thousand security alarms fired at once. The room was pierced with a light like Hiroshima, brightness that annihilated. Gatsby slammed her hands over her ears in agony, squeezing her eyes shut against the explosion of white light and sound. She felt a hand grope at her ankle, heard screaming, smacked her head against the metal arm of a chair, and spun to the floor. Her head was imploding. The room was blanketed with a kind of dusty fog, and the blast wavered down through decibels and octaves, descending into a buzz as deep as the earth's core.

She coughed in the swirling fog. "Gruedin, where are you? Clive?!"

A hand punched into her vision, nearly clouting her, followed by an arm and torso. Gruedin crawled to her, hair escaping in all directions, shirt askew, a swath of blood under his nose. "*Christ!!* A bomb?"

They heard groans and swept their hands around by their feet. The other techs were shaking and coughing, their ears ringing.

"Where—" Gatsby fanned her hands over the counter, frantically looked around the room, and moaned as despair swelled. "The Disk! Affiato *and* the Disk, they're both fucking gone!"

"Where did he go?"

"What the hell happened?"

"Shut up, everyone!" Gruedin struggled to his feet and dug a phone from his pocket. "Orr? Gruedin. I'm with the team in Test Lab 2. There's been an explosion…yes, just now…an *explosion* and a theft." He whirled on Gatsby. "Name?"

"Macèo Affiato."

Gruedin repeated it. "He should still be in the building."

An emergency alarm sounded, blaring as the electronic gates began to lower across all the entrances and exits.

"We were testing an artifact and a," Gruedin rubbed his forehead, fumbling for the right word, "a visitor set off some kind of explosion. We can't find him or the artifact." He shot Gatsby a frazzled look. "The Phaistos Disk. Damn it, I *know!* We had it here in this room, and now it's gone!"

Security guards ploughed through the door. Gruedin talked with them, and the captain said, "Everyone come this way, right now. All personnel assemble in the Commons during a lockdown."

Everyone staggered down the hall toward the lifts. When they arrived at the Commons, Orr questioned each person and took notes as they described what they saw and heard. Nelson Clevis flew into the room, his hair standing on end as if electrified.

The room filled and thrummed with interns, researchers, and administrators. Gruedin pulled Gatsby into a corner of the room. He was red-faced and trembling with agitation. "You know the explaining we have ahead of us? Orr will notify the International Council for Museum Security that the Phaistos Disk was, for reasons and methods unknown, at the British Museum *and* has just been stolen!"

She dropped her head into her hands. "I know, Clive."

As Orr walked toward her, a man wearing an expensive overcoat and carrying an iPad walked into the room. He scanned the crowd, picked out Orr and Gatsby, and headed toward them. "You're director of security?"

Orr nodded. "Right."

"Uri Polichev, Crown Investigation Service." He flashed his badge and nodded toward a nearby table. The three of them sat, stiff and wary.

Polichev grilled Gatsby, and she relayed the chronology: Affiato's claim of a forged artifact, testing at the Heraklion, meeting with Cambier in Marseille, and the interview with Hobart at Bajestaros that led her to his house in Madrid.

He scrutinized her with dark eyes. "Anything else?"

"That's everything." As she ran her hands through her hair, she saw how violently they were shaking. "Am I under arrest?"

"No, but..."

"Then I'm going home." She rose.

He grabbed her arm to stop her. "I have more questions for you, so I want to meet again first thing tomorrow morning. Call this number for the address." He pulled a business card from his inside jacket pocket and pressed it into her hand.

As she started toward the lift, Gruedin shouted, "Gatsby, can I walk you to the Tube?"

She trudged down the hall without looking back.

She boarded the subway car and was still settling in the seat when her phone buzzed. A text message; the sender ID read *MA*.

COME NOW TO SOHO
TELL NO ONE

Panic and fury pulsed through her. *Affiato!*

The train sped through the darkness. In twenty minutes, she was at the Sloane Square station. She made her way onto the platform and out onto the street. Her apartment building was two blocks away.

Once inside the quiet flat, she went to her office and collapsed into her computer chair with a thud. She rubbed her neck, feeling rock-hard muscles beneath her fingers, and closed her eyes.

I will get the Disk, Affiato. I'm sick of you and this whole fucking nightmare. Now you will play MY game, because I can deny you what you want even more than that lump of clay: a challenger.

She rolled her chair closer. Her eyes fell on the disk sitting at the center of the desk—the replica that Cambier had given her. She picked it up, turning it slowly, amazed at its lightness.

(Come now to Soho, tell no one)

Why his shop? Does he want to get caught? Or is it a set up?

She walked down the hall to her bedroom and went to the closet; the top shelf held collections of sweaters, blankets, and boxes. She tugged at an item buried in the stack and pulled down a canvas tote bag decorated in geometric patterns and pastel shades, a gift received so long ago that she had forgotten both the event and the giver.

Once back in her office, she scrutinized Cambier's disk. *What can I store this in without calling attention?* As she looked around, her gaze fell on the bookcase in the corner. After a few minutes of carefully shaping at the pages at the middle of the text, she had a round cavity in the pages of Cremin's *World Encyclopedia of Archeology.* Cambier's disk fit perfectly in the hollowed-out space.

She tucked the encyclopedia into the canvas tote bag, pulled out her phone, and sent a text message to Roman.

LEAVING FOR S'S APPR IN SOHO

In the living room, she grabbed a Tube schedule from the coffee table and dashed to the front door. The tote bag bumped against her hip.

Is this suicide??

CHAPTER 28

Dacea brushed past the bleary-eyed flight attendants. They waved robotically at the exiting passengers.

As she raced through the skybridge and into the labyrinth of Heathrow Terminal 3, she remembered the message from Vlahos.

```
SHIP-1: MAD to LHR
British Airways
```

Just one day in Madrid, then back to London. What was so urgent in Spain? She scurried down the concourse, shoving past luggage carts and baby strollers toward the lot where taxis waited for passengers.

Alexandra Bashir at Ivy9. Heathrow to Holland Park, half an hour. She rubbed her fingers against her eyes, fighting for balance. *And time is running out.*

The ride took thirty-five minutes. She paid the cab driver, walked to the entrance of the townhouse, and knocked.

A woman in a Dior suit opened the door and appraised her with a chilly expression. "Pan sil dot tuz-oh." Alexandra Bashir led her into a room lavish with modern décor and motioned toward the divan. Every gesture conveyed a stately lineage. While she climbed from runway model to CEO of a global telecommunications firm, Bashir had perfected the art of destroying inferiors with a word. Few Circle members knew of her MMA training and deadly combat skills.

They sat, assessing each other in silence.

"The ARROW is in place," Bashir said, her tone subdued.

Dacea mentally reviewed the R&D of the ARROW. Circle members developed the delivery fluid—a clear, odorless liquid—that carried a nanotech GPS device that transmitted a tracking signal. The liquid passed easily through the skin, allowing the device to lodge in the dermis. The geolocator app on a STAR SEED showed the location of the device and a detailed map of the area. After seventy-two hours, the device dissolved and flushed out of the body.

"Browning did it?"

A shadow passed over Bashir's face. She nodded.

"Show me the tools."

Bashir crossed the room to stand before on a black walnut armoire. After opening the lock with a silver key, she pulled three items from the body of the cabinet.

The LILY, the glass vial containing a milky liquid.

The DOLIUM, secured in a small glass box. A microchip was embedded in it; the box opened only upon receiving a coded signal.

The FLUTE, the dagger designed by members in Algeria, all expert steelworkers who were also trained in hand-to-hand combat.

Bashir held them forward for inspection. Her hands vibrated slightly.

As Dacea's eyes moved over the serrated edge of the knife, the creature of rage rumbled in her.

(Someone wanted you in the Circle. Why, I will never know)

Bashir's eyes narrowed. She blurted, "Delivery of weapons, like some shit-brained waitress? You don't trust me in their use?"

Fury exploded through her as if her psyche were brackish water pooled under a building. She launched, crushing Bashir against the armoire. Her left fist crashed into Bashir's cheek, forcing her head to the right; at the same time, she snatched the FLUTE in her right hand and pressed it into the creamy skin of the woman's neck. A dot of blood bloomed and oozed toward her collarbone. Bashir whimpered.

"HORN. You should be dead. Do you have any idea what you just did? What kind of AXE to expect?" Dacea dropped the knife to her side.

Bashir slumped. Her hands groped at her neck as if searching for wounds.

"Show me my room."

Her eyes locked on Dacea, Bashir whispered, "Follow me." She led Dacea down the main hallway to a room that held a twin bed, desk, computer, and mini fridge.

"I apologize. I have no…"

"San-on mer." *Get out.*

Bashir lowered her eyes and slunk down the hall.

Dacea tossed her backpack onto the bed. An antique vanity sat against the far wall, the mirror above it reflecting blue-green tapestries. She felt herself drawn toward it as if grabbed by invisible hands, and as she stared into the mirror, the black qunae over her face billowed with each hot, rapid breath. *Orders to go the city where two suspected SHIPS are based. Delivery of weapons but no specific instructions on how to proceed.*

The overhead lights flared as Affiato stepped through the entrance. His gaze swept the havoc of the room: monitors, keyboards, printers, diagrams, desks, flow charts, Post-It notes, crumpled wads of paper, mazes of cables, all tumbled together with scarves, silk flowers, canes, rope, bells, trunks, cups, rings, card decks, bottles, coins, thread, velvet bags, candles, trick cabinets, books, and dice.

The room bulged with security system camera feeds. Arranged down the middle of the room were five desks, each one installed with a monitor 120 centimeters wide, along with control pads, audiovisual feeds, and keyboards customized for instant software updates.

He pressed a fingertip against the first screen. A world map flowered into view, and an icon resembling a white bird wavered over a dozen cities.

Baghdad, Iraq
Jerusalem, Israel
Tehran, Iran
Kabul, Afghanistan
Damascus, Syria
Birmingham, Alabama
Belfast, Ireland

Lima, Peru
Palermo, Italy
Maiduguri, Nigeria
Tokyo, Japan
New York, New York

The icons rippled, mutating from white to pink to blood-red. Dozens of monitors around the room launched into full operation; vibrant world maps appeared on each screen. A BANG erupted from each one, and hundreds of blood-red icons exploded, sending animated blood and feathers flying across the screens.

Affiato burst into laughter. "Ah, populus vult decipi ergo decipiatur. The illusion of the ages, the greatest trick of all time! Ladies and gentlemen, I ask you to watch closely. The magic show is about to begin." He rolled the rings on his four-fingered hand. "Our glorious rebellion has begun."

CHAPTER 29

The storm rolled into London that morning and assaulted the city. Dacea pulled her jacket tighter. Rain pelted her as she scurried toward the waiting cab and collapsed into the back seat.

A mule-faced cabbie glowered at her. As he drove down the wet streets, he frowned, seemingly flummoxed by a passenger who demanded that he drive while she fed him the directions. With each £20 note that she pressed into his hand, he nodded to show his eagerness to drive wherever she wanted.

The cab slowed at an intersection. She ran her hand over the curve of her backpack, feeling for the DOLIUM in its plastic case next to the dagger, the FLUTE, which was protected by a handmade leather sheath. She pulled the STAR SEED from her pocket and reread the message from Bashir.

SHIP-1: BOARDED NORTHERN LINE AT 21:36
SHIP-1 OR SHIP-2: ASSUME POSSESSION OF
ROSETTE

Focused on the GPS app and the blinking red dot that was tracking north, she thought, *Where is she going?*

The driver glanced at her in the rearview mirror every few minutes as the cab bumped along. The rain cascaded, and the streets alternately emptied and flooded with umbrellas, black and slick as seals.

In the Tube, Gatsby stepped from the platform into the noisy car and found a seat near the back.

Her phone buzzed, making her jump as if tasered.

"Gatsby? Come home right now. Get on the first plane you can."

It took a few seconds for the caller's identity and words to sink in.

"Gatsby??"

"I can't fathom what's behind this insanity, Livia, or your sudden *concern* for my welfare when we both know what our relation—"

(If you're on to something important, look for an ambush)

That's what she's doing. It's an ambush.

"Don't call me again. Ever!" She slapped at the key to end the call, her heart pounding.

With a greasy smile, Affiato pulled the door open. Gatsby stepped inside The Sorcerer's Apprentice, expecting to dodge the distain of Felicity, but there was no one else in the lobby.

They moved down the hallway toward THE ATHENAEUM, Affiato leading the way in a shimmering ivory jacket and trousers. A black scarf embroidered with gold thread and appliques fluttered around his neck. He held the door open for her. "Apres vous."

She stepped inside.

He pulled the door shut, whirled, and yanked the canvas tote bag off her shoulder.

"Hey!" She muted her tone to hide the flash of panic. *What if he finds the replica?!*

"You brought me a gift, I see." He opened the bag and swirled his hand through the contents.

Shit!

"A book? Pah! Useless." He snorted and tossed the bag on an end table. When it struck the surface with a thud, she felt her heart pound.

He walked to the other side of the table, and she followed while keeping him and the bag in her sight. "You undoubtedly have a phone with you. Surrender it."

"Screw y..."

Affiato's hands flashed up and across his chest in an X pattern. A blast of white smoke erupted, just like the blinding explosion at the British Museum. She leaped back with a shout, heard a rattle overhead, and dove out of the way as a steel rapier, a meter long, plummeted from the ceiling. It windmilled; the razor-sharp tip grazed her calf, and it clattered to the marble floor.

"Jesus! Are you trying to kill me?"

The smoke dissipated, and he stepped toward her, his hand held out, palm up. "Consider that a warning. Give me your phone. Now."

Skewering him with a look, she pulled the phone from the pocket of her jeans and tossed it into his hand. Still trying to catch her breath, she looked around the room. Magic props huddled in collections like high-security inmates. The Egyptian sarcophagus—lid opened to reveal the trap-door escape button—stood upright in the far corner. Drill bits, pliers, and screwdrivers were scattered around the base.

"You deserve mountains of compliments, tributes to your cleverness!" He strolled to the bar, found a bottle of brandy, poured the golden liquid into a tumbler as if time did not exist, and sipped luxuriously. He raised his free hand, directing her gaze to the back wall. She saw a heavy oak table with carvings of animals on the edges and legs; in the middle of it, a Plexiglas display case with a riser pedestal held the Phaistos Disk. He beamed like a man drowning in a sea of love. "I get what I want, always. Case in point, the glorious reward for our efforts, the immortal Phaistos Disk."

She dropped into the Chesterfield sofa. "You worked far too hard for this. No one goes to this much trouble to acquire an artifact, no matter how renowned it is, unless the reward is astronomical. What are you really after? A ransom?"

He settled on the adjacent sofa, sat his tumbler on an end table, and propped his elbows on his knees. "To start. It's insured for sixty million euro—did you know that?"

Her eyes widened.

"But financial reward is the least of my triumph. Our triumph, because there is so much more than possession of an ancient clay disk. With the impending revolution, I take control."

"Control of what?"

"The pinnacles of power. The world's most deadly terrorist organizations, their leaders and members, then their entire societies."

She snorted but felt her stomach grip with fear. "Terrorists? You?"

He walked toward the table, his eyes sliding over the Disk as if undressing it. "Mio dolce, imperialism is never simply seizure of property. It is the plundering of minds. Rulers throughout all human history know that. Empires establish dominance by destroying the old systems and their icons and replacing them. I will replace the upstarts. They have maintained power holds for decades, some for centuries, but they could never have anticipated what is about to happen."

"Empire building?" She shook her head, incredulous. "Are you imagining headlines? Something like No-Name Magician Conquers the World? It's beyond preposterous. Why did you *really* bring me into all this?"

"It is my gift to you! I am prepared to hand you what you have lusted for so desperately and so relentlessly: the glory of discovery, of unmatched recognition. I chose you because you're resourceful and ruthlessly ambitious, and I recruit only the best."

Fear propelled her into aggression. "What a fat load of bullshit, Affiato. You're even more ridiculous than I thought."

"Am I?" His expression morphed. "A bomb of cataclysm is ticking, one that detonates only hours from now. It will smash a dozen focal points of power and replace them with the forces that *I* control—a militia unparalleled in number and expertise."

"What are you talking about?"

"Don't be dim. It's unseemly. Haven't you figured it out? The agents that I have manipulated all these years are astoundingly useful and devoted to their cause."

She froze.

"I learned of the quaint little society that had formed around the Phaistos Disk. I watched as it grew in numbers— and grew and grew. It became the Circle. I saw the opportunity, saw the potential, and I did what needed to be done to take control of it. Yes, it meant sacrifices."

She opened her mouth, closed it without speaking.

"It emerged before my eyes, the seeds of a new world, managed by the most flexible and most evolved citizens on the planet: women! How do men exert their power? All testosterone and explosions, with as much noise and havoc and blood as possible. Men ejaculate with their weaponry! Bullets are sperm! Dirty, sloppy, all sound and fury, and ninety percent energy expense for ten percent effect." His face opened; his voice dropped to a whisper. "But *women*— they know the aikido of power. Silent, invisible, traceless, precise. The ghost that is never anticipated or detected. The whisper that kills. One percent expense of energy and ninety-nine percent effect. Clean. Elegant."

"You consider killing *elegant?*"

She heard Livia's trembling voice: *Tzadok, Nassarim, Bianchi...there will be many more.*

All connected to organized crime and terrorism. Her mouth went dry.

"There has to be violence in this world. It is the necessary antagonist of order. It always has been and always will be. Why should we not make it as clean as possible? My agents number in the millions, and their devotion proves that they agree with me. They have never seen their First Commander," he spread a palm over his heart, "but they believe that she is in Sao Paulo or Brussels or Taipei or some other unnamed location."

"You're a First Command...s*he?* They don't know who you really are?"

He smiled.

"Impossible! If they're that savvy and that numerous, you couldn't fool them all."

"I can with two powerful tools. One, the leverage of astounding reward balanced by the threat of punishment. Two, my infinite ingenuity. The greatest ruse of the magician is sleight of hand. Moving objects or people to the most unlikely places."

"*That* many people?" She shook her head. "That much secrecy? It can't be done."

"Of course it can. Think of those who have marshaled followers in the millions. History is full of examples. The larger the numbers, the more easily that people can be led. The world is teeming with sheep while wolves are scarce. You would be amazed at what can be achieved by offering the right incentive to the right audience."

She flashed back to Cambier's home: the hulking manservant, the smells of raspberry tea and rye bread. *All an act? Was she deceiving me the whole time?*

He folded his hands in his lap and rubbed a thumb across the stump that was once a finger. "Consider my motivations. I have my agents, my army, my empire. I have the Disk." He grinned violently. "But best of all, I have you."

"You don't *have* me!" She felt her fingers digging against her jeans. "What makes you think you could pick me for this madness?"

"I need a partner in this paradigm shift, someone of extraordinary abilities—you. I want behind my cause someone with magnificent skill and ambition, someone whose problem-solving talents match mine—you. It must be a female, so that my identity is never revealed. After the revolution, you are my second in command, my consigliore. Behind the curtain, I direct the campaigns of millions of women. The most underutilized, underestimated, undervalued force in history being commanded by a man! What a colossal deception! It's the greatest magic trick of all time!" He roared laughter. "All thanks to you, my brilliant Dr. Donovan, who is now too knowledgeable to release and far too valuable to kill."

The word *kill* made her muscles contract, but the panic burbled into high-pitched laughter. "Second in command, helping *you* rule an army of women? Right. Try the greatest *joke* of all time! You thought I would agree to *that*?!"

"What makes you think I need your agreement?" His eyes flared. "As I said, the promise of astounding reward balanced by the threat of punishment—there is no combination more potent. I offer you a type of power like no other, but I can amplify your motivation with the threat of pain." He twirled sideways, making the scarf flutter. "Would you agree to join my venture if it means the safety of your sister? Your father? Your congenial mentor at Cambridge?"

A shriek lodged in her throat. "You can't be serious. You wouldn't..."

"I can. I would. Have no doubt. When the clock ticks to zero, the bomb goes off. The revolution begins, the seats of power change hands, and the new world is born. My agents are in place to remove a dozen terrorist squad commanders and assume their places. Hunters know that in order to take down a large animal, you must kill the entire organism. The body as well as the head. The agents will eliminate not just the leaders but also their supports, parents and grandparents, children and grandchildren. Their closest friends and confidants."

She stared, slack-jawed. "Affiato...you are going to have all these people murdered? Their families and friends? Their *children*??"

"Unfortunate but necessary."

He SAYS I'm too valuable to kill, but no criminal reveals an assassination plan unless he's talking to a target. Her stomach flared with panic. And if he needs further leverage, one who has living relatives.

She bolted to the door and jerked on the handle.

Locked.

As he slid closer, his voice rumbled through her like an inchoate avalanche. His eyes glittered. "Do you want to know what immortal glory feels like? Would you choose it over destruction?"

CHAPTER 30

Affiato gave her a chary look and slid through the doorway. The lock connected with a metallic snap.

Gatsby stumbled back to the sofa and dropped into the cushions, breathing so hard that they breathed with her. Fear writhed through her as she scanned the room. *Is this place secured, like a federal building—no phones, no Internet? And now that I know who he is and what he's planning, what stops him from killing me?!* She remembered the text message to Roman: LEAVING FOR S'S APPR IN SOHO. *What if he doesn't see it until it's too late?!*

A spasm of panic forced her from the couch. She scrambled around the room, searching under furniture, inside cabinets, behind framed artwork and posters, under and behind magic props, running her hands across the marble floor and over the velvet-papered walls, looking for wiring, cables, electrical panels—anything that might lead to a phone, computer, or Internet connection. When she dashed past a low table, she smacked her knee against it hard enough to drop her to the floor, panting against the pain and rubbing her kneecap. "SON of a bitch!"

Her gaze roamed over the offending pedestal table, which was octagonal. The surface was filled with a resin-coated diagram that resembled a chess board. Rather than an even grid of squares, she saw a spiral pattern divided into segments, each three centimeters square, that alternated black and white. The tokens, five centimeters tall, that rested on the squares were not kings, pawns, or bishops. The top of each token was flat, about the size of a U.S. dime, and depicted a symbol from the Phaistos Disk.

Her eyes darted over the tiny numbers engraved on each square.

I know this pattern. The piece at the beginning, near the edge, and the piece at the center of the spiral...the order is wrong. The BOW should be at A11, not A5. The CHILD piece at A11 should be at A5. She toyed with the other pieces, considered moving the errant ones, reconsidered it, and then switched the BOW piece and the CHILD pieces. She heard a deep rumbling. At the far end of the back wall, a door that was camouflaged by artwork and a wide Florentine mirror began to slide open.

"What the hell?"

She quickly moved the pieces to their original locations. Now halfway open, the door stopped, reversed direction, and began to close.

What if...

She switched the pieces again but this time allowed the door to open fully. Spots of light, like those of running computers, glowed in the darkness. She crept toward the entrance and peered into the room.

"Holy *shit...*"

CHAPTER 31

As the cab rounded the corner onto Charing Cross Road, her STAR SEED vibrated.

"Report?"

Browning said, "The ROSETTE was delivered to the British Museum. The next day, SHIP-1 and SHIP-2 came to the museum lab to supervise the testing, and the ARROW was placed. The TL test confirmed authenticity." Her breath quickened. "SHIP-2 created a diversion, and he and the ROSETTE are missing."

She felt her face flush with anger. "What kind of *diversion*?"

"An explosion. The BOAT is scoping his business in Soho."

Dacea lowered the phone to look at the screen; the GPS tracker glowed. *She's a kilometer from Soho now.* "ARROW is moving that direction. What is the BOAT doing?"

"Unpacking a message received an hour ago. Anonymous and no IP address. It's not a private address or subnetwork. The content has two parts. There's a short message and a description of a person the sender claims is the HAMMER. The attachment was a photo."

"Anonymous message about the HAMMER? We've got spam like this before. Hoda will deal with it. Who has seen the message?"

"Only the BOAT."

"Routed to the BOAT but not me? Who fucked up?" Her body tensed. *Even if a PEDESTRIAN attempts to hack or spam us, Hoda knows that a potential OAR threat requires alerting the SWORD. This is a serious violation.*

"I don't know," Browning said. "Hoda is scrubbing for the host now. It's a unique system—IPSec and AIDP data embedded deeper than Vine13 has ever seen. She says the chances of this being benign are remote."

The cab driver glanced up at the rear view mirror. "Excuse me, lady, do you…"

"Keep driving." She flipped another £20 into the front seat, and he cleared his throat and refocused on the road.

Dacea started to ask her what Hoda would do to track the sender and identify the threat, if any, to the OAR. *Browning won't know or understand. Not her field. Hoda is our Swartz Child. She'll know if it's spear phishing or packet sniffing, if we're dealing with a DDOS, a Smurf, whatever.*

"There's more. The message contained some strange content. Someone is claiming knowledge of personal, historic information about the SWORD. The subject key is 'Design of the SWORD.'"

She pulled in a breath. "Fuck. It means we're dealing with a RUNNER or a SHIP, obviously not a PEDESTRIAN." *Personal historic information about the SWORD. That could apply to anyone who held the role, but it's not...*Fear stabbed at her. "Do you have it open?"

A pause. "Yes."

"Read it."

Browning recited. "Design of the SWORD. Begin THISTLE training at age five. Apply behavioral methods that install skills of the dog..."

Skills of the dog—escapes, weapons, poisons. The toolset and mind of an assassin.

A color image began to fill the STAR SEED screen.

Did she say begin THISTLE training at age five??

(a heap of discarded clothing and rags)

(someone's garbage, but we saw it move)

(you were wrapped in a fabric bearing the image of the ROSETTE)

(Someone wanted you in the Circle)

As the pixels appeared, the face emerged: bushy black hair, a Van Dyke beard-mustache combo, licentious eyes.

She froze. *SHIP-2?*

"It can't. That's..."

Manage dissemination, containment! Browning saw SHIP-2 at the museum, she could identify him, and she knows about this message but not *the photo. Don't let her connect the dots.*

Her fingers tightened on the STAR SEED. *Why the hell would some RUNNER try to tell the BOAT that SHIP-2 is the HAMMER? And how could this RUNNER know what happened to me when I was five? Who could be behind this?*

From the deep web of her mind, a name surfaced. *Cambier.*

CHAPTER 32

Gatsby stepped into the dark room. Overhead fluorescent lights flashed on, making her gasp. As she looked around, her eyes slowly adjusted.

It looked like a bomb had exploded in a government war room. Documents, computers, cameras, and monitors, peppered with magic props, scarves, silk flowers, computers, canes, rope, monitors, bells, trunks, diagrams, cups, flow charts, rings, desks, card decks, Post-It notes, bottles, coins, velvet bags, crumpled wads of paper, candles, cabinets, torn pages, books, dice, mazes of cable—all amalgamated in mayhem. A sorcerer's acid trip. A Jackson Pollock nightmare.

World maps covered the walls and filled the displays of a dozen computer monitors. The back wall was taken over by a huge whiteboard plastered with photos, and below the top row of headshots, she saw three name tags.

Benjamin Tzadok
Abdul ben Nassarim
Rico Bianchi

On the left side of the board, there were more headshots, also with laminated name tags below.

Rahim Jazazi
Ezra Kalish
Hafiz al-Naid
Suhrab Murrk
Asu Wahin
Eldon Young
Patrick O'Connell
Jorge Ramirez
Aldo Cavallaro
Atiku Botha
Hiro Tokada
Dante Bonazzi

She swallowed hard. *I know these names.* The stories of Jazazi, Kalish, al-Naid, and Murrk had peppered the international news for more than a year. Rahim Jazazi, known as "The Demon," was the infamous guerilla leader of Kata'id Force, a group closely allied with Al-Queda that frequently used women as suicide bombers. Ezra Kalish had barely escaped being assassinated by his own troops in the Brotherhood of Halah. He reportedly had a stable of women; they were kept as slaves in locked compounds and made to serve the men.

Only a month ago, a bloody coup had put Hafiz al-Naid in command of the Jamaat e-Musra Army, a cabal said to be based on Hezbollah. When he learned that his sister had been raped by opposition troops, he ordered that she be publicly flogged for adultery. She spent the next eight months in the hospital and never recovered the use of her hands.

The general of the Tatulla Liberation Front, Suhrab Murrk, a distant cousin of Ali bin Qureshi, was known to have eleven wives, some as young as twelve, and had fathered at least three children with all of them.

To the right, she saw a dozen more photos and name tags.

Amira Jazazi
Rachel Moskowitz
Sabeen al-Naid
Farida Sharraf
Ishtar Wahin
Carol Young
Devin Blaine
Maria del Scorro
Franca Volante
Marta Obsanje
Jun Tokada
Rose Perrin

Are THEY all terrorists too? If so, willingly or by force? Who are these women—girlfriends? Captives? Targets? What is HIS role in all this?

She stumbled forward as though navigating earthquake rubble. When she approached the nearest computer, her eyes zipped over the screen. White icons hovered over a dozen cities. The desk at her left held another computer, and on the monitor, she saw a familiar image: something clay-colored and imprinted with a spiral of symbols. *The Disk!*

His voice rumbled through her: *I learned of the quaint little society that formed around the study of the Phaistos Disk...it grew in numbers...I saw the potential and took steps to take control of it.*

How could he possibly manage to single-handedly infiltrate and marshal a global, FEMALE network from a magic shop in Soho?

She jumped at a clank, her heart pounding, and glanced at the door.

Locations that no one ever guesses, Hiding in plain sight.

Kicking at jumbles of silk flowers and ledgers on the floor, she pulled the chair away from the desk and sat, quickly assessing the maelstrom of electronics.

Find an Internet portal or phone line, but he must have protected everything with passwords, firewalls, all that cryptographic shit I know very little about.

Two desks over, a computer beeped, and she looked up and saw a message on the screen.

```
wo-2mu san-ril? suz-pan-dil on&
   mer ter5 wan-!ruz-ker mot
```

The mystifying syntax tugged at her. She was astounded to find herself torn between the drive to escape from Affiato's lair and the need to identify the language.

An open line!

She scrambled to the desk, dragging the chair with her, sat, and fumbled around the workspace until she found a keyboard, buried under a swatch of red silk.

Affiato said that he infiltrated this organization—the Circle—and took control of it, and that a world-wide massacre will happen in a few hours. He said it will smash the focal points of power in terrorist organizations and replace them with his own forces. This message must be related to that. It's intended for him. He and the sender understand the language, and the sender expects him to reply in it.

Another message appeared on the screen.

mer-suz-wan+

Her fingers hovered, quivering, over the keys. *I can't make a GUESS that gets someone killed!*

The message flashed again, now with a question mark.

mer-suz-wan+ ?

She wants an answer NOW. Shit!

Palms slick with sweat, she sucked in a deep breath and quickly typed:

X X X X

A new message scrolled down the screen.

```
BA 14-87 Y
JE 84-89 Y
KA 45-20 Y
TE 23-81 Y
DA 84-03 Y
BI 97-04 Y
BE 10-48 Y
LI 28-61 Y
PA 58-64 Y
MA 46-30 Y
TO 93-72 Y
NE 61-85 Y
```

mer-suz-wan+ ??

Wait, those look like...

She glanced over at the computer she saw when entering the room and focused on the icons. *Baghdad, Jerusalem, Kabul, Tehran, Damascus, Birmingham, Belfast, Lima,*

Palermo, Maiduguri, Tokyo, New York. Jesus…this is some war game or fantasy, or he IS organizing a worldwide…

"I expected nothing less."

She jumped with a gasp.

He leaned against the doorjamb. "What a fountain of skills you are!" Affiato snorted. "I commend you for your initiative. It will be such a pleasure to use it."

She glared. "What are you going to do?"

As he walked toward her, the fluorescents reflected in his eyes like last-second headlights. "For espionage? Intruding into my secret space? A punishment, certainly, but what type? What tyyyyype?" He rolled the rings on his four-fingered hand.

In her mind, she tore him into pieces, but she managed to give him a belligerent stare. "You don't scare me."

He perched against a desk, and his eyes moved from the waves of her hair to her neck, breasts, belly, and crotch—as if deciding whether the painting is a genuine Monet or a forgery and weighing his moves. "I don't need to. Fear is a waste of time."

Watching her squirm under his microscope, his smile widened, and he strode forward until he stood behind her. The back of her head pressed against his chest—rustling near her ear, a fingertip lightly brushing her cheek—and he grabbed her in a head lock. She was amazed that his round body concealed such strength.

She bayed as he dragged her back into THE ATHENAEUM and shoved her onto one of the couches. While she tried to catch her breath, he walked to the pedestal table and switched the BOW and CHILD pieces. The door to the hidden room chugged closed.

She panted as he moved to the oak table and removed the Disk from its pedestal. He returned her stare as he crossed the room and stopped at the main entry. "This is for your treachery." He disappeared through the door and closed it behind him.

She ran to the door and tugged violently on the handle but only bruised her hands. Hidden gears began to grind, mechanical noises as if the room were coming to life. She whirled. The walls began to ripple.

The posters of famous conjurers—Alexander, Carter, Malini, Kellar—were changing, images melting like water paint in a hard rain, the faces twisting, distorting. She felt herself hyperventilating when she saw that some of the faces were no longer those of magicians—it seemed to be Livia's face, her lips curled, sneering or screaming. On other posters, the face was her own.

Music erupted from hidden speakers, and "Toccata and Fugue in D Minor" blasted at ear-splitting levels. Something plunged from the ceiling and sizzled by her right ear, slicing the skin.

"Shit!"

An instant before it crashed to the floor, she saw what it was: a seven-centimeter throwing dagger.

One hand pressed to her ear to stop the bleeding, Gatsby dropped to the floor and the cover of an end table as a set of steel handcuffs dropped from the ceiling and crashed near her foot. A mechanical dove screamed toward her, its papier-mâché mouth chomping as if in death throes. When the end table began bouncing, she lunged forward to dash across the room. A life-size prop resembling a woman in a glittery sequin tunic rattled directly into her path. She smacked into it and heard the maniacal titters made by novelty store laughing boxes. The mannequin tumbled sideways, and its plastic arm collided with her forehead as it crashed to the floor.

Rubbing her forehead, she darted toward another corner of the room. Rose petals drifted from the ceiling, becoming slippery as ice as they landed on the marble floor.

(PUSH HARDER!)

(NO MATTER WHAT IT TAKES, you little stoat, do you understand??)

When she realized that the words were not in her mind or coming from her lips but from the demonic posters that were now Livia's face, she felt her pulse triple, hammering so hard that pain stabbed at her chest. A high-pitched buzz filled her head.

The poster blaring *Kellar's Greatest Wonder; The Most Daring Illusion of the Age!* fell off the wall and flew at her as if fitted with jet engines; it wrapped around her body like a wet sheet, tight a straightjacket. She tore through the paper and howled when it burst into flames, lighting her sleeve on fire, and a jagged snake of fire burned up her forearm.

How is he controlling this?!

The music intensified, each bass note so powerful that primary-color jars and plastic cups on the shelves rattled.

She ran toward the claw-foot Chesterfield sofas at the center of the room but caught a split-second glance of something screaming toward her. She ducked to grab the lip of a milk can, half a meter tall and made of heavy steel, and swung it up in front of her face just as a wooden block smashed against the other side. When she crumbled to the floor and wriggled under the sofa, she realized that the milk can had wedged into the space between the floor and the bottom support of the sofa.

(Never settle for second best!)

Her fingers had cramped onto it and would not release. Chained to the heavy, cumbersome can, she was trapped. The only way to move was on the floor. She shoved the milk can to one side with a grunt, and as she rolled onto her knees, the side panel of a multicolored trunk snapped open, and a blast of fire roared toward her as if from a flame thrower. A scream erupted from her at the instant that her fingers opened. The milk can spiraled toward the other side of the room, and she scrambled, crawling toward a collection of boxes, trunks, and tables that huddled against the east wall of the room. Near the base of a tall prop, her foot snagged on the edge of the thick rug, and as she wrestled it free, the prop shuddered, emitting a metallic whine—steel against steel. At the instant that she looked up, she realized that it was the guillotine prop. The razor-sharp blade screamed downward and slammed into the base with a crash.

The warmth and acrid smell was urine. As it seeped down her leg, pain flashing through her hands, arms, and legs, blood dripping from her ear, the horror stabbed at her.

She heard herself whimper, "He wants me dead..."

CHAPTER 33

Roman rolled his neck, muscles pinched from hours of drafting syllabus notes in long hand. He walked to the end of the bookcase clutching *The Lost Cities of Africa* and pushed the book into place on the shelf. His gaze moved across the books until it fell on the ceramic replica of the Phaistos Disk, at eye level, stashed between *The Great Egyptian Pyramids, Vols. I–II.*

He wandered to his desk and dug into an old-fashioned Rolodex, searching for Gatsby's numbers. When he found the card and his cellphone, he dialed. The line rang until he heard the recorded message. *I'm not in. Please leave a message.*

He hung up and tried her alternate number but, after twelve rings, hung up with a heavy sigh.

GM, what are you up to? His heart raced. *If anything should happen to her, I would lose my mind…*

He sat back, turning the gold rings. The order screamed through the OAR network to the WHITE BIRD agents.

```
RESCIND RAN-MER0
DEPLOY TUN-MER01
ADDED TARGETS
```


Baghdad, Iraq

Amira gave her husband a smile as she handed him a fresh pot of Ceylon tea and the morning newspaper. Rahim read *Al-Mendhar* and sipped.

She walked back to her bedroom, opened the top drawer of her dresser, and felt around until her fingers moved against the small glass box. The day before, when an explosion rocked the city, she jumped, panicked, and almost dropped the box. Even if she had, she knew that it opened only when the microchip embedded in it received the signal from her STAR SEED.

Jerusalem, Israel

Rachel closed one eye, squinting, as Ezra shouted at his commanders. She was not allowed to participate in the meetings, so she listened and watched through a peephole in the next room. They were arguing about how to distribute a cache of weapons and when to send the captured activists to Syria for training. She thought, *They do not know they are training for their own deaths. They will be taught how to make suicide bombs.*

She walked down the hall and entered the kitchen. The upper cabinet held her many canisters of tea leaves, including green tea. Ezra hated it because it gave him diarrhea. She pulled the canister from the shelf and found it, buried at the bottom. The small glass box.

Sighing, she thought of Rabbi Tzadok and Bet-El. *The synagogue burned to the ground.*

Tehran, Iran

Sabeen wriggled in the subway seat, eyes lowered, trying to ignore the passengers: construction workers, ragtag students, and professionals with briefcases. She adjusted her hijab.

A tall woman in a dark blue jacket flopped into the seat next to her. She began pulling falafel balls from a white bag and eating them. They pointedly ignored each other. The woman swallowed the last bite, crumpled the wrapper, and stuffed it in the bag.

The train continued. Passengers stared out the windows or sent messages on their smartphones.

The tall woman leaned forward to place the grease-stained bag on the floor by her boots. Two stops later, she stood, walked to the nearest door, and got off the train.

Sabeen picked up the bag but did not open it. She sensed the weight of the small glass box at the bottom. When she glanced up at the clock on the front wall of the car, she thought, *Hafiz will not be home until midnight.*

Kabul, Afghanistan

Farida pushed against the door and stepped inside, glad that she had been allowed to return to her classroom a week ago. The last school had been ransacked and burned. All the students were boys except for Kazim's sisters, Laala and Nasima.

Suhrab, the man her family had made her marry when she was twelve, told her that she was now allowed to uncover her face while teaching but not when she walked down the street to school.

That evening, her meeting with Nalah lasted just long enough for them to exchange a cloth bag containing the small glass box. She took the bag home and hid it at the bottom of a box filled with baby clothes.

Damascus, Syria

Ishtar huddled in a corner of the bakery. A man with a long grey beard stood at the doorway, looking out onto the street. "Don't go yet," He whispered, and after a few minutes with no firing, he said, "Okay."

Ishtar exchanged glances with the wrinkled woman behind the counter and then crept out into the cobblestone street. The temperature had risen to 45 degrees.

She gripped the woven bag to her chest and darted toward the Greek Orthodox church that she had been told was safe. *Safer.* As she pushed against the door, she pulled out her phone and prayed for a signal. She went through options in her mind and selected a hiding place that Asu would never think of.

Birmingham, Alabama

"Here you go, Casey. Eat it up. You're a growing boy." Carol handed her teenage son a plate heaped with pancakes, ham, and hash browns.

Her husband sat at the table in the living room, muttering under his breath, amid stacks of posters for the rally. "'Spose to rain on Saturday—hey, Carol, you hear me?"

"I hear you, Matt."

She went to the kitchen window and refilled the birdfeeder, thinking of the cabinet drawer in the upstairs bathroom. She had hidden the small glass box at the bottom of a seemingly unopened box of tampons.

Belfast, Ireland

In the mud room at the rear of the house, Devin scrubbed harder at the stains on the shirt, humming to herself to drown out the havoc.

Patrick was shouting into the phone. "What the fuck do you think this is, a press conference? Tell Jack to meet me there with the launchers, now, before I kick his sodding butt to the gutter."

She moved her hand, rainbowed with soap bubbles, to the front pocket of her pants. Her fingers rubbed over the key. It opened the safe, hidden where her soldier boyfriend would not find it. Inside the safe, she kept the small glass box.

Lima, Peru

She knew how quickly the cocaine money would put the machine guns in the hands of the soldiers. Because of her staunch backing of the Sendero Luminoso squads, Maria was one of only three women chosen to train with the guerillas.

Even though Jorge was still recovering from bullet wounds, he would not ignore her birthday and gave her an expensive bottle of Malbec, smuggled in by comrades in Argentina. He filled their glasses and made a toast to the success of the attack on the British embassy.

While he undressed for bed, she went into the bathroom, opened a cabinet, and took out the small glass box. The label read *extraer de maca*. As she cupped it in her hand, the box almost felt weightless.

Palermo, Italy

As Lucia was ushered to her private room at the back of Civoleva, the manager pulled out his phone to discretely inform Signor Cavallaro that his mistress had arrived.

The windows faced Piazza Generale Cascino; she saw bustling city streets and caught glimpses of the ferries heading out to sea toward Naples. Waiters silently graced her table with wine and antipasti as she sipped the Conterno Monfortino and took a deep breath.

A waitress with blond hair approached. She gave Lucia a nod as she delivered an exquisite silverware roll of ivory linen, secured with a silk cord.

Lucia unwrapped the roll and placed the napkin, precariously balanced, at the edge of the table. It fluttered to the floor. The waitress knelt to retrieve it. While she crouched, she dropped something into Lucia's purse: a pouch containing a small glass box.

Maiduguri, Nigeria

Marta sat silently in the car, waiting for Atiku to return. In a moment, she saw him creeping down the street toward her, carrying a Kalashnikov rifle.

It was too dangerous to be on the street—it was littered with metal, concrete, tires, and broken bottles and windows. Dogs sulked past, digging through trash piles for food. He had ordered the military to patrol the housing buildings and compounds, and they were being emptied one by one.

Earlier that morning, she had managed to sneak out to Fara's herb shop to pick up the small glass box, knowing that it would be her last visit.

Tokyo, Japan

Jun watched her husband hustle down the sidewalk toward the Chiyoda line Metro station. Hiro preferred the subway to navigating Tokyo in an expensive car like the other *gurentai*.

Moving away from the window, she went to his office. All his paperwork was scattered chaotically on the desk.

There. She read down the list of names of *yakuza* confirmed for the meeting. Her heart beat faster as she thought back to the night before: he came home early and almost caught her loading the small glass box.

New York, New York

Rose killed the engine and sat immobile, breathing hard, looking around the near-empty parking structure. A red-haired woman appeared out of the darkness, yanked open the passenger door, and scrambled in.

"You have it?"

Panting, Val held out a cloth bag containing the small glass box. "Dante didn't see you? You sure?"

"He walked out, didn't even notice me. Way too distracted. Tonight he's serving his soldiers a dirty dinner." Rose gave a dry laugh. "He won't be home until late."

"How soon until..."

Rose peered at her watch. "Less than an hour."

CHAPTER 34

The cab driver grunted his thanks, and she looked around, assessing the environment. The street was mostly empty of people but overflowing with storefronts. The glare of neon signs and all-night sex shops alternately turned the wet pavement orange, red, and blue.

Dacea pulled her jacket tighter and adjusted her backpack. As she pulled out the STAR SEED, the map popped up on the screen. *63A Brewer Street, five blocks south.*

She dashed down the street, squinting against the rain, until she stood in front of a weathered two-story building. The adjacent shops—a pharmacy and a clothing boutique—were dark and closed for the night. A decorative rod attached to the brick held a hanging sign; the spidery lettering read THE SORCERER'S APPRENTICE.

She spotted a red phone box on the corner and ran to it. Huddled inside, the STAR SEED pressed to her ear, she pressed the CALL icon and said, "Schematics. Send them now."

Images began downloading. The rain assailed the glass while she scanned, frowning. "Hoda?"

The voice floated over the phone. "Go to the end of the block, take two lefts. There's an alley. Walk four meters, and you'll see a fire ladder."

"How fast is the LILY?"

"Eighty seconds."

Dacea ended the call and clambered out of the phone box. She passed a bookstore and a tea room, and at the end of the block, made two left turns. The alley held trash bins, bicycles, and a pile of tattered furniture, all seemingly abandoned. She scanned the building to her left and spotted the fire ladder. She took her time climbing from the street level to the roof, placing each foot slowly and silently.

The long, narrow roof was spotted with puddles from the driving rain. At the far right, she saw a structure about 3 meters square; the door sign read MAINTENANCE. She checked the schematic image. *Access panel on the floor.*

She reached into her pack and pulled out a pair of light-weight neoprene gloves and the glass vial—the LILY. With slow, meticulous movements, she removed the double-bolted lid made of a copper-acrystine alloy, peered into the vial. It contained a few ounces of liquid that looked like watery milk. A nozzle attachment was affixed to the side of the bottle, and she tugged it off and fitted it onto the lid. While kneeling before the door, she held the nozzle against the lock, turned her head, closed her eyes, and sprayed. The liquid sizzled and began working through the metal.

Forty-five seconds later, she tried the handle. It caught a few times but then turned.

She jerked the door open and peered into the building. Alien-green eyes glowed in the dark: a control panel of gauges and pumps that regulated air flow. It provided just enough light to reveal the access panel on the concrete floor. She tugged it loose, set it aside, and pulled the entrance door closed, now working in total darkness.

The space below was black, but she could see just enough to gauge the distance to the floor. She wriggled through the tight opening, dropped down to the surface below, and landed with the shock absorption of a cat. She looked around. *Buckets, boxes, shelving, wall-mounted electrical panels...*

She pulled out the STAR SEED and typed "Access to ground level." In a few seconds, an image appeared on the screen.

Dacea spotted the air vent in the corner. Her waistpack held a pouch of small tools, including a screwdriver. She unfastened and lifted the metal cover, again peering into a dark space and assessing its dimensions.

Maybe seventy centimeters wide and sixty tall.

She slowly slid into the heat vent and into a shaft. Warm air floated over her as she began crawling through it toward the west end of the building. She pulled her elbows against her sides to avoid raking them against the metal walls and nudged her backpack into place when it started sliding to one side.

She heard crashes and shouts from below. Muted strains of classical music, punctuated by bass notes so deep that they made the walls of the vent rattle, echoed around her.

Light filtered through the rectangular grate in front of her; she shoved on it until it popped free and fell to the floor. She wiggled forward head first, pulled her legs out, allowing them to dangle as she gripped the ledge of the opening, let go, dropped three meters, and landed with a grunt. After glancing around the dark hallway, she checked the STAR SEED for the interior schematic.

She crept forward, and the shouts intensified.

CHAPTER 35

Gatsby collapsed onto the Chesterfield sofa, dragging her forearm across her eyes. A bead of sweat fell from the curve of her elbow and into her mouth. Each breath was a gasp, bringing a stab of throbbing pain in her chest. She raised a hand to her right ear and saw bright red smears on her fingers.

A squeal sang out as the door opened. Cradling the Disk in his nine-fingered hand, Affiato stepped into the room. He floated toward her, clucking his tongue, face dreamy.

She watched him advance, heart pounding.

"Will it be your immortal glory? Or your destruction?" He moved toward her and circled the sofa, looking down at her as if preparing to deliver last rites. "Perhaps both. Rest assured, mio caro, that you will achieve eternal glory alongside me."

He's going to kill me! The scream crashed through her. She wanted to roll off the sofa and sprint for the door, but every atom of energy had been burned away.

His trousers whispered as he walked past her and approached the ornate table. He placed the Disk back on its Plexiglas pedestal and then stepped back, gazing at it with a satisfied sigh.

Still panting, she looked around the room. *Where is the bag?* The canvas tote bag lay on the end table where he had tossed it.

"The Disk. Ahh, everything depends on the Disk. The recruits, the language, the weapons, but most important, the mythos. Nothing bonds an army of zealots like an icon, the symbol of the emerging paradigm."

"Even if the icon is meaningless." Gatsby's voice was a rasp. She pulled herself up on the sofa and drew an extended breath, frowning down at the floor as if grasping a brilliant realization for the first time. "It doesn't matter! If they believe it, they flock. They ignite." She let her gaze travel, inconspicuously glancing again at the tote bag and finally meeting his eyes. A smile tugged at her lips. She stood, groaning against the pain, and took a halting step toward the ornate table.

"Ah ah!" He shifted forward, shaking his head, to stand between her and the table.

She shrugged and limped toward the back corner of the room, looking around at the multitude of props: the guillotine, the Egyptian sarcophagus, the dented milk can, the rose petals fluttered across the rug like murdered snowflakes. "So now I'm part of this global syndicate? The second in command to—"

A psychopath!

"—the man who has pulled off the magic trick of all time?"

He perched on the table, smiling widely. "Pandering to my ego. Good move."

Nodding toward the bar, she said, "I need a drink." She held up her hand, turning it to show him the spots of blood. "And some gauze."

Eyebrows peaked, he brusquely pushed past her and walked to the end of the bar counter. With his back to her, he reached up to the stemware on the top shelf.

Only when upright. The panel opens OUTWARD. Now!

She barreled into him, spinning him to face the sarcophagus. His mouth popped open to bellow, but she bashed her fist against his windpipe. With the full force of her weight, she shoved him inside it, slammed the lid shut, and bolted the locks. She braced herself against it, her hands planted on the epicene face, and pushed against it as if tipping a megalith at Stonehenge.

Inside, Affiato pounded, howling. "Agggghhyou*BITCH!!*"

The sarcophagus teetered, fell sideways, and hit the floor with an earthshattering CRASH.

The voices of Cambier and Affiato melded into one, psychotically, and blasted through her.

(These will bring you immortality or destruction)

She ran to the end table, fumbled inside the tote bag, and grabbed the encyclopedia. Cambier's disk was intact.

Affiato raged. "I'LL KILL you!!"

If one brings immortal glory, does the OTHER bring destruction?

Hobart's disk on the pedestal, Cambier's disk in her hands—her eyes ping-ponged between them, her heart raced. *How do I KNOW that Cambier's is a fake? Even if Hobart's disk seems authentic, what if it isn't? The TL test was never validated by a specialty team. That's required to confirm authenticity!*

She ran her hands through her hair, streaking it with blood.

Having the real Disk may bring immortality, but CLAIMING to have it and then finding out that it's a forgery is professional suicide. Destruction! But what else could she have meant?!

Affiato's screams tore through her. She saw the sarcophagus rocking wildly, and her heart fluttered. *Move!*

She dashed to the oak table, slipping on rose petals, and skidded to a stop. Her free hand gingerly wrapped around the disk on the pedestal.

Affiato shouted curses; the sarcophagus churned as if possessed, hammering the floor.

With Hobart's disk in one hand and Cambier's in the other, she felt something stab against her spine and froze.

At her ear, a whisper. "On your knees."

She sensed the solidity behind her, felt the pain in her back digging deeper, and began to kneel, at the same time lowering both disks to waist level. As her knees touched the floor, she gently placed the disks on the marble and turned her head, trying to get a glimpse of the attacker.

Female?

The woman whispered, "Give..."

Gatsby whirled, pulling her legs in tight and snapping them forward to smash against kneecaps...

The woman tumbled...

A twenty-centimeter knife with serrated edges clattered to the floor...

The momentum of the rocking sarcophagus propelled it onto one side, and with a *snick*, the escape panel popped open...

The woman grabbed Gatsby, locking her in a neck chokehold...

Affiato tumbled from the sarcophagus, drenched in sweat, eyes bulging as he spotted the identical disks on the floor and Gatsby wrestling with a slim woman wearing skin-tight lycra...

Gatsby planted her knee in the woman's midsection and wriggled out of the chokehold...

The woman whipped sideways, pinning Gatsby face down...

Affiato dashed to the bar and hunkered behind it, groping frantically at the harness under his jacket...

When the woman slammed her elbow into the small of Gatsby's back, she rolled to her other side, and they thrashed into a knot of violent grunts and flailing legs and arms.

They crashed against the disks, and both shot across the floor like projectile hockey pucks, zigzagging toward the far side of the room until they both collided with the base of an armoire and wobbled to a stop.

Flipped into a kneeling position, the woman froze, her eyes locked on the disks.

Gatsby pressed her upper body up from the marble, tasting the blood that oozed from her lip, and froze, her eyes locked on the disks.

CHAPTER 36

Hoda pushed back from the keyboard to look out the living room window. The townhouse overlooked Metaxourgeio Square. The usual throng of urban Athenians bustled, dropping in and out of coffee shops as they headed to their offices. She rubbed her eyes and turned back to the monitor to read the incoming codes.

```
BA 14-87
JE 84-89
KA 45-20
TE 23-81
DA 84-03
BI 97-04
BE 10-48
LI 28-61
PA 58-64
MA 46-30
TO 93-72
NE 61-85
```

Miranovski shifted in her chair. "What are you doing?"

"Final confirmation." She typed a string of commands, eyes fixed on the screen. The timekeeping app at the top of the screen ran down by seconds. A table with twelve fields began to fill. The data poured in rapidly but in random order, and to the right of each item in the column, a red delta appeared.

```
DA  ▲
MA  ▲
NE  ▲
KA  ▲
BE  ▲
NE  ▲
```

A beep signaled an IM. Hoda glanced at the ID.

"Volante, the THISTLE in Palermo. Wait, she confirmed

ten minutes ago. What's she want now?"

ASSOCIATE TARGETS
3♂ 6♀ 2✋

She frowned. "Three men, six women, two children? That's not right."

Miranovski leaned toward her, her eyes wide. "That's off protocol, directly contradicts RAN-MER0. What the hell is she doing? Since when..."

Another message flashed on the screen, this one from Tokada, the THISTLE in Tokyo.

ASSOCIATE TARGETS
2♂ 4♀ 5✋

They stared at each other. Hoda grabbed the keyboard and typed; the keys clattered like bullets.

DOT-WER-PAN +EN ??

The next message was from Sabeen al-Najdi in Tehran.

ASSOCIATE TARGETS
3♂ 5♀ 7✋

"What the fuck is going on?!" Hoda smacked the keyboard so hard that it flipped off the desktop and cartwheeled to the floor. "Specifications of RAN-MER0 are confirmed at every level. There is *zero* room for misinterpretation. A dozen THISTLE agents can't go insane at the same time!"

Miranovski's STAR SEED buzzed. Usually dry and monotone, Dhar's voice was about to crack. "Are you seeing what I'm seeing?!"

"I'm seeing it, but I can't believe it."

"No one has the authority to rescind RAN-MER0!"

Miranovski panted. "I know, not even the SWORD, no one but..."

"The HAMMER?!" Dhar was shouting.

Hoda and Miranovski searched each other's faces, looking as terrified as if picking which body to cannibalize. "I can't believe this is the HAMMER. Last minute, no direction? It doesn't make sense!"

"It's not even possible?" Hoda whispered.

Miranovski looked up at the screen again, hyperventilating.

Dhar bellowed, "What's going on??"

She spoke slowly while trying to work through disastrous possibilities. "The HAMMER has lost her mind, or the HAMMER is a SHIP."

Hoda's eyes were huge. "Or we've been fucking hacked."

"A PEDESTRIAN? From the outside?" Miranovski said.

"From the inside."

Miranovski shook her head. "That's not possible."

"Think of what's fucking *possible*, Tess. Invisible and everywhere, right?"

Their eyes darted to the timekeeping app, methodically ticking down to WHITE BIRD.

11:01:37, 11:01:36, 11:01:35, 11:01:34...

"An-wuz-wil oh kuz-dil-wer-ser. Ker-pot in mil-on-pan, sil-wan! Dan-mer!" Livia paced the empty conference room as she shouted into her phone.

Rain pelted the students and faculty who scurried across the Grumheller Fountain quad. On Presidents Day, classes at the University of Washington were cancelled, and all offices were closed; only the security gatehouses and parking garages were staffed. Earlier that morning, after parking and then dashing past the physics, chemistry, and architecture buildings, she hadn't seen a single person. The Loen Arts building that housed the classics and philosophy offices was equally empty.

A dozen padded chairs were arranged, like squat pall bearers, at the mahogany table. Her voice echoed in the narrow room. "Man-ruz ser oh man-ril London kan?"

The female voice was robotic. "Oh kan-wil un. Ser-mot en."

"But wil en ker-tot-suz ran-til en duz Donovan. RUZ WER DAN!"

There was a long pause.

"Til-pan. Tuz un."

The line went dead.

She slammed the phone against the table, breathing hard, her eyes darting. *This is BAD. Gatsby...*

CHAPTER 37

"What's this? An intern?"

Gatsby and Dacea pivoted toward the voice. Gatsby winced as terror gripped her stomach.

Affiato slid from behind the bar, his pace suggesting the impenetrability of the room. He raised the weapon—a pistol made of an organic material that looked like bamboo—and trained it on the human knot crouched in the middle of the room. In his other hand, a smartphone glowed.

Dacea blinked. *THIS is the HAMMER?! Impossible!* Then: *The TIARA, the same toxin as the DOLIUM, and he knows that, or does he?*

"We seem to have two treasures, but only one is genuine." He checked the smartphone. "Identify the real one in the eleven minutes that remain before I launch the revolution and decide what to do with you. One extraordinarily well-trained SWORD and you, our lovely and brilliant SHIP. How useful you have both been!"

Dacea's eyes flared.

Gatsby glanced at the disks and then met Affiato's gaze. "You can't take either one to a museum without being arrested, and you *know* that, and you can't kill me, because I'm the only person who can tell you which one is real."

Dacea rose to her feet, breathing hard. *The HAMMER would know the fake. We made it!* Her eyes darted from Affiato to Gatsby to the disks three meters away on the floor.

"You're wrong, and time is running out." He inched closer.

Gatsby flashed to the younger woman; her eyes zigzagged across the black fabric that covered the lower part of her face. Something small and round bulged under her shirt near the breastbone.

The woman seemed to be assessing her at the same time. Her eyes flicked over Gatsby's torso and up to her face. "En-san muz-sil an."

Affiato sucked in a sharp breath. *Don't do it? The order was to acquire the ROSETTE at any cost! What is she thinking?*

As the sound of the words reverberated in Gatsby's mind, panic surged. *That language! Why does it sound familiar?*

Dacea repeated, "En-san muz-sil an!" *Don't do it!*

Will she run with the ROSETTE? Affiato glanced at Dacea, his face constricting.

Questions burned through Gatsby like a firestorm. *He KNOWS her! He knows the language she's speaking, and they both want the Disk! What do they want from each other??*

Dacea turned to Affiato, skewering him with a stare. "RUZ WER DAN."

RUZ WER DAN! What?! What is it?

She saw the micro twitch in Dacea's face, and primal instinct took over. In the same instant, Dacea and Gatsby pounced.

When they skidded to a stop, they saw that they held the same disk. Like ninjas at opposite ends of a *bo*, the weapon of *bojutsu*, they rose to their feet, eyes locked, legs quivering.

Gatsby stared into the woman's dark face. A minute eye movement seemed to transmit a message. *What is she trying to tell me??*

Dacea whispered, "San-wach. Tuz on ran-mer." *End it now. Let it go.*

CHAPTER 38

Dacea saw the faces burning with anger, felt the Maratti tear her skin, heard Badra growl "not important enough." The creature of rage roared again, seeking to...

(How do I fucking get OUT *of this life?!)*

...destroy the never-ending nightmare of her life.

This is no life. This is slavery! Electricity shot through her muscles and into her head, making her ears ring. *No. It's MY life! I won't be a slave! I won't be an obedient lap dog, a mindless foot soldier, leading the massacres of the Circle. I AM important enough!*

Looking into Gatsby's eyes, she released her grip.

As the solidity of the disk transferred to Gatsby's hand, it felt heavy as a continent.

Dacea and Affiato stared at her. The second hand of the cosmic timepiece stopped.

Gatsby's heart pounded, lungs hitching for oxygen.

Something glimmered on the surface.

She brought the Disk closer to her face. A viscous amber fluid was seeping from the edge and oozing down the B side. As it coated the surface, tiny symbols materialized, glimmering like fireflies—*new* symbols.

She turned the disk a few degrees, peering at the edge, cautiously pulled a fingertip through the liquid, and spread it around as if finger painting. Staring at the emerging symbols, she gulped. "It can't...I, I don't believe it. *I don't believe it.* It's Linear B."

Affiato snapped toward her. "What?"

"Linear B, proto..."

"What does it say?"

"Christ, you think I can decipher..."

He roared. *"Tell me what it says!"*

A lifetime of linguistic research whizzed through her. *Etruscan? Cypriot? Phoenician? Aramaic? Egyptian hieroglyphics? Is it actually a language or an elaborate joke?!* Sweat rippled down her neck as she concentrated on the lines; her forehead bunched in a tight frown. "Wait! No, more like a kind of bastardized cuneiform, closer to Akkadian."

Dacea swallowed. *A message hidden on the ROSETTE? How the fuck could we have missed that?!*

The squiggles formed syllables. The syllables formed three words.

Gatsby felt her knees shaking, her heart at full throttle, as stunned as if the Phaistos Disk had grown hands, gripped her by the throat, and hissed into her ear. She looked up at Affiato to see the wild hunger, the need to know what she knew as desperately as an addict needed a fix. *This DEFINES him.*

"It's three…" Her mouth dropped open as she pulled in air. "Three words that change everything about your assassination plot, everything about your recruits, everything about the Circle—all of it! The first one begins with the diphthong pronounced *mo-ah*."

"What does it mean? Tell me!!" His body shook with spasms.

The scales of power just tipped, Affiato. Now I have YOUR *immortality on a clay platter.*

"Call off your massacre. Let us go." She glanced at Dacea and turned, shoulders square, to face him fully. "And I'll give you the rest."

His eyes locked on her. She saw, almost palpably felt, the twitches of his lips. The four fingers of his left hand clutched at the air, and his chest billowed as he seemed to run through alternatives.

"How many options do you think you have, Affiato?"

"Far more than you imagine."

"In the next ten seconds, you have exactly one choice to make." She looked back at the flowing lines on the disk. "Three words. This is the most important sentence you will ever hear. I'm going to tell you something, and I want you to really listen."

His expression shifted, as if he were preparing to consider surrender. "I'm listening."

"The message contradicts what you told Cambier."

His eyes bloomed with panic.

Dacea jerked toward her. "What?"

"No, it *reverses* it."

His eyes ping-ponged between them. His hands—one holding the TIARA and the other the smartphone—jittered violently. He began to shake with laughter. "Welllllllll, now you want to *negotiate* with me, like a fruit stall vendor? That is rich. My dear Dr. Donovan, you are delightful, but *you* are not an unbreakable code."

(NEVER LET GO!)

The voice crashed through her. Rather than cringing, she moved toward it, focusing on it with such intensity that desire materialized before her as if written on the air.

(PUSH HARDER!)

(Grab them before someone else does, hear me?)

(NO MATTER WHAT IT TAKES, you little stoat!)

Livia's face swirled through her mind, the phantom that haunted her, the Iron Maiden who made her hold a dish or figurine or book or anything heavy and awkward.

She felt her heart thudding madly. A precipice, a point of no return. *Am I nothing but this drive for immortality that I inherited from you? I fed the neurosis that kept your voice alive for decades, but if I stop feeding it and kill the beast, will it kill the drive that propelled me? The obsession with achievement? Who would I be?* What *would I be?*

She squeezed her eyes shut, hyperventilating so hard that dots danced in front of her eyes. *You couldn't control your world, Livia, so you had to control mine. What YOU couldn't let go of was ME.*

While her fingers clamped onto the Disk with a force that would shatter it, a pathway unfolded before her, the one that led to the refuge she had been seeking.

"I am unbreakable, Affiato. I have what you don't and never will."

She opened her hand.

CHAPTER 39

The disk fell, flipping like a wounded animal.

Affiato scrambled forward. "Cazzo! Vaffanculo, figlio di putana, cazzo, CAZZO!!"

When it hit the marble, shards sprayed like flying insects. He dove to the floor, keening, "No no no no no no NO!!"

Gatsby ploughed into him, and he bellowed as the TIARA and smartphone catapulted from his hands. She spun toward Dacea, panting. "Hold him!"

Dacea dove onto Affiato, pinning his arms while he kicked wildly, and Gatsby raced across the room to the cabinet with shallow drawers, the one where Affiato stored the Okinawan Death Trap. She yanked the top drawer open, grabbed the finger trap and the gold key, and ran back. She spotted the second Chesterfield sofa—one arm connected with the back support, the front leg, and the lower support but left an open space. "Help me move him over here!"

They shoved Affiato, writhing and cursing, toward the sofa, and Gatsby grabbed his arms and twisted them around toward the arm of the sofa. "Get his hands up here!"

Dacea helped her wrangle Affiato's hands into position. He thrashed violently, but she managed to get one hand through the opening and the other up by the padded arm. While he lurched at her, she jammed both index fingers into the finger trap, effectively cuffing him to a piece of furniture that outweighed him several times.

She spotted his phone about a meter away on the marble floor, grabbed it, and glared at the screen. "How do we stop it?" She locked on Dacea. "You want to stop it, don't you?"

Affiato twisted against the sofa like a straightjacketed lunatic. "Ti ucciderò! I'LL KILL BOTH OF YOU!"

Dacea snatched the phone from Gatsby's hand, grabbed her shoulders, and spun her until her back was to Affiato. She slid the phone into the front pocket of Gatsby's jeans and whispered, "Trust me."

She waved for Gatsby to follow as she walked toward Affiato and knelt by his side. "One disk is genuine and one is a fake. *You're* a fake, and this is all a ploy! You're not the HAMMER."

His cheeks flushed. "No? Who else could maneuver all the pieces of a living puzzle as I have? No one. No one could take that sinking ship of rats that was the Circle and save it! Only a *genius* could liberate millions of women, free them from lives of misery and persecution!"

"Who's persecuting them? Who the hell is liberating them? If you were the HAMMER, you'd know that three days ago, all Circle communications and codes were transferred from the HAMMER to the SWORD."

"Transferred? To *you*? A stupid lie." His eyes blazed.

"You'd know that Miranovski, Hoda, and Dhar were ratted out. They're all RUNNERS."

He scoffed, laughing weakly.

"You'd know that every DOLIUM manufactured in the last month has a reengineered toxin that makes the original look like a mosquito bite."

His mouth opened and closed wordlessly.

"And at the first sign of a SHIP, you would have called the Argonaut Law for the SPIN TEMPLE."

"Ha! You silly HORN!" Affiato grunted laughter. "I thought you were better trained than that! The SWORD knows the HELMET commands better than her own name, knows that the Argonaut Law is SPIN *HELMET!*"

Dacea walked to Gatsby and pulled the phone from her pocket.

Gatsby felt her stomach clench. "What are you doing?"

Dacea shoved the phone into Affiato's face. The screen had gone black except at the center, where a digitized image of the Phaistos Disk rotated slowly. "Your lies uncovered, your precious ROSETTE in pieces. WHITE BIRD was just aborted. *You* just gave the SPIN HELMET order, the command to destroy all Circle networks, all intelligence, databases, servers, vaults, including everything on the HAMMER's system."

A thread of saliva twirled from Affiato's lip toward the floor. Pupils huge, he blinked.

Dacea scanned the keypad of Affiato's phone to compare it to the STAR SEED. "And you know that after it wipes out all data, it destroys the hardware."

Out of the corner of her eye, Gatsby saw Affiato staring at the finger trap, a focused look creeping over his face. Using a precise level of relaxation and a subtle twist, he coaxed the finger trap to flower open. It tumbled to the floor. He scrambled across the room and dove behind the bar.

Dacea dashed toward him but skidded to a stop when she heard a cabinet door squeal and the click of a pistol hammer being cocked.

He rose with a break-top Webley .455 trained on Gatsby and moved across the room until he stood before the octagonal table. He slowly switched the BOW and the CHILD pieces with his free hand. "I wasn't sure that you could discover the intricacies of my chess board, but no surprise. Precisely the smarts that I need in my first commander." He glared at Dacea. "And now we see just how wrong *you* were, whether all the training effort was worth it."

Gatsby and Dacea peered at each other as the rumbling started and the door at the far end of the back wall began to slide open. He walked back across the room and stopped before the widening entrance to the war room. He waved the gun, signaling for them to come toward him. "In here, both of you. Move."

As they walked forward, keeping their eyes locked on him, he took a step inside the room, and his face crumbled. The papers and magic props smoldered or had burst into flames; black smoke billowed from the sputtering computers. Explosive electrical flashes made them all jump. Affiato lurched toward the closest one as if he could save it from destruction. "No!"

The door! Gatsby sprinted to the octagonal table and switched the pieces again, frantically asking herself, *Can I can trap him in there? Is there a second control switch or device in that room? There must be!* The machinery gave a scream as the steel door reversed. Affiato swiveled between the closing door and the sparks and flames arcing from the hardware.

The sliding door mechanism was computerized. From inside the war room, the only way to open the door was by launching a software program—the program installed on a computer that was melting into a sticky, dying beast of plastic, aluminum, and copper wires.

He dashed to the door. The opening was only forty-two centimeters wide, but he thrust one arm and one foot through the space, struggling violently for the freedom of THE ATHENAEUM. There was no safety catch, no mechanism that stopped the door in case of an obstruction. He knew this; he had installed it.

"AAAAAGHHHH!!!!"

Gatsby tumbled back as blood shot through the air and bubbled down the front of his ivory jacket and pants, forming a candy-red puddle on the marble. It ran from his mouth and nose as he flailed, a screaming beast captured in a snare. His words disintegrated into a moan and sobbing, punctuated by coughs, and then gurgles. He slumped, eyes glazed.

Gatsby felt her stomach lurch, tasted the bitterness of bile.

Dacea inched closer, her eyes darting between Gatsby and Affiato's crushed body. She navigated around the puddles, moving close enough to grope his neck for a pulse. After a minute, she stretched across him to peer into the war room. The fire was spreading, engulfing all the computers, photographs, magic props, and schematics. She whispered, "Οι ένοχοι δε θα γλυτώσουν." *The guilty are not spared.*

Fighting back the nausea, Gatsby managed to whisper, "How do we get out of here? How did you get *in*?"

Dacea pulled her smartphone from her pack and dialed 999. She held it forward, motioning for Gatsby to speak into it.

"Metropolitan Police. What is the emergency?"

"63A Brewer Street, Soho, I'm trapped inside, and the place is on fire!"

"Don't worry, we'll be right there."

Dacea ended the call. She circled the room, retrieving the TIARA and the FLUTE and stowing them in her backpack.

Her stomach still cramping, Gatsby walked over to Cambier's disk, still on the floor, and carefully placed it by the Plexiglas pedestal on the oak table. She crossed the room, picked up the tote bag that Affiato had tossed aside, and pulled out Cremin's *World Encyclopedia of Archeology*. While gathering the shards of the disk and moving them into the hollow space inside the book, she peered up at Dacea. "Who are you?"

Dacea stared at the mangled body, crushed between the edge of the steel door and the wall. "I thought I knew who I was. Who the HAMMER was." She turned to gaze at the supports of the guillotine prop and down at the glittering blade that had slammed into the base.

"What you said about the Circle, about RUNNERS, the DOLIUM—was it true?"

"Does it matter?" She met Gatsby's eyes. "When the police arrive, you'll say you were taken hostage."

"I was, but..."

"You'll be questioned and released. Then look for an email from phoenex.ac.uk. It will have instructions."

Gatsby heard the howl of a siren and glanced toward the main door. After checking that all the fragments were securely stowed, she sat the bag on the end table and turned back to Dacea. "Instructions for what?"

She looked around the room—the bar, the doorway, the props, tables, and sofas. She was alone.

CHAPTER 40

It was as surreal as first time she entered THE ATHENEUM—Affiato's fiery smoke-and-mirrors illusions, the snifters of Courvoisier, the velvety Chesterfield sofas. As she looked around, dazed and drained, the room was familiar and utterly alien at the same time. "Toccata and Fugue in D Minor" danced through her mind.

Kellar's Greatest Wonder; The Most Daring Illusion of the Age!

"Populus vult decipi ergo decipiatur." Her voice shook. It sounded childish and robotic in the silence. "The people wish to be deceived, therefore, let them be deceived." Still looking around for the girl who had attacked her and then helped her, she whispered to the air, "Where did you go?"

Was she even here? Did any of this really happen? She looked down at the smears of blood on her fingers. *It happened.*

Agonizing fatigue pushed her down into the nearest sofa. *He thought he could murder to bring on a new paradigm. He thought he was a savior, rescuing these women around the world. What did he call them? The most underutilized, underestimated, undervalued force in history, but it was all illusion. Like he said, the greatest magic trick of all time.*

She thought of the underestimated force, and their faces rose in her mind—sad, defiant, angry, determined, relentless. The women who had nothing to lose by following the HAMMER's route to salvation but unaware that the HAMMER was male and an unequalled expert of deception.

Who are these women?

With a groan, she pulled herself from the sofa and stumbled across the room. The door to the hidden room was still open, leaving an open space about forty-two centimeters wide. As she stepped over Affiato's mangled body, she felt her stomach lurch but wriggled through the opening and into the war room. The scene was apocalyptic—mayhem, fire, destruction, ash, smoldering piles of indistinguishable metal objects that were once hardware.

The poisonous cocktail of illusion and the drive for power was so strong that it obliterated everything in its path—everything except them. She wandered to the back wall. As her eyes moved over the whiteboard plastered with photos, she read the name tags aloud. "Amira Jazazi, Rachel Moskowitz, Sabeen al-Naid, Farida Sharraf, Ishtar..." At the name *Franca Volante*, she swallowed hard and felt a shiver run up her spine.

These men, all known terrorists, were singled out for death, but not just them. His voice rumbled through her. *To take down a large animal, you must kill the entire organism...the agents will eliminate not just the leaders but also their supports...parents and grandparents, children and grandchildren, their closest friends and confidants.*

A global coup. Scores of women tricked by his lies, and a dozen signed up to carry out execution orders. What made them consider killing? What was the tipping point?

A computer sputtered, sending out a spray of sparks. She jumped, turning toward it, and noticed a light glowing at the bottom edge of the monitor, indicating that the system was in sleep mode.

What if...there might be...

Careful to avoid the cables and fires on the floor, she moved toward the computer and searched the desktop for a keyboard, a control device of any kind, but found none. On impulse, she brushed her finger across the screen. The monitor flared; a horizontal strip appeared along with four columns of multicolored icons. Her eyes raced over the screen and stopped when she saw an icon that looked like a camcorder. Breathing hard, she pressed it.

A fresh panel slid open, and the black square at the center slowly filled with the image of a woman's face. Behind her, Gatsby saw cabinets and dishware. The jerkiness of the image made it clear that the woman had made a video of herself by holding a smartphone camera at arm's length. Her head and neck were covered by a white hijab, her skin light olive, her face etched with worry lines. She spoke in rapid Arabic, her voice a whisper, her eyes shifting quickly between the camera and something at her right. "I am Amira.

There are still shootings outside. Rahim may come home soon. I don't know…I don't know if he is still with the soldiers or has gone to the south. The jets are so loud. Every day there is firing, people are being killed. Her lip trembled. We cannot stay in Bagdad, we must go, I must take my children to…"

The image fractured, blinked from black to random images, and then resolved into another face. She stood in front of a public bathroom in a park setting. Coarse, curly black hair swept around her cheeks. She stared into the camera with smoldering eyes. "Perrin. I met the FORK last month, an she says I'm in the ninety-fifth percentile." Her accent was outer Brooklyn; her smile was that of a prison guard. "I know what I can do for the BEEHIVE, and my scores freakin' prove it. I'm know ready to…"

What are these, interviews? Audition tapes?

Perrin's face dissolved into black-and-white pixels; the play speed shifted to fast forward, and female faces appeared rapidly, interspersed with visual static. Gatsby jabbed her fingertip against the icon several times, and the video speed returned to normal. The woman on the video looked like she was in her early 30s. Prints on the wall behind her were stylized block prints of water, trees, birds, and temples. She did not look up at the camera but stared down into her lap, and her hands moved slowly as she smoothed them over her pale-blue dress. Her features were Asian; a jagged scar ran from one corner of her mouth and under her chin. She spoke in halting English.

"It is not good. My husband gone all the time, but he will not let me go outside. Yakuza will not let wife do anything and too much powerful for me. I cannot work to make money. My family cannot help me. I want to go home, I cannot be with Mr. Tokada. There is frightening…"

They're hostages in their own homes, and they join Affiato's army because it's better than the prison of their own lives.

Heart pounding, she looked across the room to the wall where the photos and name tags of the targeted men had been mounted. The wall was black with ash, and most of the photos were burned, but fragmented pieces of two remained: Rahim Jazazi and Atiku Botha.

Jazazi the Demon. Botha the Destroyer.

A lifetime of work and challenges raced through her— accomplishments, disappointments, the images of award that had played on the screen of her mind for years. She remembered her conversation with Roman just before receiving Affiato's invitation.

(It's an Aeon, the most prestigious award in antiquities sciences. Big Athens party, funding for life.)

A sigh moved through her. Her gaze flowed from the dark eyes in the photos to the chaos in flames on the floor.

(What is YOUR place in history?!)

As though Roman were there, deconstructing an argument over a glass of chardonnay, she said aloud, "What was yours, Livia? Some people their lives obsessed with glory. These people—these women—are living in destruction. They're trying to survive. They just want see the next sunrise."

Cambier's voice floated through her: *What you will risk for glory, what you will destroy.*

Affiato's first message: *Open your eyes to the truth. The scribe is a liar. The world has been deceived.*

The world HAS been deceived, but not the way that he thought. Not that way that I allowed myself to think. Livia tried to force me to fight for glory, to hold on to it no matter what. I let the Disk be destroyed. I let it go, but what matters is what you choose to hold on to.

CHAPTER 41

Banging and shouts startled her. A male voice barked from the other side of the door, "Metropolitan Police!"

Gatsby dashed toward the door and wriggled through it back into THE ATHENEUM. "In here!"

The handle shook as it was twisted back and forth. "Are there any other entrances?"

"No other doors, no windows." She overheard muted conversation and a voice crackling over a radio or phone.

"We're going to cut the lock! Move at least five meters away, understand?"

She darted to the far side of the room. "Yes. Ready."

Bickford, the senior officer, dug into the Emergency Escape bag and pulled out goggles and fireproof gloves. A tall potted ficus partially blocked the door, and he pushed it to the other side of the hall.

Another officer steered a wheeled caddy toward him that held an acetylene cylinder and an oxygen cylinder, side by side like Spartan sentinels and connected by colored tubing. He checked the pressure of the gauges, grabbed the valves atop each cylinder, and started the flow. He picked up a silver-and-gold torch and held the striker a few centimeters from the tip of the torch.

"Move back."

The other officers stepped back as he squeezed the sides of the striker together. The spark ignited a flame that shot out from the torch nozzle, dancing like a demon set ablaze. He reached to the valves and turned one to decrease the oxygen, and the flame shrunk to about ten centimeters. As he knelt before the door, eyes scanning the dead bolt below the handle, he held the torch up and traced a rectangle around the dead bolt. The others watched while the flame sizzled and hissed.

Bickford turned the torch off, secured it at the side of a cylinder, and reached back into the bag for a rubber diaphragm attached to a chain. The flat side of the diaphragm was covered with a protective sheet, and he pulled it off to expose a sticky surface. After pressing the diaphragm to the loosened area around the dead bolt, he pulled hard on the chain. The rectangle popped free and fell to the floor.

Another officer tried the handle, stood up and kicked at it, and the door swung open with a bang.

Four policemen stepped into the room. Their eyes widened at the maelstrom of THE ATHENAEUM, the litter of posters, fabric, the red rose petals scattered across the floor, the assortment of bizarre magic props and, at the back wall, the Rorschach spray of blood.

Bickford and Gatsby met in the middle of the room. "Are you okay?"

She pressed a finger to the wound on her forehead. "Banged up, but I'll live."

The other officers pushed past her toward the carnage at the second doorway and pulled on latex gloves. One scanned the mangled body, rivulets of blood, and contorted face. "Jesus, Joseph, and Mother Mary. Who is this? Did you know him?"

She explained.

He shook his head. "Hell of a way to die."

Another officer, his nametag reading O'HARE, walked toward her with a phone in his hand. "This can't be a coincidence. An hour before you called, we got a missing persons call from a Bella...um..." He shouted to the others. "What was the caller's name?"

An officer crouched next to the guillotine shouted, "Balasubramani."

CHAPTER 42

The police scoured the room, taking photos and notes about locations.

O'Hare looked the stainless steel door up and down. "What's behind this?"

"A control room, or a war room, I guess you'd call it. A shitload of electronics, documentation, photos."

He pushed against the exposed edge, seeming to gauge whether he could slide through the space, and shook his head. "You know how to open this door?"

"Over here. There's a remote control."

She crossed the room to the octagonal table, showed him the BOW and CHILD pieces, and switched them. The door rumbled as it chugged open and the body dropped. In chorus, the officers let out an "awwww!" of disgust when it hit the floor and blood splattered the wall. Bickford and O'Hare carefully stepped over it and into the second room, looking around with stunned expressions at the photos of well-known terrorists and the chaos of burning electronics. Coughing from the smoke, they pulled their shirts up over their mouths.

While an officer named Fischer sat with Gatsby to dress the cut on her ear, Bickford stepped back into THE ATHENEUM and knelt next to the body. He pulled out his phone to call David Cook, the medical examiner and head of the Metro crime lab.

The younger officer's nametag reading CHESLER. As he walked toward her, his twitchiness screamed rookie. He herded Gatsby toward one of the Chesterfield sofas, pulled an armchair closer, and began writing on his iPad with a stylus. "From the beginning, please, Dr. Donovan."

She told the story. Affiato helped her acquire a priceless artifact. When she found it and had it transported to the British Museum, he stole it. He told her to come to The Sorcerer's Apprentice and imprisoned her; as he tried to get out of the hidden room, he got trapped and was crushed by the door.

The long monologue had made her voice hoarse. "Talk to Polichev with the CIS. He showed up at the British Museum just after Affiato took off with the disk. He asked me most of these questions." She coughed. "I was supposed to call him this morning."

"Polichev, CIS, okay."

While Chesler scribbled notes, Bickford walked up. "Tell me about this area on the floor. Looks like something broke."

"It did." She retrieved Cremin's encyclopedia and opened it, motioning for him to take a look. He peered at the shards that she had arranged in the hollowed-out space. They lay flat next to each other, clearly out of order. He looked up at her, eyebrows raised.

"What is this?"

"It's," she paused, "it *was* a priceless artifact called the Phaistos Disk. He claimed that it had been stolen and asked me to help him track it down. I found it." She grimaced at the body. "And then he revealed his real plan."

Bickford frowned. "If it *had* a price, how much?"

"Sixty million euro, or so he claimed. It was originally stored at the Heraklion Museum in Crete. After I recovered it in Madrid, it was transferred to the British Museum for dating and preservation, and it needs to go back."

He shook his head. "We don't know what happened here—a homicide, suicide, whatever—and this is material evidence, so it all goes to the crime lab."

"You can't just bag the pieces, Bickford. Sixty million euro, remember?" She turned on him angrily. "They have to be transported by specialists. Call Talbot-Wei in Southwark. They are the only people qualified to transport the pieces to your lab, and when your investigation is complete, they need to deliver the fragments to the British Museum." She rubbed her aching neck. "Clevis will shit kittens."

"Who's Clevis?"

"Nelson Clevis, the curator. He was beside himself when he saw the intact disk, but when he sees it in pieces..." Her voice trailed off. "And there's this." She picked up

Cambier's disk from the Plexiglas pedestal. "This one is a replica, but it should still go to the museum."

"Artifacts. What a racket. People stealing ancient bits of junk that someone says are worth a fortune." He began dialing, shaking his head.

While Chesler and the other officers worked through the room, adding notes and photos, Gatsby wandered back to the other side of the room. As she approached the octagonal table and ambled past it, she drew her hand forward. When it was in reach, she picked up the CHILD piece and quietly slid her hand into her pocket.

"Everyone ready?" Chesler barked.

Nodding, the officers finished packing their equipment and laptops.

"Let's go. Dr. Donovan, I'll take you home."

He ushered her to the lobby and out into the darkness of Brewer Street. It was just after one in the morning. The buzz of the LED street lights was both alien and oddly calming.

The police car was parked in front of The Sorcerer's Apprentice. Chesler pointed to the passenger seat, motioning for her to climb in. "Where do you live?"

She stumbled up the front steps of her building, thoughts tumbling.

The pieces will be reassembled. It will never be completely returned to its original state, of course, but it IS the real Phaistos Disk. Now the question is whether I spend the rest of my life trying to understand it.

She crossed the lobby and inner staircase, dragging herself to the second floor and the door of her flat. Her legs felt like they were encased in concrete, and the cut on her ear still throbbed. It would be long a time before the nausea dissipated and she could eat.

Without other samples of the glyphs, the chances of that? Astronomical. Impossible.

She thought of THE ATHENAEUM, the demonic posters, the guillotine, the rose petals fluttering like confetti, the pandemonium of Affiato's hidden war room, the terrifying moment when she released the Disk and let it shatter on the marble floor. His hideous death scream. The faces of the terrorists, targeted for death, and the haunted faces in the video-recordings. *The jets are so loud. Every day there is firing, people are being killed...*

Tossing her shoulder bag on the loveseat in the living room, she walked into her office and turned on the overhead light. She settled in the chair and booted the computer.

(Look for an email from phoenex.ac.uk)

Her email service flowered on the screen. As she scanned the new messages, she saw the domain name, phoenex.ac.uk. As she clicked READ, a knock made her jump. Her heart pounding, she walked to the front door. Dacea stood slouching in the hallway, hands stuffed in her pockets. After an intense staring match, Gatsby pulled the door open.

Dacea walked into the living room and dropped onto the sofa. As she straightened the qunae over her face, she said, "SHIP-1. So you're the American, Gatsby Donovan. You're famous in some circles."

Gatsby settled on the loveseat, eyes fixed on the wiry young woman. "You know who I am, and you knew Affiato. Who the hell are *you*?"

"You don't need names." She paused. "Tell me this. Just before you let it go, you said you saw a message in an archaic language."

"Linear B."

"You translated three words and said it changed everything about the Circle. The HAMMER was screaming to know what it was. Not a very original bluff but effective."

"No bluff. It *was* Linear B."

She frowned. "Then what was the message?"

"I have no idea." Gatsby gave her a tight smile.

Dacea seemed to process this for a moment and then nodded. "How did you find the ROSETTE?"

"I went to see Cambier."

Dacea's body froze, but her eyes gave away the force of her reaction. "Cambier, the RUNNER? She's been..." She stopped, seeming to weigh options and level of disclosure. "Where?"

It was Gatsby's turn to weigh what she should say. *Because of what I have told you, the Circle will find me...they will take my life.* "In France."

"What did she tell you?"

"She told me about the Circle but didn't give specific details. She also told me about being accosted years ago by a street performer. From the description, it had to be Affiato."

"SHIP-2?"

"Yes. After the Disk was analyzed and dated, I went back to The Sorcerer's Apprentice—that's when he locked me in that room and told me that he infiltrated it, took control, manipulating all the members and orchestrating a massacre of terrorist leaders. Men like Rahim Jazazi and Atiku Botha who have been on Most Wanted lists for years."

"The THISTLE agents in a dozen cities were ready."

"THISTLE?"

"THISTLE, RUNNER, HAMMER, SHIELD, ROSETTE—notice a pattern?"

It registered instantly. "Godart sign names."

"Also called Kameroff Coding. The WHITE BIRD operation was set, the planning perfect, but with no warning and no explanation she," she caught herself, "*he* added targets. Family members and associates."

Gatsby nodded.

"Even after the SPIN HELMET command, some overeager agents took matters into their own hands and finished the targets. That sort of insubordination requires a serious response."

(I learned how the Circle protected its possessions and enforced its rules)

Gatsby cleared her throat. "I can't condone any of this, but the question has to be asked. Isn't the world better off with these leaders dead? Men who kill innocent citizens? Who exploit and brutalize women?"

Dacea looked toward the wall, eyes dark. "A moral nosebleed? The ethics of murdering murderers? In a few days, we'll know."

"That's it? *That's* your response?"

"You don't know the first thing about this world. You're treading on dangerous ground. Let it go." The look in her eyes was fired metal.

Gatsby took a deep breath and a conversational U-turn. "Then…Affiato. Without him, what happens to the Circle?"

"Unless a cohort was named, the HAMMER's role transfers to the SWORD." She drew a sigh. "I don't want it."

"He said it was a militia of vast numbers. That's an astounding cache of human energy and power. Why walk away from it?"

Dacea crossed the room to the picture window and stared out at King's Road—still, dark, empty. "The SWORD is always handpicked. The previous HAMMER was ready to transfer the role and supposedly gave the SHIELD to the selected woman, but no one knows who she is. We don't even know who has the SHIELD." Her head tipped; she seemed lost in doubt. "The Circle is the most protected secret in the world, but even it has secrets. Plots within plots."

"Tell me about the SHIELD. What is it?"

Dacea tugged on a chain hanging around her neck. She pulled a round pendant from under her shirt and walked toward Gatsby. "This. It has these symbols from the ROSETTE—otherwise not very impressive. This one is a replica."

She showed Gatsby a flat stone, about the width of a shot glass, with two engravings: a circle with seven dots, a flower with eight petals.

The shock hit her. Gatsby's hand flew to the chain around her own neck and the hematite pendant she had worn since high school. She pulled it from the V of her shirt and held it up.

Dacea's eyes bulged. "How did you get that?"

"Cambier asked me the same question. It came in a package when I was seventeen. Unmarked, no packing slip, no letter, so I have no idea who sent it."

"Seventeen? And you're the SHIP-1 that the HAMMER sent me to finish?" Dacea's eyes darted as implications barreled through her. "Fucking hell. Do you see what this means?"

Her heart skipped a beat. "I don't...."

"*You* are the selected one. You are the SWORD, you are RUZ WER DAN!"

Heat exploded in her chest; she felt like she was suffocating. "I've heard that phrase all my life, come across it too many times to count in completely random circumstances. My mother-in-law said it to me and told me to *not* try to translate it, because the day I did would be my last. What the hell does RUZ WER DAN mean?"

"RUZ WER DAN is reserved for the SWORD and the HAMMER. I don't have time to explain the WATER language—it would take months—but simply, it means *Circle Protected Eternal*. Safe from any level of harm from the Circle. For life."

"You said it to Affiato. Why?"

Dacea snapped toward her. "In the moment, distraction, something to knock him off balance." She stopped, panting lightly. "And instinct. I knew immediately that you weren't a threat to me but were both valuable and a threat to *him*. You are the SWORD, the protected one."

"Protected from what?" She heard Cambier's cracked, despairing voice: *I learned how the Circle protected its possessions and enforced its rules. Obscene measures. I learned of those who had been killed.*

"Ruz-sil pot wer san!" Dacea blustered as she paced across the room, hands fluttering madly. "Unbelievable...but there will be a breadcrumb trail, so the BOAT has forensic work to do. Who was local when you received the SHIELD, who held posts in the BEEHIVE..."

"Are you saying that you could trace who sent it to me? How?"

"PEDESTRIAN." She turned with a dry laugh. "The unicorn of the Circle. It's easy to forget what you don't know. We are air—invisible and everywhere. You'll soon learn the import of these words, Donovan." She paused. "But you still have the ROSETTE? The pieces?"

"The police have them now. They'll eventually go to the British Museum for restoration."

Her eyes clouded. "You have no idea what the ROSETTE symbolizes to the Circle. Our members number in the millions, probably close to *billions*. If the BEEHIVE learns that the ROSETTE—the real one—was recovered and then destroyed, I don't know what kind of anarchy this could ignite!"

They stared at each other, wide eyed.

"What are you going to do?"

Dacea shoved the SHIELD replica under her shirt, yanked her jacket zipped, and walked out.

White Russian in her hand, Gatsby sat at the desk in her office. She stared into the living room where furniture pieces huddled in the dark like sleeping animals.

The Circle will find out that the Disk is being restored at the British Museum, and here we go again. The realization that she used the first person plural—including herself in the Circle—made her pull in a sharp breath.

(RUZ WER DAN...you are the selected one!)

She groaned. *Impossible. I'm not their recruit, not their convert. My only objective was to find the real Disk, and I did. What now? With Affiato dead, does the Circle NEED to possess it? If it's taken to the British Museum or any museum, I won't have exclusive access, no rights to the research.*

She sipped.

Letting it go was the ONLY answer, the only way to exorcise her. No immortal glory without destruction. The Disk was destroyed. She blew out a shaky breath. *YOU are destroyed, Livia.*

The images rose in her mind: the inexplicable amber liquid oozing from the edge of the disk, shards scattering across the marble as if tumbling in slow motion.

A thing so craved but so brittle. There was no other choice.

She searched the desktop for a pen and paper. As she drew the symbols that had emerged in the liquid, the three words inscribed in Linear B, the translation flowed through her.

Glory

...Cambier's care-worn eyes, the weight of sadness in her voice...

through

...*It does not belong to anyone, even me*...

destruction

She dropped the pen onto the paper. The room seemed to spin. She felt herself swimming in fear, wonder, chaos—a ghostly sense of becoming a different person. Stretching her hands in front of her, she squeezed them closed, then open. Closed, open. Closed, open.

Closed.

Open.

CHAPTER 43

Dacea bent over the coffee table, picked up the carafe and refilled her mug, and went back to the computer humming on the desk. She clicked the videoconference icon; the webcam images loaded. While she finished adjusting the volume, the BOAT members logged on and gave their passwords.

"Hoda. Dan nil sez."

"Miranovski. Wat pan on."

"Dhar. Pot dot wer."

"Ready for your reports."

Miranovski cleared her throat. "The SHIP-2—" Her hands flew in arcs. "Tchyo za ga'lima!! I can't believe it! How did this fucking mu'dak get..."

Dacea cut her off. "We were hacked, you're outraged. Let's move on. ID is now a top priority. Dhar?"

Dhar spoke in her gravelly monotone. "A new version of the ARROW, this one for identification. It's an antigen. Once it's injected, it stimulates production of antibodies, and we test for them routinely and at random. The lab at Ram2 is working on the mechanism, but it will probably be a cheek swab that turns a bright color. If it doesn't, we have a PEDESTRIAN."

Dacea nodded. "Good. Effective."

"And all members get an annual booster."

"What if they don't get it?"

Dhar's eyes narrowed. "Call the dog."

Miranovski lunged toward the camera. "We can't do that!"

"Call the dog as far as the BEEHIVE knows—maybe it does, maybe it doesn't. Christ, settle down."

"This is a good start," Dacea said. "R&D will be tricky, so keep me updated. Hoda, what's the status of the new tech?"

Hoda moved closer to the lens, the image of her face filling the feed screen. "It's in beta, but the skeleton is in place for the upgraded STAR SEED. Fifteen-digit PIN that updates every twenty seconds, an adjunct password that updates every ten seconds. If she's breathing and wants to continue doing so, she carries it 24/7. That includes the SWORD."

"Good work. You all saw my message and agenda. Requests from eight of the WHITE BIRD THISTLE agents. Three requested transfer to another city, four request transfer from the role. One wants TATTOO."

Dhar said, "Become a RUNNER by permission? We've never seen th..."

"You have now," Dacea broke in. "Approve them."

"Which requests?"

"All of them."

Dhar's eyes widened. "Done."

"Next. The rogue HAMMER is dead, and the role of the SWORD..." Her voice trailed off.

Miranovski spoke up. "If you're thinking of the investigation, it's already launched."

"Don-muz. I, um..." Dacea found herself struggling to organize her thoughts as her desperate desire to leave the CIRCLE was becoming a reality. It was a shock of stinging and relief at the same time.

Hoda seemed to sense her disequilibrium and seized the opportunity. "SHIP-1. What's her profile?"

The question shook Dacea back in familiar territory. "PEDESTRIAN, of course. All the usual naiveté, but there's resilience in her. Determination, intelligence. She risked everything to find the ROSETTE, and then she outmaneuvered the SHIP-2."

Hoda shook her head. "What was his profile?"

"What we've seen before. The member who goes rogue, thinks she's powerful enough to reverse the magnetic poles, dying to launch a jihad for some righteous cause."

"Except this time, the rogue member was a *he*. Mu'dak..." Miranovski jabbed a fist at the webcam as if ready to rampage but then dropped back in her chair.

Dacea closed the meeting. They all logged off, and the panels went dark.

She drummed her fingers on the desktop, thinking. *Donovan as SWORD? A dual-edged sword, that. Ingenious but unknown. A fighter, but what is she driven to fight for? If she's inducted into the BOAT, would she follow or rebel, clamoring to lead? Is she an academic, a drone, a builder, or a hidden tyrant?*

She shut off the computer and stood. *Only one way to find out.*

CHAPTER 44

Roman stood near the steps, his briar pipe wobbling between his lips. "Have you called CNN?"

She laughed. "I'll let my publicist handle the press."

They climbed the stairs, navigating the marble columns of the British Museum's portico entrance, and dove into the dazzling architecture and bustle of the Great Court. They turned toward the lift near the South Stairs.

"Nelson only knew what I was billing the museum for travel, so when I tell him we recovered the Phaistos Disk—*twice*—and then hand it to him in pieces, he'll piss himself."

The door opened, and they stepped into the cab. The lift jerked to life, dragging them up to the third floor.

"And then what?"

"The mother of all political battles. That is to say, the usual. Stephanos will claim ownership and insist that the pieces be returned to the Heraklion, and the British Museum will assert right of possession. The rancor of bureaucracy, Roman. You know what it's like."

Without a word, he leaned forward and gave her a tight hug. It was unexpected and surprisingly long. Her cheek pressed against his chest, Gatsby mumbled, "Um, thanks, Roman...Roman? The door?"

He released her and stepped back, a nervous teenage-boy's smile on his face. They moved out of the cab and into the corridor. Gatsby nodded toward the right. "The, uh, Conservation Lab is this way. Let's go."

Nelson Addison Penn Clevis was regularly mistaken for the American actor Bob Balaban. He wore frameless glasses, and the slim burgundy tie had been his trademark for decades. The creases in his grey suit screamed. He had no tolerance for badly prepared steak, lateness, or children.

He cleared his throat. "I want the pieces retested and verified by the specialty team...x-ray, radiocarbon, and spectrometry." He turned toward Gruedin. "Clive, who was the Brazilian we called in about the Vesuvius? The forger?"

"Barajas," Gruedin said.

"Yes. Get him. I'm sure CIS will want a look as well. I'll speak with Alexiou…"

I'm sure you will, Gatsby thought.

"But for the time being, they remain here."

She glanced at Gruedin. "And Clive? Test for liquids."

"Why?"

"Before it broke, I saw a liquid seeping from the edge."

He frowned. "On an artifact of that age? Not likely. Did something spill on it?"

"No. It was there, Clive. I touched it. Amber color, the viscosity of honey. Sh…" The word *she* almost made it out, but she clamped her lips. "It may be a resin or some kind of cellulose."

"How much?"

"Twenty-five or thirty grams."

Eyebrows raised, he said, "I'll get Browning on it. That's her bailiwick."

The last of the museum staff had left for the evening, headed for their cars or the Tube. Gatsby stepped inside Test Lab 2 and flicked on the lights. She looked around at the electronics. The tech's excited shouts flowed through her mind.

(How the hell did you acquire it?)

(We have our sample from the edge—about a hundred milligrams)

(Thirty-three to thirty-eight hundred! Holy shit!!)

The annihilation of sound and light, crawling across the floor, coughing up smoke, scrambling to find the other techs, Gruedin's hair escaping in all directions, shirt askew, patches of blood under his nose...

"Are you okay?"

She jumped. "Clive! Good god, you scared me."

"Sorry." He leaned against the doorjamb. "This was a rattling…" He rubbed his chin, seemingly at a loss for words. "I didn't have a chance to say it earlier, but congratulations."

"Thanks. I think."

"I'm glad you're all right." He gave a nod and disappeared down the hall.

Gatsby listened for a few minutes, entranced by the rhythm of his footsteps, then switched off the lights and closed the lab door. Just as she started toward the lift, her phone buzzed. She spotted the caller ID. *Seattle. Don't answer!*

"What do you want?"

A beat of silence. "Gatsby, listen to me carefully. I was recruited in my twenties. At thirty-one, I was a RAM. A regional manager, charged with overseeing a territory."

She felt her palm sweating, slippery against the phone case.

"When I met Thomas, you and I became enemies. It was intentional."

"What? For fuck's sake, Livia, why are y…"

"I saw your fascination with the Disk. Innate interest, not forced. When the time was right, I sealed the package and had it delivered to our house. Anonymously, of course. Possessing the SHIELD was a deadly prospect. You had no idea of its magnitude and how it would change the trajectory of your life. I hounded you, taught you to always look over your shoulder, to always be wary, to trust no one, especially women. I thought I could ensure that you remained a PEDESTRIAN, but of course, that was impossible. We are air—invisible and everywhere."

"You…this, this can't…"

"It sounds trite, I know, but my intentions were good. I know how I caused you to suffer. I didn't want that. I wanted to protect you, Gatsby. I'm so sorry."

With a beep, the line went dead.

Her knees buckled. Her back pressed against the wall, she slid down to the cold tile, unable to breathe.

CHAPTER 45

Gatsby rounded the corner of the walking path and settled on a park bench on the north side. Wellington Arch, erected to celebrate Napoleon's defeat, cast long shadows over the expanses of grass. A clutch of German tourists ambled by, chattering and taking photos.

She sensed someone approaching and looked up.

Like a small pirate flag, the qunae swayed against Dacea's face. She sat down next to Gatsby. Her face and body betrayed no emotion, as if feelings of any kind were synonymous with pain. Gatsby pondered how old she was and what kind of daring or tragic stories she had to tell—if she revealed anything about herself to anyone. *Perhaps she too was steeped in suspicion from a young age.*

"The police? CIS?"

"I was called down to Met headquarters to make a formal statement. Spoke with a Chief Inspector Rausch. He said they confiscated the electronics and documentation in Affiato's war room, but the fire destroyed almost everything of investigative value." She paused. "But if you're in line to be the SWORD, I doubt this is anything you don't already know." *Don't even think that I want the role.*

Dacea's eyes flickered.

"They'll do an investigation, but it sounds open and shut. Affiato was the beginning and end of his own obsessive world." She stared up at the towering columns, the chariot and four stampeding horses atop the monument. "What megalomania. When his grandiose plan of destruction imploded, he *wanted* to die. That's my take."

Dacea shook her head. "He was a PEDESTRIAN who turned SHIP. What he wanted doesn't matter."

She shook her head. "It mattered to the THISTLE members and all the other people who were targeted." She paused. "What will happen to the Circle?"

"Reorganizing. The THISTLE division has been eliminated." She pulled in a deep, slow breath. "It's time. There are better ways."

"And you? Do you step up and become the SWORD?"

The breeze picked up, and the qunae flipped. For the first time, Gatsby saw the extent of the disease that had destroyed the woman's face. Below the serious eyes, her nose jutted to the right, but where there should have been nostrils, there was a gaping hole. The lips had rotted away, permanently exposing the teeth and gums. Her tongue flicked rapidly to prevent saliva from trickling down her chin. The skin of her nose, cheeks, chin, and upper neck was black and scabby, scarred with pocks that might have been from injections.

"Oh my god, what…"

Dacea quickly wrapped the fabric over the face and tied it behind her head, eyes darting rapidly.

Gatsby felt the wooden piece nudge against her thigh. She slid her hand into the pocket of her jeans, pulled out the piece, and held it forward. "A5. The CHILD. Take it."

Dacea's chest began to pump, and a gasp burst from her mouth. As tears swelled, she took the small, wooden piece from Gatsby's hand.

Gatsby whispered, "Will you tell me your name?"

"Bayoumi." She curled her fingers tightly around the piece as she looked away. "Dacea Bayoumi."

Gatsby took a deep breath. "My stepmother, Livia Rudden. She told me that she was part of the Circle. What was the term? A RAM." Her right hand rose to her chest, and her fingers brushed across the pendant. "All my life, this has been a mystery. I never knew who gave it to me or why. I never knew anything about the Circle, never knew that all her insanity and my years of obsessive study were interconnected. Now I know that she gave it to me, and I'm starting to understand why." She searched Dacea's eyes for understanding, even simple acknowledgment, but what she saw told her that controlling forces held the young woman with an iron fist.

"I know."

Dacea stood. As she turned, Gatsby glanced at the midpoint of the young woman's chest. At their last meeting, she wore the replica of the SHIELD, and the distinctive bulge had been clear under her cotton shirt. The bulge was now gone. She walked away, headed toward Serpentine Bridge.

Curled on the loveseat in her flat, Gatsby looked across the living room, staring into the vacant black eye of the television.

The SHIELD.

She pulled the pendant from under her shirt and slipped the chain off her neck. Rolling the hematite piece in her hand, she stared at its rune-like markings.

(one unique image is the labrys or axe. It represents slaughter of enemies. It's thought to be a symbol of death, of destruction. On the B side, the symbol of the lily correlates to the olive branch that was given to the victor of a battle, alluding to praise or glory...)

(You had no idea of its magnitude and how it would change the trajectory of your life)

Run or do nothing? Forward or retreat? Roman would say "you're at a crossroads, GM."

She slipped it back around her neck, walked into her office, rolled the chair toward the desk, and turned on the computer. Five minutes later, she had clicked "Confirm" and booked the round-trip flight to Seattle.

EPILOGUE

The wheeled suitcase trundled beside her as she entered Caffe Fratelli. Standing at the counter, Gatsby ordered pasta salad and a latte. She shifted her weight from one foot to another as she waited. A couple with a fussy toddler approached the counter, chatting about the little girl's upcoming birthday party. An elderly woman, sitting alone at a table, sipped tea and read the *London Evening Standard*.

After wandering to a table at the right side of the room, she dropped her shoulder bag onto the tabletop and sat, reviewing her pre-flight list. *Ticket, cash, phone charger, melatonin, trail mix...*

The elderly woman lowered her newspaper and stared intently at her. As Gatsby gave her a *mind your own business* look, the details registered. The wool scarf around the woman's wrinkled neck. The wide-set, blue eyes and mottled hands. The old woman tipped her head toward the empty chair at her table. Furtively glancing around, Gatsby snatched up her bag and approached.

"*Cambier??*" she hissed.

The woman raised her arm and shook Gatsby's hand as if warmly greeting an old business associate.

"But...but you...I..."

"Sit so that we can have a quiet conversation."

She understood that it was a command, not a request, and slid into the seat on the opposite side of the table, stunned.

Cambier calmly folded the newspaper and lay it on the table. "I did take the real Phaistos Disk from the Heraklion. Everything else was fabrication. Ivan Hobart thought he had the genuine artifact. So did you. So did the HAMMER."

"That's not..." She swallowed against a gritty taste. The room began to spin. "We did the TL test with a freaking *team* of experts, and they confirmed the age. Thirty-eight hundred years—that is the original artifact!"

Cambier pushed away her teacup. "We made the replica. Only two people knew, myself and a woman with deep knowledge of museum lab processes. She knew how technicians would collect a sample for analysis. She removed material from the real Disk and applied it to the outer edge of the replica. She was old then. Dead now." She gingerly folded her wrinkled hands. "Hobart hid a fake. His bad judgment put him in jail."

She dropped her head into her hands, breathing hard. "I can't believe this. You gave Hobart a fake? You gave *me* a fake?!"

Cambier nodded. "Ker-suz ran." *I did.*

"But all this...then where the hell is the real Disk?"

Cambier reached toward a dispenser on the table, tugged out a paper napkin, and wiped her hands slowly and thoroughly. "When I was the SWORD, I learned that the upstart HAMMER was a man. No one else in the BEEHIVE knew. I was ready to call the dog on him but then considered the advantages. He might be useful. I waited. I watched his patterns for a long time and saw that he was the type to make a rash move. He did when he contacted you and began his hunt for the ROSETTE. This gave away his full identity and location. I knew that the new SWORD would track down a SHIP. You led her to The Sorcerer's Apprentice and the HAMMER. The operation is complete."

Gatsby shook her head, swirling in confusion.

Cambier dug inside a 1950s-style handbag and pulled out a device that looked like a customized smartphone. It booted into operation as she held it across the table. Gatsby took it from her hand, amazed at the incredible lightness. Her eyes zigzagged over an array of unfamiliar keys and functions.

"What is this?"

On the glowing screen, she saw a live webcam image of a living room—*her* living room. She saw the artichoke-green loveseat, armchair, and media center, sunlight filtering through the picture window that faced King's Road. On the coffee table, a brushed-metal container was propped open to reveal a clay disk, about twenty-five centimeters wide, covered with a spiral pattern of familiar symbols.

Cambier said, "The SWORD will dismantle the webcam. She will teach you how to use the STAR SEED and the OAR. Both are safe from the best hackers, because we *are* the best hackers. You will be given access to the database, all the critical names and locations, the terminology, our history from the beginning. Start by studying the WATER manual."

"No, I don't...you..."

"Read a file marked AM. Anya Manez, an archeologist. In 2011, she was working at an excavation site in Göbekli Tepe, Turkey. She uncovered a dozen artifacts with symbols identical to those on the ROSETTE."

"A cache of samples? The key to unlocking..." She closed her eyes, wrangling with the implications. "With no examples for comparison, decipherment has been impossible, but with them..."

"The Champollion of the new millennium?" Cambier pushed the soggy napkin into her handbag. "That remains to be seen."

The café filled, customers ate with gusto, and baristas prepared drinks. Couples laughed and bickered. College students flipped through books or texted on smartphones.

"Oh yes. Take this." Cambier reached into the side pocket of her handbag, pulled out a small carved item, and held it out for Gatsby. "She said this has served its purpose. She says thank you."

Gatsby took the CHILD piece from the older woman's hand, too stunned to reply. She slowly ran her fingertips across the smooth wood.

Cambier said, "And I disabled the ARROW that Browning implanted."

Her eyes widened. "What?"

"When we shook hands a minute ago. Dimethyl sulfoxide on my palm. I transferred a chemical that dissolves the GPS transmitter."

"GPS...what the hell are you...wait, Ruth Browning, the tech at the lab?"

(Oh, sorry. Ruth Browning, Forensics)

Gatsby raised her hands. Her eyes darted over her palms, looking for traces of liquid. Heart pounding, she looked into Cambier's blue eyes and whispered, "Cambier, who *ARE* you?"

A phantom smile tugged at the woman's lips. "I do not know that name."

She stood and shuffled down the aisle to the front door, pulling the strap of the leather handbag over her shoulder.

Gatsby sat, mouth agape, holding the humming device. She bolted toward the door.

As Cambier stepped out onto to the sidewalk, a charcoal-grey Audi rolled up to the curb and stopped. She opened the passenger door, climbed in, and turned toward the driver, a well-dressed woman about Gatsby's age. The driver shared Cambier's petite body type and blond hair. A florid, blue-green tattoo of a phoenix rippled on her left bicep.

Gatsby couldn't hear Cambier's voice but focused on the old woman's lips. She seemed to say *Helena.*

The driver gave a nod.

The car pulled away, moving south on Berkeley Street.

THE WORLD OF THE CIRCLE

WATER LANGUAGE

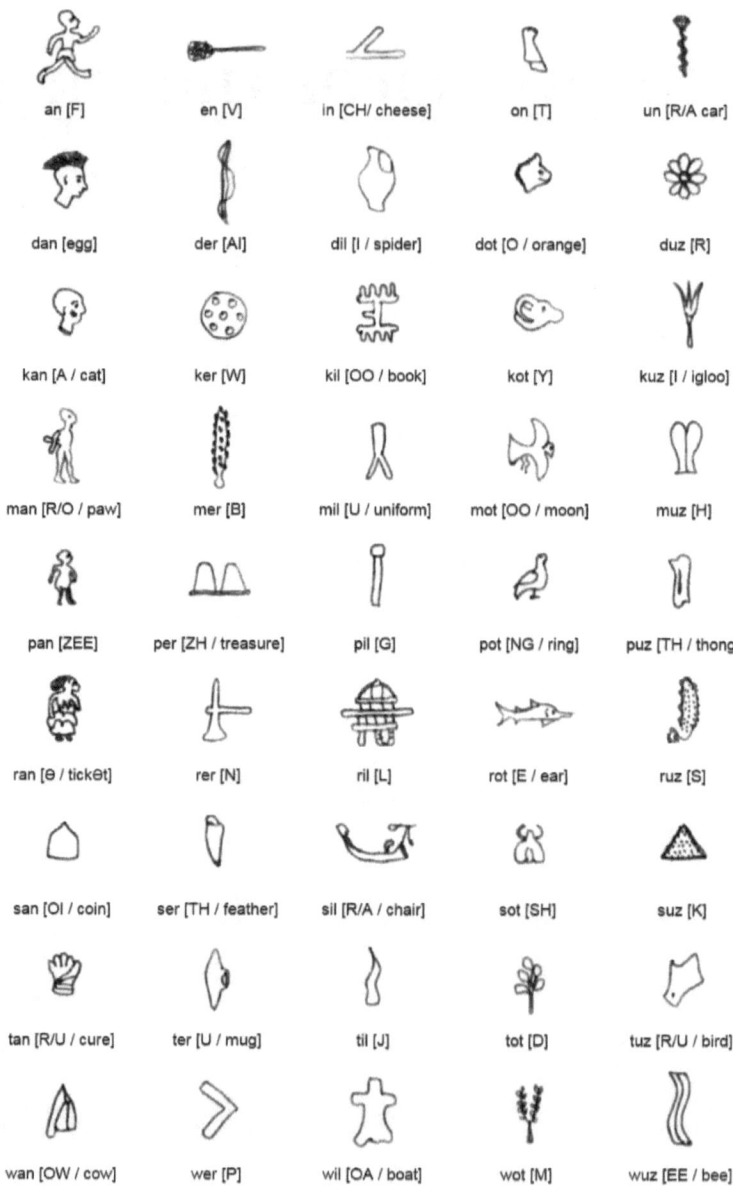

an [F]	en [V]	in [CH/ cheese]	on [T]	un [R/A car]
dan [egg]	der [AI]	dil [I / spider]	dot [O / orange]	duz [R]
kan [A / cat]	ker [W]	kil [OO / book]	kot [Y]	kuz [I / igloo]
man [R/O / paw]	mer [B]	mil [U / uniform]	mot [OO / moon]	muz [H]
pan [ZEE]	per [ZH / treasure]	pil [G]	pot [NG / ring]	puz [TH / thong]
ran [θ / ticket]	rer [N]	ril [L]	rot [E / ear]	ruz [S]
san [OI / coin]	ser [TH / feather]	sil [R/A / chair]	sot [SH]	suz [K]
tan [R/U / cure]	ter [U / mug]	til [J]	tot [D]	tuz [R/U / bird]
wan [OW / cow]	wer [P]	wil [OA / boat]	wot [M]	wuz [EE / bee]

Diacritic Symbols

3 br	/ gr	(sl
& bl	0 j	— st
< ch	! kl	% th
- dr	2 kr	\ thr
? fl	[pl	* tr
5 fr	> pr	6 v
+ gl	7 sh	= z

Diacritic Application

mer-suz-wan<	*Construction:* mesuwa**CH**
dot-pan-ker7	*Construction:* dopake**SH**
ker-pil-dot-ruz—	*Construction:* kepidoru**ST**

TERMINOLOGY

ARGONAUT	Argonaut Law—term for the SPIN HELMET command
AXE	Punishment for sloppy work or insubordination
BEEHIVE	General membership of the Circle
BLUE CAT	Code for ABORT
Call the dog	Code for assassinate
CAT	A newbie, new recruit
Circle	Global women's network; name based on the shape of the Disk and the spiral pattern of symbols.
Circle motto	"We are air—invisible and everywhere."
FORK	A new recruit's mentor
GAUNTLET	Code for THREAT
GRASS	Reward for work well done
HELMET	Command for *MOVE IMMEDIATELY*
HORN	Worst insult / slur within the Circle
LIONESS	A "data mule" (undercover messenger / courier)
OAR	Circle-exclusive network server
PEDESTRIAN	Anyone who is not a Circle member
ROSETTE	Code for the Phaistos Disk
RUNNER	A woman who deserts the Circle
SHIELD	Pendant that identifies the SWORD

SHIP	Someone who tries to infiltrate or undermine the Circle
SHIP-1	Code for Gatsby Donovan
SHIP-2	Code for Maceo Affiato
SPIN	A last-resort "kill switch." At the SPIN HELMET order, all agents around the globe destroy all digital information about the Circle; this action destroys everything on the HAMMER'S system as well.
STAR SEED	Circle-engineered smartphone-like device
TATTOO	An allowed RUNNER (permission to defect)
WATER	Circle-engineered language. The symbols of the Phaistos Disk are the basis of the language—invaluable for communication b/c only Circle members know it
WHITE BIRD	Code for the planned assassination of terrorist leaders (operation later amended to include families and associates).

Leaders

HAMMER   First Commander: The unknown leader
SWORD   Second Commander: The known leader
MAIZE   Metro Commander
RAM   Regional Commander
SHELL   Country Commander

Divisions

BOAT   The ruling triad
          Tess Miranovski (Executive Lead, Dove4)
          Anastasia Hoda (IT Lead, Dove4)
          Jayna Dhar (Tactical / Weapons Lead,
          Spindle5)
          Aria Vlahos is Lead LIONESS (courier)
TEMPLE   The IT/tech force
THISTLE   The assassination force

Weapons

ARROW   Circle-engineered nano-level GPS transmitter,
          implanted via liquid. Members developed the
          transmitter and delivery fluid. A clear liquid
          carries a nanotech GPS transmitter. The liquid
          passes easily through the skin, allowing the
          transmitter to be planted in the dermis. The
          transmitter sends a tracking signal to a STAR
          SEED. Software on the STAR SEED screen
          shows the location of the transmitter and
          navigational directions. After 72 hours, it
          dissolves.
DOLIUM   Circle biologists developed a patch that
          mimics the action of the sea wasp jellyfish.
          The patch is 2 inches square and loaded with a
          Circle-engineered toxin (TUNNY). It causes
          sharp pain, respiratory and cardiac depression,
          and death within minutes. When it is attached
          near a vascular area, needle-sharp hooks
          pierce the skin. As the victim attempts to pull
          the patch off, the movements aggravate barbed
          threads that inject the poison. The harder he
          struggles, accelerating heartbeat and
          circulation, the quicker his death.

A microscopic recorder that detects the pulse is embedded in it. When no heart beat has been recorded for 120 seconds, the patch dissolves, leaving almost no trace (sometimes, a subtle abrasion that looks like a minor burn is seen on the skin).

FLUTE   Assassination dagger with serrated edges.

LILY   Circle-engineered acidic liquid. Members developed this corrosive liquid that damages metal; it is used to open locks.

TIARA   Made of bamboo (lightweight, easy to hide). It is projectile at short range (like a gun) but silent. It kills by exposure to the same toxin used with the DOLIUM. There is no antidote, making it more deadly than traditional weapons.

TUNNY   The Circle-engineered toxin used with the DOLIUM and the TIARA.

Safe Houses

Cat7	Berlin, Germany
Crab6	Kolonaki (Athens), Greece
Dove4	Plaka (Athens), Greece
Ivy9	London, England
Ram2	Vancouver, BC
Spindle5	Messina, Sicily
Vine13	Palo Alto, California
Vulture11	Dublin, Ireland

PHOTO & ILLUSTRATION CREDITS

Front Cover: No changes were made to the image as shown on the cover art other than minor enhancement of shading and sharpness. Courtesy of Wikimedia Commons, the free media repository.
https://commons.wikimedia.org/wiki/File:Phaistos_disk_B.jpg

Description	*English*: Phaistos Disk. Side B. Heraklion Archaeological Museum. Greece. 2010 July 22. Русский: Фестский диск. Сторона Б. Археологический музей Ираклиона (Крит, Греция) 22 июня 2010 года.
Date	22 July 2010
Source	Own work
Author	Aserakov

Page 5: Courtesy of iStock.com
Page 7: Courtesy of Lori Stephens
Page 17: Courtesy of Lori Stephens
Pages 133–134: Courtesy of Lori Stephens
Page 228: Courtesy of Taylor Gilmore

ABOUT THE AUTHOR

Ellery Stone is the pen name of the American author Lori Stephens, pNLP, CCP. Stephens earned a BA in English literature and creative writing at the University of Oregon. Her career in the publishing field began in 1988, and she has edited over 200 books on topics as varied as cancer research, dating for seniors, music therapy, Neurolinguistic Programming, software security, and zombies.

The research for the *Paradigms Lost* series was extensive. In addition to visiting England, France, and Italy, she researched Egypt, India, Peru, Australia, Greece, Crete, and Spain. While writing *Deep Structure*, she spent five years learning about archeology (specifically the history of Stonehenge) and quantum physics. *Alpha Omega* required research into the structure of ancient languages, and she drew on her own experience with NLP and hypnotic language. *Viral Glyph* took her into studies of the Phaistos Disk, theories of its decipherment, and the history of cryptography. Descriptions of the world of stage magic were drawn from her association with a professional magician.

The author at Stonehenge (Wiltshire, England)

ALSO BY ELLERY STONE

DEEP STRUCTURE
The Stonehenge Quantum
Where are the mysterious symbols coming from? Why have they appeared in an Egyptian tomb, a Peruvian palace, and a shape created by a fakir's squirming snakes?

Dr. Gatsby Donovan's career at the British Museum has made her an expert in decoding ancient glyphs, but solving this linguistic puzzle is the greatest challenge of her life. Will her knowledge unearth the answers, or are they secreted within the very source that she dare not decipher? As she spirals into the universal "deep structure," she finds herself dangling from the edge of everything she once believed about reality.

ALPHA OMEGA
The Holy Drug
In a London suburb, a cult disciple gasps, dying in a pool of his own blood. The only clue is the holy scripture that he clutches.

Who would kill for the Librah Vaeta? What secrets are hidden within its pages? Do the leaders of the Omega cult know of the terrible violence it can spawn, or was that the intention?

Dr. Gatsby Donovan's abilities to decipher ancient writings pull her into the vortex of a treacherous mystery. Revealing Omega's most powerful secrets will be deadly—the question is not the salvation of her soul but whether she will survive the night.

www.ellerystone.com